THE DRIFTWOOD BOYS

in Ocean City

jimboY fitz

CONTENTS

prologue to a story

This is a fictional story of youth, friendship, and life in a little ocean city town in a mid-Atlantic USA state which sometimes dances on the edge of pleasantry. The story takes place during the summer of 1976 with just a bit of truth mixed into the fiction creating *(what I hope is)* a sweet and sometimes-messy storyline. But there was such a time and place. And there were some characters who lived life together in a driftwood-like bungalow that's long since been covered over by time &

space although to such characters, this moment will never be completely dismissed from their memories any more than youth itself can be completely lost; it just gets older and a bit dusty & dingy with time but when you've been young and in love with life, how can such a time be completely forgotten?

Now this story is told through a more semi-disjointed story-telling-like chain of events with bits & pieces of short stories dancing through the pages instead of in (what I might consider) a normal sequential storyline; it uses narratives from several characters to tell a story that's augmented with a few *story detours* and previously written *chitter-chatter*-like short stories. Moreover, the initial chapters are dominated by character & location development whereas the later chapters concentrate on the stories themselves. So if the story appears at times to be a bit disjointed in its presentation or even repetitive at times, hopefully it rounds itself out and tells a complete story by the end of the book.

If I had to give a movie-like rating to this book for its content type (i.e. 'G', 'R', etc.) then I'd probably have to give it a 'R' rating cause there's a little bit of *camouflaged risqué-ness* in the storyline that could offend some uptight *make-believe* religious types who are more offended by sexual innuendos rather than *da trumpers'* ungodly caging of immigrant children at America's southern border during the detestable 45th reign of stupidity & heartlessness. But that aside, there is nothing problematic in the story's scenes or dialogue.

On a few occasions I will utilize the phrase *'in the Pleasant Land of Living'* to define a place where this story takes place. Also, I will occasionally reference a few words cited in popular songs, movies or sitcoms which invaded my thoughts while writing this story I'm telling, but I always try and make the appropriate references (explicit or implied) to all such sources whenever I can, so *'credit is given where it's due'*. In most cases, whether explicit references are made or not, I've *italicized* the phrases for identification purposes although it doesn't mean all italicized phrases are borrowed phrases from other sources, just some.

And yes, occasionally I'll misuse the English language in my dialogues but it's usually done in an attempt to lend *street cred* to some of my storylines although as my one younger brother used to tell me when I talked such shit, "don't bother doing it cause you *ain't got no damn street cred*"... Fair enough! ...but I do it anyway(s), so take 'that' *brother-dearest*. Besides, what the hell does he know anyway(s)? ...'*absolutely nothing, say it again...*' where I think we've heard such words sung somewhere else before; think '*War*' from the album '*War & Peace*'; written by Edwin Starr & released by Motown in 1970.

And *sooo*... with all *that being said*... and without further delay, I say... '*and awayyy... we go*'... to story-telling land...

Note: The phrase '*in the pleasant land of living*' used throughout the book is a take-off on the Natty Boh commercial line '*in the land of pleasant living*' used in the Maryland region during the sixties & seventies.

...in the beginning

There is a black empty screen and out of it comes a deadpanned monotone high-pitched voice from the background...

"My name... is... Jose... Jimenezzz..."

...and then there's laughter from the crowd at the antics of the show's now seen host & guest...

Now... if you're old enough to remember this dude's elongated introduction on the Ed Sullivan Show then maybe you get my gesture... and NO, this line is NOT meant 'here' as a derogatory comment on ethnicity or anything else so negative; it's just a light hearted introduction to the story I hope to tell so I'd like to step around the mine-field of political-correctness for just a moment here, to see where it takes us...

So I'm driving along this small tree-lined two-lane road when it veers towards this lone guard shack and as I come to a stop... a guard comes out and says to me "State your name and purpose"

And I say... in a deadpan monotone high pitched voice like this dude on the Ed Sullivan show, trying of course, to be funny... *"My name... is... Jose... Jimenezzz..."*

...and I giggle just a bit cause this routine has recently played inside my head during my drive and I think it's funny when said in a high-pitched voice like the guy on TV did... and for some reason, I think this guy might laugh with me cause I'm funny<??>... and it's supposed to be a light-hearted intro before I get serious with him and state my real name and business.

But he just looks at me for a minute with blank eyes before they turn rather piercing; his eyes are piercing through me like daggers might do, like penetrating spikes shooting through to the back of my head like laser beams might do... and then he says to me straight-faced... "State your name and reason for your visit..."

And of course, I shake just a bit now cause I'm a little afraid of this guy... and then I stumble just a bit more on my words for a moment too long... and suddenly he points a gun at my face, just inches away from me or so it seems to me at the time... and he restates his query... "State your name and the reason for your visit..."

So now... with this Jose Jimenez sound track still running through my head, I blurt it out in a bit of my own self-deprecating humor... "err, okay... my name is... Jimmy-boy... *Fitzzzbaggg*... and... *ahhh...*" where of course, I've elongated my *ha-ha 'Fitzbag'* bit just a wee-bit more than necessary... and I've failed to finish off my stated purpose for the visit as well, *ughhh*.

...and still nothing... not one reaction from this stone-faced guard... just his beady eyes piercing through to the back of my head...

Okay, I'm finally starting to get it... I'm just not all that funny or the line isn't all that funny... or both... but unfortunately, that's me... *drattts*; what's the world coming to?

"*ahhh*... my name is jimboyfitz... and, *ahhh*... I have a storybook I'd like you to read... *Please*"

And this dude says nothing at first... he just looks at me with those piercing eyes of his... with a gun almost buried in my face as I sit there fearing I'm going to wet myself due to an uncontrollable fear that grabs at every fiber of my being...

"This here, is a Magnum 44... [one ass-kicking] powerful hand gun..." and *blah-blah-blah...* or *etc.,... etc.,... etc.,...* or something like that... almost like Clint said it in his San Francisco thriller so many years ago except, this dude isn't Clint... and I'm not 'that

psycho'... and this isn't 'that movie'... cause it's a book... or a *book-want-to-be* if you will...

...and he continues, much like Clint might do with some adjustments made *here & there*... but with his teeth clenched just like Clint... "*so tell me punk... do you feel lucky?*"

And of course, I want to giggle cause I know these lines oh-so well, or at least, somewhat well... so I think to myself... 'Am I a *monkey grinder* or what? ...cause I grind & I grind... and all I get in return is ground-up used words from someone else's bits'... I mean, wtf?

...and apparently, I take just a bit too long to acknowledge this *Clint-like-wanta-be* guard's query cause he says to me again, in an ever-deeper teeth clenched *sorta* way... "*well, punk... do you?*"

And then suddenly, I'm swimming in a light-yellow flowing stream of warm fluids that contains just a bit of... *ahhh, how shall I say this*... a bit of yucky smelling stuff which just aromatizes things for a bit... and I think to myself... 'what *da f*<k*... something must be wrong here... cause all I want to do is offer up a book in a catchy *kinda* funny way and 'this' - is how it goes<??>' wtf???

So I think to myself, there's *gotta* be another way... cause this just seems like a *'fake f*<king news' kinda* situation where I utter nonsense and then cover my tracks with accusations and foolishness just to avoid the truth; the truth being... that maybe, 'I suck... big time'... and maybe I blow too many chunks of foolishness out too damn often, too...

Okay... I get it now... I see the light... I suck... but still... I have a story to tell... a story of camaraderie... a story of stupid naive youths playing at being too damn young... a story of sadness at lives wasted for no reason other than some lives never get to finish their own songs but who none-the-less, are remembered for the light they were... a story of gratitude to those who enriched *'the mediocre'* with such bright colors of hope... and it all occurs somewhere in and around, give or take a bit or two, in an Ocean City town somewhere out on the east coast in the mid-Atlantic region of the USA in a place some people like to call, *'the pleasant land of Living'*...

...somewhere... overrr... the rainbow... where skies are [mostly] blue...

...damnnn, that almost sounds rather familiar too, doesn't it<??>... *'Monkey grinder'* I say, a *friggin' monkey grinder,* am I...

Well, obviously this thought pattern of mine has taken too damn long again, and this impatient guard again repeats his message of hope and love to me in an ever-deeper voice with his teeth clenched in an even deeper *sorta* way...

"wellll... punk... do you?"

"ahhh... well, *yesss...* I do, I think<??>" ...which I say with a *shit-eating kinda* grin...

...and again, another stolen line from somewhere or other... but that's what I do... cause what else can I do... but leap... and jump... and twirl... and play, as I do... like in a *'monkey grinder' sorta* way.

...and then... there's a blast of light which flashes across the skies and blinds me for a moment or two with a magic that's streaming by...

...and yes, there's a magical click of some kind before the flash of light... and as this blasting sound containing this loud *banggg-like* noise echoes around the globe and through my head which fortunately for me, is just fictional and NOT real... and which oddly enough, now seems to start our race forward at a quicker pace than before... and we, in mass, we shutter and shake as we blast forward from the start line I've drawn in the sand, and on-downwards we go towards a long dragstrip we rush, down towards a bright light at the end of the road...

"Yes sir... *I do - feel lucky today...*" I say.

...although you<??> ...maybe not<??> ...or maybe so<??>

So... the only remaining question, I fear, is where to start this story I want to tell beyond where I've already been... *ahhh... 'Ohhh, say can you see... those enlightened blue stars waving so bravely above... giving proofff... through the night...'* that I have no damn idea what I am doing...

Now... don't be(s) all mad at me for including a bit of our musical history in those words because I'm just a rambling-boy in search of a way to kick-start this show-off on-down da road... sooo... with a little more foot dragging... I've decided to start at the beginning...

...for in the beginning... there was nothing, but maybe space... one big vacuum of space with nothing but gaseous stuff stirring around, as some people like to say, although one has to ask, 'how did the gases get there?' Spontaneous? Or planned? Or maybe, 'it just is'?

But 'that point' aside, there are gases somewhere in space and then, for some reason... there's a big bang... and then... after some more time has passed, maybe there's some dinosaurs and such... and then... maybe a 'voice' or a hand uses some kind of drink-straw to stir things around just a bit more... or not... with a multifaceted 'seven days' thing going-on here or there where time seems irrelevant, I guess... and somewhere within this sequence of events, as some others might say, there are some people of some sorts, who appear on earth, and they are walking around, some of which are bent over a bit more than not, ape-like or not, but people of some kind who seem to get a bit prettier with time, if you like such a form although 'smarter' is questionable given our recent past & current status... and then – there were kingdoms... big kingdoms and small kingdoms... fair kingdoms and unfair kingdoms... and in some of the more fair kingdoms there's a *kinda* noble chivalry among some of the good knights of the round-table who make the world better than it was before they were present... and within these kingdoms there are little villages which are influenced by some of these good knights of the round-table... which - is where we start our story... cause in the beginning, somewhere on the southwest side of one *Charming-like* city-like kingdom, there were several small villages from which our boys danced out of... and into this story...

So welcome... to this story of the *'driftwood Boys'*....

Notes: The line *'This here, is a Magnum 44... [an ass-kicking] powerful hand gun...'* was triggered by a famous line in the Clint Eastwood movie *'Dirty Harry'*. Ditto, the line *'wellll... punk... do you [feel lucky]?'*. The *'somewhere over the rainbow...'* phrase was triggered by a famous line in the movie *'The Wizard of Oz'*. btw, *Israel IZ Kamakawiwo* does a great job singing this song. The words *'Ohhh, say can you see...'* were triggered from the Star-Spangled Banner.

Going 'down de ocean'

So within these villages there was a *village of violets* where there were all kinds of *birds of various colors* and billy goats too, etc., and they ran and flew *up & down* and around those violet-filled fields that coated our steps with many hopes and dreams... and within this village, there *came a leaping* out of it, a shaggy-ass billy-goat of a dude who was *kinda* like a bird of a different feather, a tall slender *sorta* dude with a bluish tinge to him which when seen from a certain light, made him look like a Jaybird might do under similar conditions which is why some kids called him Jaybird although there were other reasons as well, I suppose, as we might see later... and yet oddly enough, in another dimmer *kinda* light he may even have appeared to take on a more grounded slower image often mistaken as a slow-moving turtle-like dude which is why some may have even called him turtle-dude... sooo... all-in-all, it's pretty-*friggin'* weird-ass sight, indeed.

Anyway(s), in this story... Jaybird is sitting in his basement this one day just reading some text when he gets a call from dirty Dan.

"Hey, what the hell are you doing?"

"Nothing, why?"

"When you going *down de ocean*? You're out of school already, right?"

"Yeah, but our place isn't ready for another week or so... so I'm thinking of going down with Bobby when things have cleared up"

"You chickening-out then?"

"What??" asks a surprised Jaybird.

"You're chickening-out, aren't you? You going to dump on the guys? You said you were leaving the nest this summer, going East..." and he chuckles to himself just a bit cause he's thinking of an old slogan that's been reversed just a bit here: *'Go East young man, go East'.* "So you're not go *down de ocean* with them, are you?"

"None of your damn business"

"I knew it"

"F*<k you"

"You got a job yet?"

"No... why?"

"Well, get down there and get one while you still can"

"And where am I supposed to sleep?"

"Figure it out... unless, you're chickening-out? You going to dump on the guys, aren't you?"

"F*<k you" ...click...

Now dirty Dan's lines had kicked Jaybird in the face just a bit because he was pissing on him a bit. But in fairness, Jaybird had started chickening-out on their grand summer adventure on *down de ocean* which is a rather mundane 'grand adventure' if there ever was one, so dirty Dan was semi-right about Jaybird's equivocating...

So now Jaybird faced a dilemma, 'if not now - then when?' ... and if he waited, would it be any different then, than it was now, minus his living quarters issue... so he quivered and quaked for a bit while sucking on some of those lemons he'd been *eating-on* as he contemplated converting this bitterness into one large sweet glass of lemonade... after all, he was the first of the guys to be out of school this spring and therefore, he could be the first to head east if he wanted to, but should he? ...or should he wait and maybe even equivocate? ...so in this moment of indecision, he makes a decision; he'll leave his cozy nest and head east, escaping the usual summer routines of the mundane for what he hopes will be some *fun in the sun on down de ocean... and with that, face some 'unpredictability' as well.*

...so he decides to grab onto a ride *'going east, young man', 'down de ocean'* for the summer of 1976, the summer of America's *happy bicentennial* in *'the pleasant land of Living'*... and he packs a duffle bag with the clothes he needs for his great escape although just enough so he can easily carry them in the duffle bag, so not so much... and he gathers together a few dollars he has left from past reindeer games he's worked at... and I mean, just a few cause that's all he has ringing in his ears... and he leaves home, flying eastward toward opportunity & fun but *not upon the wind under his [jaybird] wings* does he go either, where again, such words seem like a line that's been sung somewhere else before, up on the silver screen, now doesn't it<??> ...but the truth is: this Jaybird just can't *'fly so good'* as they say, so he's a more grounded *sorta* bird. So he hops onto a bus heading downtown to *Charm City's* core where he catches a *Greyhound* of a dog blazing the *Trailways* heading eastward, going *down de ocean...* to Ocean City. *'Go East young man, go East'* say some ornery old crows watching from above.

...and of course, there's going to be *costs* for such an escape cause there are always *costs* to be paid for the rides we take. It's just that we don't often consider all those costs or understand them completely until the moment has come and we're part way down the road... but then again, there are costs for not taking the plunge as well. *Que sera, sera,* as one silver screen legend once sang.

So anyway(s)… when Jaybird gets down there, in Ocean City, he walks off the bus onto an empty parking lot where there's just him. There is no money for temporary housing. There is no credit cards either cause there were few of them available in this day & age, especially for young people… and there was no job to go to yet cause he didn't have one yet… but he's there in one piece ready to dance to the music of *the unknown*.

So Jaybird stands there without a place to live at temporarily because their rented apartment him and the guys had planned to play at, was still unavailable for another week or so, but it just so happens he knows a dude whom he'd met at school this past spring who's living and working down here in Ocean City already this spring… and this dude had told him to stop in sometime when he wanted to… Sooo… Jaybird takes his invite seriously enough today cause of his lack of other options, plus he's a friend; a friend with space for one more<??> So he hotfoots-it on up the streets towards the burbs of Ocean City to see this dude with duffle-bag in hand.

And when he arrives at this dude's door, he knocks on the door weeping rather pathetically for a temporary place to hide at until his apartment opened up in a few days. Well, he doesn't really weep as much as he's standing there rather pathetically sad with little other opportunities to go to if not for this guy. And lucky for him, this dude takes him in like he's a lost puppy dog of sorts.

"You want to smoke with me? I was just about to light up"

"Sure"

…and they dance for a bit on the edge of a ride while talking shit to each other like young guys sometimes do. And it's somewhere within this conversation when Jaybird lets it slip that he's houseless for a couple of days between puffs on the smoker and this good-hearted dude takes in this hopeless, clueless *'homeless Jaybird'* for just a bit... which *kinda* sounds like a *'shoeless Joe Jackson' sorta* story except Jaybird isn't shoeless although he's *without a home* for the moment and without work too... so a charity-case, at least temporarily... and so they smoked some more weed... and they drank some beers... and they talked some shit... and *whaaa-laaa...* this dude tells Jaybird about a job opportunity he knows of because this dude knows someone who knows someone working in a restaurant kitchen where they are still looking for seasonal help... and once he gets caught on, well, he dances the whole summer long there like *a tick hanging onto its host...* So like they say, there's nothing like a *'little help from your friends'* I suppose... or the *'old boys network'* or so...

So Jaybird and da crab-shack up on 21st street were *pair-ed* together for the summer... and he's hidden away *'in the back of the restaurant'* where he probably belongs... hidden-away and unseen by anyone other than those who need their plates and eating utensils cleaned... and they, the bus boys and waitresses, stand on one side the racks while Jaybird and da 'other' birds like him, stand hidden-away on the darkened side of the kitchen racks, hidden away from the light of day while cleaning pots and pans and knives and forks so the crab-shack food can be cooked and served to all those beautiful OC tourists who are hungry for more.

...now you might ask in a stage of wonder, if at all... how can a Jaybird fly free when it's caged inside a darkened space full of pots & pans and knives & forks and other such stuff?

...well, as we've seen, grounded jaybirds don't fly so well. But grounded or not, the first of the *driftwood boys* was *down de ocean* and ready to start the boys' *summer of fun*. And thus, *'da summer of da driftwood boys'* had started *down de ocean* in a little Ocean City town on the edge of the Atlantic Ocean, hidden away in *'the pleasant land of Living'*.

the boys' driftwood abode

So in the summer of 1976, four or five boys, more or less, lived in this old slightly rundown-like *yellow submarine* of a driftwood-like motel down on the shore side of downtown Ocean City that had regular motel rooms as well as some motel apartments on 2nd street, or there-about(s)... Now the apartments were especially functional for summer help looking for *cheap-ish* rooms to spend the summer in although it was only affordable to these boys, and to most working youths working the summer *down de ocean* when they were sharing costs with multiple roommates. Most of the summer help were doing this kind of thing somewhere or other in Ocean City.

So this small apartment is maybe 250 square feet of space; it's a one-bedroom flat with a double-bed sized bed with a small combined kitchen and living room space containing a small kitchen table with three old kitchen chairs right next to a living room with its old lazy-boy-like chair and rundown sofa... but it's clean enough for these runaway boys hoping for some fun '*down de ocean*' and so the apartment's décor was the least of their concerns.

Now one of these boys' more-fastidious brothers once described the bedroom inside this place, after our summer of fun, as a dirty beach where a messy brown wave of sand had washed *up & over* a dirty pile of damp bedding and old unwashed clothes cast about(s) *here & there*, which was probably about right; we weren't the neatest group of guys in the world and we certainly kept that part of the deal up.

And usually one of the guys used the bed to sleep-in although on occasions when sleeping arrangements were tight, two guys had to suck-it-up and sleep in the bed. The others were left to scramble about(s) for sleeping arrangements on the couch or in the living-room lazy-boy-like chair and when all other options failed, there was the floor... and *we-all* took a time or two sleeping there too, during the summer. But we were young and full of life so *we did as we did* with little in the way of complaints.

So obviously, there was little room to be had... but housing prices in this summer paradise could be quite expensive even back then so that's what you could get for the money most of us summertime kids had... So the boys shared it all by sucking in their belts and having a good time, at least, the best they could.

As I said, the summer at the driftwood revolved around four or five boys who made up the core of the *driftwood boys*: Johnny-boy, Bobby, Big-Al, and me & Jaybird... and then... there were the other strays who were part of this dance where these *'American kids [were] doing the best they can'*... sounds vaguely familiar, doesn't it<??>... *monkey grinder?*

Anyway(s), there was JD (briefly) and then little gorilla-Tea (later on), both stray-ass *driftwood boys* on the edge of things... and somewhere further-out along the edges there were a few other stragglers who joined us briefly, all who should get mentioned somewhere *'over the rainbow'* and down along the riverside... and yet there were even others whose aura was certainly a part of the story I wish to tell in some sense or another but who may slip-by without much color although they will always be in our hearts just the same... And yes, as has been said, this story is *'partly truth... and partly fiction'*... as some musical lyrics once *played-at*, where again, I may have borrowed these slightly fine words from a much more illustrious writer than I... so *monkey grinder* again<??>

But a fictional story it is...

So it was these boys who formed the core of this *sorta* simple-minded *'band of* slightly disturbed *brothers'* who functioned as 'one' at times... and not, at other times... although in fairness, we were much less cool than those more famous *'band of brothers'* in the 'made for TV' WWII movie called a *'band of brothers'* cause those brothers were freaking awesome for many damn good reasons... but regardless, we were a slightly disturbed *'band of brothers'* just the same; a much less cool *sorta* Ocean City *'band of brothers'* but a band just the same... and the band largely revolved around the steady hand of Johnny-boy... and then Bobby... and then the rest of the boys just seemed to spin around the edges in some way or other, and it seemed 'okay' with us cause we were a *'band of brothers'*.

Now I usually managed the sofa to sleep on if I was home in time; I left the bed for the others to fight over after all, it was a sandy mess of a room with a wall-to-wall wave of sand washing up and over the bed so *ughhh*... and the third or fourth guy grabbed the chair to sleep in while others were left scrambling for space on the floor... nice and cozy like; like the Beverly hillbillies... but without all the oil... or money...

So in a word, it was... 'filthy'... a *'teenage-wasteland'*... (again, sounds awfully familiar, doesn't it<??>)... but with laughter and fun most nights; beers and bullshit in spades... and I guess, it could have been a whole lot worst although it would have taken some effort to get there. But I imagine many of the other such apartments were pretty much the same.

Now I remember this one time during the summer when someone cracked an egg on the floor and it just sat there until it dried out and turned to dust... disgusting, right? But each one of us boys thought of the problem like this... 'I didn't do it... so... I'm not cleaning it up. Let the pig who did it, pick it up'... except of course, the dude who made the mess apparently didn't care all that much about it either... So whoever he was, he didn't pick it up... and neither did the rest of us boys.... And the dried egg finally turned to dust before our eyes. So you see, dirty & dusty were we although somehow we were neat enough to avoid bugs

& rodents so we weren't the worst..

But what made this situation even funnier to me was this: not one of the boys ever addressed the issue; we didn't yell and scream or kick-up a fuss saying *'someone is a pig and they should pick it up'*... nope... we just acted like it wasn't there... so *we-all* just walked past it like it wasn't even there for weeks until it turned to dust... and whenever anybody else came in, they'd just look at the spot and sometimes maybe, they might even point at it and ask 'why'... and then we'd all laugh... and nothing else more was said about it or done about it either.

Later during the summer in the mess that was our summer house... Bobby noticed his clean underwear was disappearing faster than he was wearing them out... or maybe cleaning them up, I don't know... but regardless, he was clueless as to what was happening to them other than his underwear seemed to be disappearing quicker than he could wear them... but the fact this place was so messy meant clothes could disappear unbeknownst to any of us which, in retrospect, seems very sad... but again... there were no fights... the boys just acted like nothing was happening out of the ordinary and we went on with our business. I found out later in time that little Gorilla-Tea was the one grabbing what he hadn't cleaned-up for himself, his own underwear. So instead, he grabbed Bobby's clean underwear as he needed them. So Bobby's missing clean underwear mystery was finally solved many years later.

Now I know the house wasn't any worse than other *'teenage wastelands'* and maybe even cleaner than some of the other waste-holes that were out there in space... after all, we were more messy than dirty, but it was all a freaking mess just the same.

This one weekend during the summer, three young ladies and two guys dropped in on us; where they all slept is a wonder cause I've blocked it out I guess, but *we-all* managed it somehow and had some fun. Anyway, these young ladies were so disgusted at the status of the house that they pitched in and helped clean it up as payment for staying for free I guess, or out of disgust, maybe. And one of our many disgusting spots in the house was the shower where our shower drain developed a mess of clogged-up hair which was so disgusting they felt compelled to at least try and clean it all up before using it since it disgusted them so... and when they had completed the shower clean-up task, they'd pulled out this huge string of mucked-up hair and stuff from the shower drain that looked like an alien life form or so; I guess some of us were already losing our hair, think me... *ughhh*. There's nothing like being bald eagles before one's time.

But again, compared to other young guys our age, we probably weren't so much worse than they were but it definitely wasn't a place to be featured in some 'Good Housekeeping' type story. So the picture of our humble abode is now complete... the boys were a bit of a mess and so was our place. So what about the main characters in this story?

Well, Bobby worked the counters and tables up at some cafeteria-like place up on 17th street or there about(s) and he'd worked there the summer before too... and he usually started just before lunchtime and he ran all day long until closing time late in the evening although he did mornings too when he was called upon to do it.

And Jaybird & I, two feathers of almost the same kind despite our different strips, we worked up at some crab-house nearby on 21st Street in the dishwashing section, cleaning pots and pans and knives and forks and other stuff... So the only girls we saw most of the time were the waitresses running in and out of the kitchen area with food in their hands too busy to notice us... So not too much action there and besides that, there seemed to be an inferred social hierarchical order at the crab house: waitresses & waiters, busboys and cooks were the 'somebodies' in this establishment while the dishwashers were at the bottom of the barrel; the kitchen help supplied what was needed but we were not to be heard from or seen as the dirty bottom of the barrel... and we worked from mid-afternoon until late at night... or until everything was cleaned-up and closed down for the night.

So the kitchen help's *'beach time with pretty young ladies'* was infringed upon in a big-big freaking way as were some of the late night parties at the jumping clubs & bars and all other such parties... mostly because we were a bit tired by the end of the night despite our youth and energy... tired, wet and dirty by the time our shifts were over, so partying wasn't always something at the top of our list of things to do for some of us when the end of the night rolled around... although we made time sometimes... but again, our dreams of the ocean fun was infringed upon just a bit by the work that had to be done.

As for big Al, he was a baker... and even though he didn't want to do it *down de ocean*, he had to settle for it because that's what his talent was; that's what he could trade for money and the hope of parties and girls although he was up at 3 or 4 in the morning and he worked all day until early evening so not too much social activity there either despite his coinage...

...and somewhere in all this, there were the others too.

So *'much of our expected late-night fun with all those pretty young ladies up on the beach'* scene wasn't as easily attained as we'd originally thought it would be although not all was lost upon us cause there was always a bit of time somewhere out there to carve out a bit of uneven fun in this Ocean City town.

And last but not least, there was Johnny-boy who worked all week up in *Charm City lifting those boxes and totting those barrels* as the saying goes, but come Friday night, after his evening shift work was completed, he was off to the races and *'down de ocean'* he'd come for a weekend of fun where we'd fill in times between shifts of work for what late night fun we could carve out with him. And with Johnny-boy, you had to be on top of your toes when he was around cause he was a hand full of activity when he was up… and he hung low when he was down. But he was the heartbeat of the driftwood boys even though he was only *down de ocean* during the weekends. So when he was there, he often times set the tone for what *hummed* during this driftwood ride of ours.

Notes: The *'American kids…'* line was triggered by a line in John Mellencamp's song *'Jack & Diane'*. The words *'teenage wasteland'* were triggered by the song & lyrics *'Teenage Wasteland'* by *'The Who'*. The *'yellow submarine'* reference is from *the Beatles*.

driftwood delights &
one sexy young lady

Now the *driftwood motel* had its delights which went along with its everyday Ocean City life... and the summer work dwellers were all part of the attraction cause people usually are.

Right next door to us there was a dude who lived there for part of the summer and he was an artist of some type, or at least, an *'artist in training'* from some art college... and he was working up on the boardwalk sculpting caricatures of the tourists, for the tourists... and when he told Jaybird and I this... we were like... "Oh while... so cool..."

In retrospect, I don't think it was so cool for this *artist-dude-in-training* as it seemed to us at the time cause I imagine, it was just as uninspiring an experience for him as our kitchen help experience was for us; 'less than thrilling'... but at least, when he was asked by the girls at those Ocean City parties 'what do you do down here?' ...he had a cool answer... whereas, Jaybird & I, *ahhh*, not so much; in fact, 'hell no'... cause it was no answer at all... cause 'kitchen help' was the bottom of the barrel when it came to OC jobs... minus, cleaning out spot-a-pots, I suppose... so I guess, maybe, Jaybird & I were higher up the food chain than that.

I mean... when a girl asked one of us what we did *'down de ocean'*... We'd start out by saying, "well, I work up at the crab shack on 21st street" ...which was usually followed by the question... "oh yeah, you a busboy or waiter?"

"Well... *ahhh... nooo... cause... I am Spartacus!!!*" we'd say, "...*da f*<king KING... of da Kitchen urchins*" ...and that was all we'd say...

which fetched us little more than an odd look or maybe a tiny... *'what da f*<k' kinda* smile from the clueless hearts prowling the boardwalk at night... sooo... not so good for luring the ladies into our arms.

But yes sir, this we could say, ladies and gentlemen... *"I am Spartacus!!! ...da f*<king KING... of da kitchen urchins"* ...at least, in our minds... which wasn't saying much.

Now next door to our artist neighbor, just a few doors down from where we lived, there were these three beautiful young ladies who lived only a few stoops away from us... and you can think of them in terms of the old spaghetti western movie called *'the good, the bad, and the ugly'*... except in this case, it's in less obvious terms... like... *'the good, the sexy, and the full-of-herself one'*.

Of the first one: *'the good'*... she was an approachable beauty who was soft on the eyes and sweet to talk to and Jaybird wasted a rare opportunity when it came his way to see and be seen with this lovely lady. They'd talk on rare occasions and minus that missed opportunity of an evening up on the boardwalk at some outside bar cafe, nothing really ever happened there. Too bad for Jaybird, I suppose. By the way, she was probably pretty damn smart too, but we rarely saw past her beautiful outside wrapper which was our failure, not hers.

Of the third girl: *'the full-of-herself one'* of a young lady... she thought of herself as better than us as if she was too good for us which we pretty much thought was a joke cause she wasn't so spectacular... well, minus the fact we were foolish-ass slobs which she didn't actually see except when she looked into our eyes and we sang out to her as sweetly as we could... So in retrospect, maybe she was better than us but that aside, 'this' pretty much wraps-up her disguise.

But it's the *second girl, 'the sexy'*, who stole my interest even though she was way-beyond my reach. Yes, *'the sexy'* one rung my bell as in, she was a *'sexy badass'* from my viewpoint... cause she was this sexy strutting young lady with a casual saunter that made me dream of *creamed corn* cause she was a *'wowww'* ten-fold over... and even though she almost never cast an eye in our direction without an 'I'm cooler than you' distain towards us which was okay with me cause... well, she was cooler than us, by a long shot... and definitely cooler than Jaybird or me for sure... and I mean 'way-cooler' than me and I knew it too... and she knew it... and the world knew it as well, if it ever bothered to look our way to see... so no hard feelings there.

And it was funny cause while the third girl who was so *'full of herself'* and acted so aloof to us, she just made me laugh at her aloofness cause she was so pathetically misplaced in her aloofness that it was hilarious... but in the case of this *'sexy badass'* one, oh, mannn... every time she walked down the street I would watch her from the distance until she walked on by, as incognito-like as I could... but my heart was pounding out of my chest while *'visions of sugar plums danced in my friggin' head '*... actually, it was more like I had 'deep lustful desires to go scuba-diving down below the water's edge and in through heaven's gate' which made me tingle with a combustible spark of life... *Yeahhh...* 'bad', right<??>... talk about *'sins of the flesh'* or a trip to the *edge of a cliff...* but *man-oh-man...* I was a goner for her.

She looked athletic; beautiful & athletic... and so sure of herself... with a slight bow-legged-ness in her stride as if she played girl's lacrosse or something like that or maybe she cycled... but there was something definitely athletic about her stance and it turned me 'on'... cause... *man-oh-mannn*, she was wrapped-up just fine.

So while some ladies flirt with their sexuality in a manner that floats and sways out before one's eyes... some ladies like her, just ooze with sexuality; they just ooze with it and this young lady did that whether she meant to or not, at least, in the eyes of this beholder.

And yes, in retrospect, and with respect to the '*#me too*' movement of today... there is and was much more to her as a person and as a young woman than just her sexual appeal but in fairness, I never really got close enough to know the depth of (or lack of depth) within this young lady and maybe that's because I failed to see the person in her in the first place... and yes *I get it*, '*my bad*'... but with this sad fact aside, I continue with my story...

And of course, no matter how I tried to disguise it, I imagine she could see the desire in my eyes even during my incognito-like stares that I thought I hid so well... and if my existence didn't disturb her enough, I'm guessing... my longing for her probably did the trick, as in: *ughhh*. There's nothing like *the uncool* drooling over *the cool* to be horribly sad.

So after a while she'd just completely ignore me while walking past so I'd do the same with her although all the while I was hiding my stare, I was stealing a longing look under the covers of my aloof disguise...

So whenever she passed close by our front stoop after that, I'd wander my gaze over at *this or that*, anything which wasn't her while in the corner of my eyes, I'd watch her sexual 'beauty' light my fire with hot burning torches that stirred my lustful desires for her... but 'never'... would I give her the direct satisfaction of knowing how she jerked my chain... although... and I say it again, she probably knew it all too well after all, a zombie-boy with foaming lust pouring from his toothy jaws is rather *friggin'* obvious to most people and especially to beautiful young ladies who probably see it all *way too damn often*.

It was *kinda* funny though... cause this one day she actually acknowledged me just so slightly when she passed me by... and afterwards, after she'd entered her abode, she returned quickly and asked me if I had a 'screen' she could use...

Now I was speechless... cause she was talking to me... as in: 'what *da f*<k*, mannn'<??>... and since I was blindly 'in lust' with this girl, I was probably a bit breathless too cause she'd talked to me... and maybe I was so speechless because I was still on a lustful high from watching her walk-on by but regardless, I had no idea why she needed a 'screen'...

...so I told her to hold it up for just a moment while I asked my roommate if we had one, as coolly as I could, of course... then I rushed inside to see if Bobby knew if we had a 'screen' she could use... thinking, 'this is my 'IN' with this sexy young lady'... as in: 'the weak (me)... and the sexy strong (her)'... will be together at long last.

So when I got inside, all breathless and all, I said to Bobby... "Hey, do we have a 'screen' for our 'lady friend' next door?"

...and Bobby says to me rather dismissively... "No"

...and of course, I'm besides himself cause I'm thinking... 'I've finally got an 'IN' with this beautiful desirous woman' who's been tickling my fancy for a while now... and now... all I've got, is 'nothing'...

...and of course, that aside... I was just a bit curious as to why she wanted a 'screen' which I took to be a 'window screen', don't know why, but what other type screen could it be, right<??>

So I was curious as to how Bobby understood whether we were all tapped-out or so, of 'window screens'... or why we'd even have an extra 'window screen' cause that just seemed a bit odd to me... cause such a thought just never occurred to me... I mean, why would she want a 'window screen'? ...and why would we have extra 'window screens'?

So in this brief moment of silence, I ask of him... "Bobby... why does she want a 'window screen'?"

...and he looks at me in a bit of disbelief... and then laughs at me slightly... "no, she wants a screen for her pipe..."

"What pipe... she smokes pipes?" ...and I'm thinking... 'pipes'<??>... as in the ones we've all seen being smoked on TV sitcoms where those old sophisticated dudes are smoking their pipes...

...and again Bobby laughs... "where have you been all these years... her pipe... for pot..."

...and I laughed at myself during this momentary quiet for being so *friggin'* clueless... *ahhh*, yes, she is definitely too cool for me... just... *way too cool* for me... hell, Bobby was too... and just about everyone else I knew seemed that way too, at least, at this moment anyway(s)... and I was ever so grateful I hadn't asked her why she needed a 'window screen' like I almost did... cause... 'that'... would have been way too embarrassing for me... even if she never looked my way again, which was the case most times anyway(s)...

So I go on out there where she stands in anticipation of a 'screen' I'm supposed to deliver-on so she can light her way up into oblivious happiness... and I'm thinking... 'okay lady, let's make-believe here, just for a moment... that I've got your 'screen' so you can light up a smoke in your hands while I go diving down into the mists of your beauty in a non-obtrusive way', assuming such can be done, way down yonder in through *heaven's gate* where we each gets something we long for... you 'the smoke'... and me, well, the sweet 'taste of heaven'... assuming it's there, of course...

But alas... it would never to be... and I had little else to say to her at that moment or ever again either cause I'm a clueless bastard who was in love with an illusion who's way-out-of-my-league anyway(s)... so the moment just slipped away and we never really exchanged too many words after that... beyond the casual 'how-do-you-do(s)' *kinda* ways imparted with just a casual nod or so, if that<??>... *Shittt, shittt, shittt... and drattts...* and there I was... *down in the front row...* oh-so close to the action and yet, I had no cigar to finish my way...

Of course, it didn't stop my lustful yearnings for her... oh-no, that would continue to consume me whenever she passed my way and I often tried to be out there on the stoop whenever she'd walk her way back from her long shifts up on the boardwalk slinging pizzas and beers for summer customers... and in retrospect, maybe that was my mistake... cause maybe, I should have had a 'screen' waiting for her whenever she walked on home during some of those nights... and then offered to rub her feet after a long pizza-slinging shift... and then after she'd cleaned up from all those pizza & beer smells... you know, maybe I'd rub her feet again, oh-so well while she lit her way up into the heavens above, all the while I'd be finishing it all off with... *well, you know<??>* ...*with a blah-blah-blah, here & there*... Although, shit, given such words, I have to wonder here... 'what *da hell* is wrong with me?'

...although, maybe... on second thought, why even have her clean up from all those pizza & beer smells cause all that fine aroma would have been just okay to keep around at one time, after all, there's nothing like eating pizza and drinking beer together to make one whole... and if you add into the mix a little bit of youthful play, well now... how bad could it be<??>... so maybe, that too, would've been just fine...

...and again, I have to wonder... 'what *da hell* is wrong with me?'

And again I say, despite what I've written here within my implicitly-lustful *play on words*... 'women are not just sexual appetizers' and I certainly knew it then when I was younger and I know it now while I am older... and despite what's been written above, make no doubt about this... *people are people* with smarts and stuff far exceeding their beautiful wrappers that covers 'the stuffing(s)' deep inside... and I'm quite sure this 'driftwood dynamite' was undoubtedly the same... smart and thoughtful, even if a little bit aloof from me... it's just that, in this story, I had a little bit of trouble getting past her dazzling wrapper's disguise to see anything else cause... mannn, she wetted my lustful desires just by walking on by me... but... and this is important to understand too... *'that was on me'*; not her... I was the one with the lustful desires or problems, not her... she was just being herself... and that's just fine too... absolutely, 'just fine'.

...but *ohhh*, how I loved that dear sweet 'driftwood dyno-mite' in my own slightly disturbed and maybe sorted *sorta* way... but as I like to say about this young lady and all the others too... with some *sorta* dulcimer-like rhythm playing in the back of my head...

'*...women are the [finest] fruit that God ever [painted] on [a] vine...*' where of course, similar words were used in the song *Berkeley Woman* (John Denver & Bryan Bowers)

...and *ohhh*, how sweet is that dulcimer when it plays that tune... talk about lustful sounds of 'the beautiful'...

Ohhh, and smart too...

And again, I mean no disrespect to the ladies out there cause there is so much more to all those beautifully smart and thoughtful ladies out in the world than just their magnificent wrappings.

Now I should mention 'this' before finishing off the driftwood characters who danced around us this summer. There was this maintenance-man like dude who worked at the hotel and apartments which made up the 'Driftwood', fixing problems as they arose during the summer season and he was just a bit older than the boys of the driftwood and he was dismissive of all of us who weren't sexy ladies of the summer too, like my *'sexy love'* I've just been talking about... So he did little for us for that matter which was just as well cause he irritated me just a bit, maybe cause he was so dismissive of us and maybe cause I thought such an old dude shouldn't be trying to carve into the action I wanted to be part of; so jealousy was probably a reason too and when he tried to make-way with my *'sexy love'*... well, that was an unforgivable sin to me which he did and I couldn't blame him for pursuing.

...but what made it worse really, or at least, was really small of me in some ways, was this dude was missing one hand due to some *kinda* accident, I suppose... so he had a hook for one of his hands... but he'd parade around the apartments without his shirt on more times than not, trying to impress all the young ladies around the motel with his mature thirties hairy-like built-up chest, I guess... with his one good arm... and with his pirate hook too, I guess... *ughhh...*

...and since I was a tall thin boy and I mean, thin... think 115 pounds on a frame of 5'8"or so... so *friggin'* thin and naïve to boot, with jealousy for a bigger sized me... but still, I was like... 'wait... he's an old *friggin'* mannn, but me... well, I'm *da man'* ...all 115 pounds of this sterling silver diamond mine as in: *'I am Spartacus*!!! ...*da f*<king KING of da kitchen urchins'*

...hardly, right<??>

And so, there it is... and there it was... some of our driftwood neighbors from a time long time ago... those slick personalities who tickled my fancy while we lived out our dreams during our *'summer of fun' down de ocean* in our little *'yellow submarine'* hidden inside this yellow boarded motel called... *'the driftwood motel'.*

...and then suddenly for no good reason I can think of... I find myself in a cloudy mist of smoke in some rundown bar where one old dude sits alone drinking a beer as slowly as illusions might do, and I think to myself, 'what da f<k - is this?'*

...and a trusty face I've seen many times before and since such times, [he] chuckles at me before turning slightly towards me, saying... "what da f<k is wrong with you?"*

Now it is at this time when it should be mentioned that this dude is someone I call 'Patty-boy'... and he is an illusion; he did exist... and then he didn't... but I still have talks with him sometimes even if he isn't here in da physical sense anymore... much to his annoyance and mine, for that matter too.

So Patty-boy is turned my way, slightly at first, like he expected me... so I'm a bit confused and a bit surprised because I don't remember choosing to be here in this scene and yet I'm supposedly writing this piece of muckish foolishness... but I see him so I know there's 'trouble a-brewing' of sorts...

"Sooo... you didn't know what a f*<king 'screen' was<??>" ...and he chuckles his kinda chuckle like he does when he knows something I don't... which in this case, he's right about.

"ahhh... well" ...and I smirk, cause obviously, my illusion is punking on me cause I didn't know what a 'screen' was... so there's that going-on...

...and again he chuckles... "You're a dick" he says.

"ahhh, well, f*<k you, mannn... how was I supposed to know?"

...and he continues to laugh at me... "I guess you wouldn't, cause you're a dick..."

...and I chuckle slightly, cause I'm a bit embarrassed by the situation... "ahhh, and f*<k you too" I say, just a bit more cutting than before...

"...and you missed out on that fine young lady cause you just didn't know shit<??> ...you're a f*<king dick"

"How about this..." ...and I pause just a bit here for affect... first looking away like I'm about to whisper a secret to him, before looking back at him with my hidden words of wisdom... "how about this... how about... I kick your f*<king ass... is that 'dick' enough for you?"

...and again, he chuckles and says to me mockingly... "yeahhh... and that's my biggest concern<??>"

...and I smirk, just a bit again... just before I transform into a fearsome bat-flying monster who's tripping about(s) on some fearsome-like musical track... and then... there's an awful sound that's reminiscent of the Batman sitcom's ass-kicking scenes from so long ago where there's a sound of a bat busting down upon some lowly scavenger down on the dusty plains below... 'crashhh... boommm... banggg...' or something like that... you know, with the words flashing across the screen like in the old Batman shows.

...and then there's a chuckle... "what da hell are you doing?"

...and again there's a... 'crashhh... boommm... banggg' ...or something like that...

And then... all is 'quiet on the western front', or something like that... for when the fearsome bat sees his prey... there's always going to be a terrible ruckus... but then, it's all over for his prey... as in: 'all over, but the crying' from such lowly scavenger-like dudes who've been knocked down below...

"Balls!!!"

"ahhh" ...I say, with pointed authority... with my hand held straight-up pointed in a dismissive fashion in the direction of Patty-boy, like a cop's hand might do when stopping the flow of traffic... "it's my f*<king show here, boy... and that's... 'that'"

...and the curtain drops before he can say another word... and this scene... is finally over.

Notes: The line *'visions of sugar plums...'* was triggered by a line in the Christmas story *'Twas Night Before Christmas'*. The *'yellow submarine'* reference is from *the Beatles*.

detour: the eclectic
Library boys

Now one might wonder as we head into the core of this storm, 'where did this odd group of Ocean City *band of brothers* come from? Where did this simple-minded grunge-like *band of brothers* who made up the core to the *driftwood boys* originate?' ... or maybe not.

...regardless, I digress for just a bit to tell a bit of the backstory to this story.

...well, we were a little bit from *everywhere in Charm City*, a bit *here & there,* but we were all from somewhere out on the southwest side of *Charm City* in *'the pleasant land of Living'* where the sun shines so brightly during the year most times, minus winter, of course...

Now there are a lot of guys I recall from my youth although in fairness, many of those guys and the specific events we shared have become a bit fuzzy with the passing of time cause with age and time, all such crystal-clear images we had back then, well, they've just faded into something like dusty black & white photographs with just a glint of clarity sometimes... all, the benefits of old-age, I suppose... but there are a few images or events from years ago that are still remembered quite clearly...

...and most present in my foggy-ass head was the *library boys* during our senior year of high school. And the guy who held this eclectic group together most times was a boy I call Johnny-boy; the same guy who led us *'down de ocean'*... and he collected this eclectic group of misfits and put them together during the senior year in high school... and we hung out in the library when we had little else to do... and we were 'eclectic' in every sense of the word because we were quite different amongst ourselves despite our one-ness; most times 'like people' usually hang together in high school because being different is sometimes considered a curse... and for those people familiar with 'the Breakfast Club' movie from years ago, it seems to have, more or less, correctly identified normal high school groups: preppies, druggies, smart students, mediocre students, loners, athletes, wall-flowers, etc., etc., etc... even if that's a little over-simplified because among other things, such groups are often times sub-divided into smaller groups... for example, not all athletes are equal nor hang together... footballers hang with footballers, basketballers hang with basketballers, etc., etc., etc.,... with some minor intermingling... and of course, location plays a part in groupings too... some are from 'above the tracks' and they hang together... and others are from 'below the tracks' and they hang together... etc., etc., etc... and that often has a bearing on who you hang with too.

Well anyway(s)... this eclectic group was mashed together from many of those stereotypes... footballers, baseballers, lacrosse players, smart students, mediocre students, guys from above the tracks and below the tracks, and different grades even intermingled too, which was weird cause usually seniors don't mix with juniors or sophomores... but we were from all over the place... and we meshed into a single group for some reason... and it mostly had to do with the personality of our ridiculous ringleader, Johnny-boy.

...and even cooler about this group was that Johnny-boy wasn't the typical domineering leader spearheading a group of ditto-heads who always followed his lead without question or objections... quite the contrary, cause he was an all-inclusive *'get your-ass over here' kinda* guy who'd *hoot-&-hollered* in a jovial type manner most of the time with just about anyone and any time... and while this group expanded and shrunk from time to time... our eclectic group mashed together even though we often had little in common other than Johnny-boy's personality.

Now we'd usually gather in the library between classes or during free time and carry on until *Brother Library*, that's what we called him in those days, came over to calm us down... and we'd smile and engage with him in light happy banter and then he'd go off after a bit, after he'd thought we'd calmed down... but sooner or later, we'd get louder again and back he'd come... and this would go on until we were finally tossed out of the library... and then we'd scatter into the hallways laughing and carrying on until the next time we'd show-up... and rinse and repeat.

And the core of the group... as I remember it, as faded a my memory is, was driven by two footballers (Johnny-boy and big Jack), two baseballers (Lew & I), a cool nondescript lacrosse player who looked like an angel who wasn't (Mikey-boy), two guys I'll call the storybook-boys for their outlandish tales they told, and then there was Bobby whom I may never have really known if not for Johnny-boy pulling us-all into this eclectic group... and Johnny-firebird, who drove a <??> ...that's right – a firebird... And then there was this last big dude who Johnny-boy always called BO-DOE... or something like that... and he said it like it was all in caps because Johnny-boy would yell it out in a deep sounding boisterous voice... as in "you da-MAN... BO-DOE"

Now BO-DOE was too big for me to call out anything to him other than 'Big-A', and in a most respectful tone least he snap my neck like a twig... and again, I use the letter 'A' because we called him by his last name... and definitely NOT 'BO-DOE', minus Johnny-boy... but he could get away with such things.

...anyway, around this core there were a few others whom I have failed to mention with NO disrespect intended... and yet there were others who came & went, sometimes a junior or so, and even an occasional sophomore too showed up while Johnny-boy held court... and as I said... there was little in common connecting most of us cause some of us were athletes, some starters & others bench warmers (me)... and we played different sports so no natural hanging mechanism there... and some were mediocre students while others were good students (again, no natural hanging mechanism there)... and some were from 'this side of the tracks' and some were from 'the other side of the tracks'... some worked after school and some didn't work after school although we most-all worked summers some way or other cause we wanted money for cars and to woo girls with, as if that was the trick; we were more or less, clueless and *we-all* definitely weren't too damn good at wooing girls either and maybe that's what we had in common, our cluelessness. Yes, one could say that 'we were clueless crusaders for girls lost in a mist of naivete'.

So from this eclectic group under Johnny-boy's guiding hand, sprang our relationships, Johnny-boy, Bobby, and myself, who would become core members of the *driftwood boys, who played down de ocean in the summer of 1976.*

A crab shack of no return

Now there was a *crab shack of no return* up on 21st street or there-about(s) that danced behind the façade of an eclectic brick exterior which seemed oddly attractive to me. And behind those walls there was a restaurant, a kitchen of some size, special dining rooms *here & there* with regular dining spaces too, and there was even some small apartments up above the restaurant which I knew little about other than some waitresses lived there or so it was rumored to be. So heaven on earth, huh<??>

And it was behind those walls where I met Reds as he was called, for the first time. He was all business-like and yet very eclectic in style and he looked *kinda* like *a long-haired hippy-dippy sweet kinda guy freak* as such may be said, but that aside, he was *da man* behind the kitchen work and he was concerned about the work ethic of his staff although in an offbeat *sorta* way. And most nights you'd see him working in and amongst us as we washed dishes & utensils and pushed them on out into the great void where meals were made and delivered to hungry customers.

So this loose scraggily guy with long messed-up red hair & beard viewed me cautiously during his *short & sweet* job interview process when I showed-up looking for a job, explaining the work and his expectations as if it were hard to grasp. "No problem" I told him cause I needed the work. So I won him over... or he needed workers bad enough that he just didn't much care but either way, I started in the hidden corners of the kitchen in one grand ole crab shack *sorta* way down on 21st street or so.

Now within a short period of time I started to realize the kitchen help positions may be the lowest form of work in a restaurant and definitely within this restaurant given the way we were viewed. But we hustled to wash and deliver the clean dishes & utensils out onto the kitchen counters where the food was made and where it was picked up by waiters, waitresses, and busboys, etc., I suppose, and delivered with customers' meals. And they, the cooks & wait-staff, seemed to form a special click amongst themselves while we were either not seen nor acknowledged most times. There were exceptions though.

And by the way, we looked different too. The wait-staff was spit & polished in their uniforms cause they were the face of the product we delivered and they were usually our age; young. And the cooks who were usually older looking than the wait-staff or us in the kitchen, [they] were also clean-looking in their pearly white outfits minus minor food spills which developed over an evening worth of work; I suppose, neatness and cleanliness were rather necessary around the food and our customers. But we, the kitchen help, we were usually dressed in jeans and tee-shirts that often got wet and messy from the cleaning machines and the food scraps we removed from the dirty plates & utensils and cooking pots too. So maybe, we looked the part of second-class citizens, don't know. Plus, our tongues sometimes wagged in less than couth-like ways too.

So anyway(s), if we nodded at one of these waiters or waitresses or cooks then we were often dismissed as mere pests to be dealt with as little as possible and so there developed a sort of us vs. them mentality which wasn't supposed to be, but it seemed to exist in most cases although again I say this, not in all cases.

Now within the kitchen area there were all kinds of personalities among the boys working back there which mixed-in well together in general, and at first we worked together sharing the tasks amongst ourselves as Reds wanted us to do... but sooner or later, type-A personalities always seem to insert themselves into places where they usually aren't needed and unless restrained by someone, they insist on going into those spots where they don't belong and in being heard in all those places as well.

So our type-A dude turned out to be a youthful tall, intense athletic-looking type boy from a state who's claim to fame is that *'it's for lovers'* of the foxtrot or so, I suppose; a good-looking boy with long flowing bleach blond hair who I sometimes referred to as Blondie. Now he started out well enough working within the confines of the kitchen as a good team member sharing duties as he was supposed to do before grabbing onto a position of pseudo-boss whenever Reds wasn't there. Not that we needed it cause we worked okay together doing what was expected of us but type-A personalities always insist on saying to the world, 'I am here' whether we care or not, and 'I have direction for you' whether we need it or not. It's just what they do.

Now I didn't really care about his bossiness cause it was not my intent on being labeled the *lord of the kitchen* like Blondie seemed to desire… and as long as he didn't tell me what to do when I didn't need his direction, I rarely said or did anything one way or another because there was plenty to do without interfering with his mouthy directions which often left him with favored jobs over other less favorable jobs as is usual with type-A personalities; they grab the easiest and best jobs while barking orders to others doing the harder and shitter jobs. But this much I can say about Blondie, besides him being a bit mouthy and bossy where it wasn't really needed most times, and other than him *snowflaking-it* by demanding his favorite job most times which was easier than other jobs we did (he liked running the hot water cleaning machines for the dishes and utensils), he worked his ass off. He was no typical *type-A talk without work* guy cause he worked hard which I respected even if he didn't share in some of the other less likable tasks *we-others* had to do; most of the rest of us worked different tasks throughout the night but not him. Blondie did what he wanted to do and *'that was that'*.

And Blondie was not just an odd piece of work in and of itself because he was attractive to some of the waitresses who would sometimes find their way back into the kitchen area where they would talk to Blondie and of course, those of us who were working around him at the time or taking a break with him at the time, we got to dance just a bit with his sweet luck and we jumped at the chance more than not. And 'this' of course, made him popular with lots of guys in the kitchen and even allowed most of us to turn a blind eye towards his bossiness cause we liked the *cast-off* attention we sometimes got under such conditions. So his lemmings became a close-knit posse because of this situation and therefore, within the kitchen there developed a split around Blondie's persona. Some loved him and some didn't, and some tolerated him and some really didn't like him, as we shall see.

Anyway(s), I thought, 'what the hell<??>… why throw away good luck when this light followed him like so, provided I didn't have to be one of his blind-ass lemmings'. Although funny enough, I don't think he ever really grasped his good fortune or maybe he just didn't care for it for whatever reasons there might be, but for the rest of us, we relished the attention he got because we benefitted from it too.

Now there was this one long-legged blond-hair beauty who seemed, at least initially, attracted to Blondie like others were but he was so enthralled with his own mystic illusion of importance that he never really saw her so eventually she ended up befriending some of us cast-aways for no good reason I could think of. And she seemed different than many of the other waitresses too. She was less involved in their waitress clique and she saw us which was always odd because in general, as I've said, we weren't seen. She was quiet and not going to college so maybe that had something to do with her not being so clique-ish with the other waitresses, don't know. But she was sweet and nice and hot as a pepper but what do two quiet people talk about to *kick-off* the ball rolling. Who knows? But she added occasional beauty to our sterile setting and it was nice for the non-Blondie types who enjoyed a bit of innocent times together in our kitchen *den of iniquity* where hormones ran higher than reality.

Anyway(s), with time as I said, Blondie gathered a troupe of lemming-like supporters who formed their own small kitchen clique of Blondie worshippers which I couldn't follow because I'm not an *ass-licker of narcissistic popular fools too blind to see what's really in front of them kinda* guy so there was *that going-on*, I suppose. Don't get me wrong, Blondie could be charming with his *'I'm a suffer-dude'* aloofness but I'm just not a follower-type of such mouthy individuals who think they know it all so I stepped my way and he and his lemmings went their way and as long as the work got done, he, they and I were okay and we avoided unnecessary confrontations so things were okay with me even if Blondie asserted his type-A personality within the work space where it didn't belong.

So, there you have it. There's the restaurant. There's the waiters, waitresses, cooks, busboys, and kitchen help. And within this restaurant there appeared to be a hierarchy with the kitchen help at the bottom of the barrel. And within the kitchen help, there were the Blondie dudes and the rest of us who all worked furiously trying to keep up with cleaning and delivering the dishes and utensils as fast as we could to the cook-areas even if we were unseen by others most times. And then there was the late-night kitchen area cleanings which the kitchen staff was responsible for; we cleaned the floors, took out the trash and made the kitchen area ready for the next day. The cooks were responsible for cleaning-up their cooking areas though. The waiters & waitresses were responsible for cleaning-up the public areas, I suppose. But we cleaned everything else in the whole kitchen area. And those chores usually ended near midnight and were usually taken on by those wanting extra hours unless none wanted it and then we were assigned those tasks randomly which made making-it to late night parties a bit tricky to do sometimes.

JD dances 'IN' thru a gate

JD became one of what I call *on-da-edge-liners* of the *driftwood boys*; he hung-out on the edge of things that was 'we'.

I met JD up at the crab shack up near 21st street where I worked; he joined us sometime during the early summer... It turns out he was a bit younger than us but he was a bigger-sized guy whose age was hidden by his physical size, so he looked older than his high school age which we didn't realize until a bit later. Apparently, he just left home during the summer after school let out and came *'down de ocean'* as we *'in the pleasant land of Living'* like to say, for the summer... we never knew why other than he did it and we never asked anything more of him cause that's not something we did; you were what you were and unless you spoke up, nothing else was said...

So I didn't know anything about him or his past when I met him... or for that matter, later on either; he was just JD... short for 'Juvenile Delinquent'. Now JD was really a rather useless worker most times in the kitchen and it's true despite the fact we didn't have to do very many complex things in the kitchen other than wash some dishes and *da such* and deliver them back to the cooking areas for usage as quickly as we could. And we were expected to hustle but JD, he'd do somethings and then he'd just slump around for a while not even hiding his laziness after that, doing nothing but avoiding work and talking to anyone he could talk to.

But for some reason I liked him although maybe it had to do with his interactions with Blondie-boy more than anything else, I guess. Plus, he had a charming dry sense of humor which usually attracts me for some odd reason; maybe because such humor is so disarming sometimes.

Anyway, as I mentioned previously, we had this guy I called Blondie, a real type A *sorta* guy with too much mouth for his own good as in: *who made you boss?* ...and for some reason JD irritated the shit out of this guy... so Blondie, after he'd asserted himself into the role of *'lord of the kitchen'*, started harassing JD for his laziness... but JD didn't let it bother him like it did others, at least it seemed so... and JD would fire back smart-ass remarks at Blondie's verbal cuts with his own dry-humor *sorta* verbal shots which made me laugh cause he was witty...

Well, sometime while I was watching this going on, I realized Blondie was going to have-at JD cause Blondie's eyes would turn blood-shot red and his face turned purple with rage when he was mad and I thought, 'oh-shit'... although JD showed no fear... nothing... no arrogance either... he'd just drop off some witty dry humor type one-liners at Blondie-boy which just seemed to irritate Blondie even more... and JD did it with little regard for its outcome which meant he was either a damn fool or a hidden badass which in retrospect, I *kinda* doubt... but anyway(s)... during this one altercation, Jaybird stepped in to run interference between the two of them; it's not clear to me anymore what happened cause it was a squabble which had been brewing for some time but knowing Jaybird, it was a sissy-ass distraction-type approach he used to distract Blondie from the altercation... and then he got JD out of Blondie's way after talking down the situation...

But the cast was set, and Blondie-boy and JD would spar occasionally thereafter on the verge of eruption very often after that with neither wanting to back down which was amusing and threatening at the same time. Where was our illustrious leader Reds, I had to wonder? Who da-hell knows cause after a while he was less visible to us in the kitchen and maybe that's because we did the work and as long as this feud and others didn't escalate any further into the view of other kitchen workers like our cooks and wait staff, he didn't know or wasn't concerned.

Now sometime during this period, I realized JD didn't have a place to sleep anymore so Jaybird told him he could stay at our place until he found something more permanent to live at although our place wasn't really all that nice since sleeping arrangements were at a premium... but it was better than sleeping out on the streets, I suppose.

It turned out JD had been shacked up with some girl for a while before; she was slightly older than him and maybe he'd followed her *down de ocean* this summer, who knows<??>... but then she threw him out on his ass replacing him with another dandy and it ate away at JD even weeks after the fact. We ran into them one afternoon on the streets and I thought JD was going to blow-up or something although the situation was defused after a bit; JD came off as a jealous lost lover which he was and he looked pitiful in this dance but then again, I guess *we-all* do when it's our turn.

Anyway(s), at our driftwood place, new guys and 'the last' guys usually ended up sleeping on the floor because there wasn't enough beds or couches or lounging chairs to accommodate us all... but as I said, I guess inside was better than outside... so after work... *we-all* walked our twenty blocks home to the driftwood and JD spent the night on the floor with us for a bit. We let him stay with us for a few days and then it turned into more days, and then into a few weeks... Bobby used to say of Jaybird that he'd bring home all the homeless dogs from the streets for saving if he could and *we-all* laughed at it, but what the hell...

It was at this time that I started to realize we may have a bit more of a problem than I initially thought cause JD was just a bit lazy most times and although I had initially thought we could help this guy, I started to think after a while that he was beyond our help cause he wasn't interested in any damn help but I didn't know how to throw him out into the street when he was just down on his luck; it's not so easy to do especially when you know he just needs some help to get back on track... just a little, maybe...

Anyway(s)... let's say that JD had hormones which were really running high and what he really wanted out of Ocean City *'was girls... girls... and girls...'* NOT that the rest of us didn't want the same, it's just that he was so focused on girls he rarely concerned himself with working or other such things necessary for eating and housing one's self... much less wooing girls.

But he could be advantageous to have around sometimes especially when it came to girls cause he had no fear... he'd just walk-on up and talk to any of the girls at the crab shack even though most of the waitresses wouldn't have anything to do with us, the kitchen help, or him... but persistence sometimes pays off and it did for him in some ways although not as much as he wanted.

So this one day, we got up to work early enough to get some food before work; this crab shack served their workers some early lunch food when you arrived early enough to get it before business started and even if you were working later in the day, you were allowed to arrive early for lunch and get something to eat and then go elsewhere until your shift started later in the day.

...now keep in mind, there seemed to be an inferred-type social hierarchy which was held-to within this restaurant most times: waiters, waitresses, cooks & busboys were at the top of the pyramid for summer hires while kitchen help was at the bottom of the barrel... So we often kept to ourselves while the waiters and waitresses intermingled.

But this one day we got our food up in the worker's lounge and we're there eating when two pretty waitresses sit down at two open seats next to us which I can't remember ever happening before and they are talking among themselves as if we weren't even there when JD injects himself into their conversation which puts one of these ladies off... as in: 'who *da hell* are you?' ...but JD... was JD... and he didn't care...

...but the other young lady takes a bit of a shine to this interaction and eventually to Jaybird for some *friggin'* reason we couldn't fathom even though it was JD who initiated the activity and I'm like 'what *da hell*<??>... so the *put-off* young-lady departs after a bit for whatever reason it was, and the cheery one, I called her *Carolina-blue* cause she was going to North Carolina for school, [she] stays behind and entertains us for a bit longer with tales of her game until she too, is finally grabbed-up and pulled-away from us by the other *put-off* waitress and they disappear into the cavernous reaches of the restaurant... but not before Carolina-blue smiles a come-on at Jaybird, leaving him an irresistible calling card for some time out along the boards sometime later, I suppose.

...what *da hell*<??>

So JD and I sat there a bit dejected for a while as Jaybird smiled like a *chessy* cat... 'who's - da *friggin'* man now... boys?'

But as I said, such slow starts never stopped JD... cause he'd use whatever opportunities presented themselves, *striking-out as he goes* until he was rejected or accepted but at the very least, he was up there taking his swings at love with no fear of loss. Unfortunately for him, this type of *meet & greet* opportunity at the restaurant was usually too early for him most days so he rarely made it up there to cast his irresistible net of love out among these beautiful ladies. Moreover, despite his swings at the plate, he usually failed to hit the ball so he was swinging and missing most times cause he couldn't seem to reign in his charms enough to win at the game.

(cc) de omega man at the crab shack blues

Now in one of those chitter-chatter-like ways it all goes sometimes when reflecting on a memory with just a bit of 'Settings' replication going-on...

It just so happens that during this summer *'down de ocean'*... a band of gypsies played at summer work in this ocean-side town of Ocean City... and I had the luxury of working at this 'famous' crab shack down there, down by the sea somewhere in the east corner of *this* little old... *'pleasant land of Living'* of ours... and there in our mists... *[there]* was this dude we called... the *'Omega man'*... whatever the hell that means.

Now don't get me wrong, I knew about Charlton Heston and the *Omega man* from a thousand years prior when I was even younger than I was *[in this kitchen setting]*, but this was Ocean City... and in this rather famous crab shack where we worked, he was our *Omega man*.

So at this famous crab house, there was this one dude, a cook, who made me laugh on occasions... He was a bit older than most of us and he had a cool dry sense of humor about him; low-keyed but funny if you listened to him when he cracked wise at you... and sometimes when I'd drop by his food station with my stack of plates I was delivering to the food-chefs working with him... he'd say... *"I... ammm... deee... Omega... man..."* and I'd laugh... because - there I was... delivering this stack of plates to his station that was making something or other and I didn't know what the hell they were making either, but 'something'... and he was talking such shit to me while stuffing those plates with whatever he was 'making' at his station.

So he laughed and I laughed and we went on with our duties...

You see, we had food stations all over the place in the kitchen area and it was our job (da lowly dishwashers) to clean the plates and utensils in our area and then deliver all *dat stuff* back to the various food stations so the cooks and waiters and waitresses could grab and run with it-all, as was needed... and so again I say, when I'd approach his station, he'd announce to the whole damn world within earshot of us... *"I... ammm... deee... Omega... man..."* and again, I'd laugh... again... and again... and again... and it would repeat more often than not throughout the night since I suppose, I encouraged him with my laughter.

...and sometimes I'd add onto his play of words with my own words... "And I am Spartacus... KING of da Kitchen urchins" and we'd chuckle at our charming humor whether others got it or not.

Of course, after a while... how funny can the same line(s) be<??>... so I'd direct my *drop-off* activities to other areas within the kitchen so I'd get a break from him and *our bit of funny...* after all, how could I just stop laughing at this odd line he was delivering to me when I'd already approved of it with my laughter before... *or added to it with my own lines... all of which would've* seem rude, right?

Now, if I'd been a different kind of person then maybe I would have cut it off after a bit... like... *'reallly, mannn... I get it... you're... deee... Omega... mannn...* enough already' ...but that's not me... or maybe I could have sung-out even louder than I did... *'hey, I'm Spartacus... KING of da friggin kitchen urchins' but then again, that's not me either...* and so I diverted my *drop-off* activities when I could after the first few times of his 'omega man' stuff and then let others stuff his area with our stuff *for a while...* and then I'd show back-up at his station later in the evening when his line was fresher... *righttt*<??>... but it worked somehow.

Pie Face Al

The setting is a group of guys sitting around a small OC apartment drinking some beers and talking some shit like they do on such occasions. And within this group is Johnny-boy, Bobby, me, and big-Al, and a few others as well.

Now... Bobby and I met Big Al at CCC which *we-all* laughingly called USC sometimes (the University of Southern Catonsville) or UCLA (the University of Catonsville, Left of Arbutus)... funny right<??>... or not<??>... anyway(s), he'd been a friend of a friend at school there and we just started hanging out sometimes. He was a lovely person if ever there was such a person; he was nice-looking dude and a bit of a sweet-heart with a heart of gold who could kill you with too much love and kindness sometimes even if you really didn't care to see it or have it. But he was a really nice guy. A bit shy most times and a bit tongue tied around women but a really nice guy.

And he'd been a construction worker for a while and a baker too, and he'd done that for some time although he didn't really like baking so much especially with the hours being so much earlier than others because he hated waking up in the middle of the night to start the baking routines; I think his father had been a baker and thus he learned the trade from the old man. So when he heard we were going on *down de ocean* for the summer, he asked to share some time down there with us initially theorizing he'd work up in *Charm City* during the week and then come *down de ocean* on the weekends for fun, much like Johnny-boy was planning on doing. But somewhere in the march through time, he decided to quit his job up home and join us down there full time.

And when he got *down de ocean,* he absolutely didn't want a baking job but he was trained in it and eventually that's what he'd do, glamorous or not... I guess he could have done the stuff I was doing cleaning pots and pans or waiting on tables like Bobby was doing... but I guess not, so he took the early morning hours and he always thought he was missing-out on all of our late-night parties which just didn't happen as much as he thought was happening for us.

Now this one night while we were talking shit together after a few too many drinks had loosened our tongues, this friend of big-Al tells us-all one of the funnier big Al stories which ultimately earned him the label 'Pie Face Al' with us...

You see, one night as the story goes, big Al had been at some high school party and he ended up being with some young lady in some *kinda* intimate *sorta* way for a bit, just eating some pie with her; they went upstairs for a bit of youthful glory and then he went downstairs for a bite to eat on what he thought was some fruit-filled pie, I think... which oddly enough, turned out to be somebody else's sour cream pie... So, there he was, face down eating someone's else's cream pie which he'd failed to recognize for some reason while he was there. Nope, cream pie is not fruit pie and when it's someone else's sour cream pie... well then, it can be very messy.

And of course, at the time he didn't know he was eating someone else's sour cream pie but it turns out this sweet heart of a young lady had worked these two guys into her schedule in consecutive type order in some *kinda* different *sorta* way and poor old Al was second in line, face down in all that sour cream-pie.

Sooo... if we assume I'm not talking about any *sorta* regular type cream pies here, or fruit pies, then you probably see big Al's dilemma... cause otherwise, it's not such a problem depending on your taste buds, I suppose... but this kind of sour cream-pie is just a little bit too far 'out-there' for most of us to eat upon and that was certainly the case for poor old Pie-Face Al.

Anyway(s)... when we heard this story about big Al's pie eating on someone else's sour cream-pie situation while we were under the influence of some alcohol-laced laughing gas that was coursing through our system... well, besides a brief moment of complete silence and disbelief at the story's conclusion, well, we erupted into grand laughter... cause hell, it's funny, right<??>

Now big-Al had stepped out when the story was first being told but he stepped inside the room at just about this moment when the story was concluding... and he heard the finishing lines and I imagine he knew the damn story all too well... and all the while we busted loose laughing at poor big-Al's dilemma, he got redder than an apple at our laughter which is understandable cause he was embarrassed by the story and we were laughing at his poor unforgettable situation... and for a while, we really howled and crowed on about it as he got redder still...

...but amusingly, he didn't kick our asses which may have crossed his mind cause while he was a sweetheart of a dude as I've said before, he could drop the hammer down on you too, when the time arose.

It turns out that during the night of his cream pie eating situation, the other dude found out about poor old Al's dilemma and he busted-on big-Al's chops for eating his cream pie in front of all these other guys at the party which was a mistake because despite big-Al's sweet disposition, 'he was no one to f*<k with' as they say on the streets... so big Al busted that mouthy boy's chops up real bad which just goes to show, be careful of the fool you're busting-on cause he may have crocodile teeth, 'all the bigger to bite your face off with' which is what big-Al did to that dude.

But for us, he didn't do it. He just got redder than before and maybe there were reasons for it and maybe not. Anyway(s), it must have been tough on him that night but after the initial exposure, we didn't abuse him about it all that often afterwards although we'd laugh at the story occasionally when he wasn't around sometimes... and sometimes, we kid him lightly too, but only within our group cause we weren't the types to embarrass each other in public like that; we kidded each other but we didn't embarrass each other with others outside our circle.

But it was a funny story to us... and sometimes, we'd indirectly kid him about it by calling out to him on occasions... "hey, pie-face Al"... or we'd say some 'idiot-like' stuff like... "hey Big Al... did you get pie-faced tonight?"... or even... "hey Big Al... we(s) going to get pie-faced tonight, you want *in on it*?"... and other such stupid-ass stuff even though we weren't going to eat somebody else's sour cream-pie or at least, if we could help it we weren't... in fact, I think you could say, we preferred fruit-pie instead...

Now this kidding routine was especially active when Johnny-boy had gotten a few beers in himself cause he'd kid big-Al about it but again in fairness, not *denigratingly-so* cause we weren't that way with each other. But Johnny-boy definitely messed-around with big-Al... and Big-Al would always get a little red and probably felt like kicking Johnny's ass for it but he never did... he'd just get a little red and maybe laugh in embarrassment and that's all.

But like I've said, Big-Al had a heart of gold... and when you were his friend he'd put up with a lot of crap if you weren't cruel... and despite it all, we really loved him, *we-all* did.

We'd always slap him on the back after such a mess-around and say... "*ahhh*, Big Al, you *da f*<king* man... *one pie-eating f*<king man from la muncha* maybe, but *da mannn*" ...or some such shit... but again, we only said it amongst ourselves and not out among others who didn't need to know... and like I said, we didn't mean it in any denigrating *sorta* way either cause we weren't like that to each other, never, at least as far as I knew. That's not to say we didn't kid each other cause we did, but we just didn't denigrate

each other especially when we were outside our group.

Yes, we'd hoot and holler at each other's messes but then we'd always end it all by saying something like *"shit mannn, you da friggin' mannn"* ...and we'd all laugh and carry-on some more about something else, usually going-on in another direction. But our laughter was never about making someone feel bad about themselves cause that wasn't us; you just took your abuse and the next time it was someone else's turn, but never... did we ride a guy into the ground cause it wasn't our style and again, we never opened anyone of us up to any kind of denigration especially in front of others either, nor for a cheap laugh. We were brothers of a sort, and *'that was that'*.

...and that's, how Big-Al - became known to us as *Pie-Face Al...*

da driftwood dangler
emerges from the dark

Speaking of our messes... A bunch of us were outside our apartment this one night just talking with some girls who were passing by; you see, we'd hang-out on the front stoop sometimes... maybe just one or two, or more sometimes... and we'd talk... and if a few of God's finest creatures just happened to pass us by... well, we'd try our opening bit on them usually with poor results but on occasion, someone(s) would actually stop and talk with us for a bit... and this was just one of those nights... a small group of God's finest creatures dared to stopped and talk with us.

Sooo... there we were... talking it up with a few lovely young ladies when one of our crew stumbled to the door cause he'd finally realized there's activity going-on outside the door and I suppose, he wanted to join in on the fun... so this *'Jaybird of a fool'* stumbles to the door stretching his neck out like a long neck goose to see what's going on outside...

...and there... in all the glory of this partially lit screen door with the corner streetlight casting it's shine down in his direction, up against the darkness of the night, stood our dude in just his underwear draws...

...and after a moment of silence... *we-all* laughed a bit at him... or chuckled... at the unexpected sight of him... and Johnny-boy calls out to him, in-between our laughter... "hey dangler... put your damn pants on, boy..."

...and again, *we-all* laughed... well, I don't know about the young ladies cause they were probably suspicious of us all-along... but we did... cause *da dangler* didn't mean anything by it all, it's just that when the Jaybird thought he smelled this activity outside the door he must have thought in a moment of glee that maybe he should join in on all the reindeer fun, forgetting he was not quite in vogue for such a meeting.

So anyway(s)... *da dangler* looks down at himself and in a deprecating chuckle at himself, trying to dismiss the foolishness he'd created, he says... "well hell... they're as long as my bathing suit, right<??>"

"Well... then..." says Johnny-boy... "...your bathing suit is too damn thin... so go put some damn pants on, boy..."

...and again, *we-all* laugh at him, at least, the *driftwood boys* who were standing outside... and *da dangler* stumbled back into the apartment looking for his pants like a blind man in a hurry to find some gold... cause *'there's gold in dem hills'* as they say except of course, the only gold here were the charms of a few beautiful specks from God wonderful hands.

Meanwhile, the girls say to us they'd better be moving on... and we plead with them to stay and have a drink with us... cause... well, we were loved-starved fools looking for love or attention at least, and they were just the kind of attention we were looking for...

But... they do a sweet dance around us and excuse themselves from our clutches and move on down the sidewalk... out & up towards the boardwalk... and we chirp a bit at each other and them as they walk away, throwing last minute sweets into the air as they make their way up the street which probably sounded more like boyhood 'foolishness & desperation' which it was...

...and then out into the night stumbles *da dangler* with his pants on but still with no shirt, I guess he didn't have time to get fully dressed or maybe he thought his skinny-ass torso would be so intoxicating good to at least one of those beauties that he'd be swept away into her arms for a night of love unlike any he'd ever known before.

...but they were gone... almost out of sight on up the street...

So *da dangler* yells out into the air where we stood... "*whattt<??> da hell*" ...with his hands swung up in the air while he looks their way... "why did you leave?..." he asks.

"You, numb-nuts... what the hell were you doing..." asks Johnny-boy... "we were dancing a nice dance until you screwed it up"

Well, that was only partially true cause we weren't very good at dancing any kind of dance most times even though we often tried... but *da dangler's* dangling didn't help things either, I suppose...

So *da dangler* calls on up the street anyway(s), after his chuckle with the guys, and out towards those intoxicating fine beauties floating along up the street... "*heyyy*... sweet ladies... I didn't mean nothing... come on *backkk*..."

But they were way-up the street and though they turned and laughed and waved, they just kept on walking on up the way...

...and Johnny-boy chuckles at Jaybird late words and says "You're okay Jaybird, no matter what others say". And all the guys laugh at their plight.

"Okay... but if you change your mind... we'll be dancing on down here awhile longer..." yells *da dangler* up towards those young ladies.

...and he puts his one arm up in the air again as he calls on up to them... making the two fingers *'hanging sign'* so often associated with the Hawaiian surfers... I guess, he was trying to be cool despite his un-coolness... and of course, *we-all* laughed... cause that's what the *driftwood boys* did when one of us screwed up... we laughed at the absurdness of the other... and then we slapped him on the back and said... "well done, numb-nuts...

well-done" ...which we didn't literately mean but despite all our screw-ups... we usually had each other's back.

And so that's how Jaybird came to be known as *'da dangler'*... and how... and why... we sometimes responded to each other's 'what *da hell* you doing now' query with a...

"...just dangling, brother... just dangling"

...and we'd do it with his old *'dangling surfer' like* sign *'da dangler'* had stolen from those Hawaiian surfer-dudes... so you see, sometimes... stolen signs can be a blessing... cause we weren't too damn cool but those surfer dudes were [cool]... so maybe, we thought, it would rub off on us... Of course, *cool - we never were* regardless of any cool surfer-signs we tried using but it never stopped us from trying...

...but still, one has to admit, or not, I suppose... that the two fingered 'hanging' surfer sign is just plain cool... at least, I think so... and since I'm writing this foolishness... it's *friggin' cool* within this mess.

...and then suddenly for no damn good reason I can think of, I find myself in a cloudy mist of smoke in some rundown bar where one old dude sits alone drinking a beer as slowly as illusions might do, and I think to myself, 'what da f*<k - is this?'

...and a trusty face I've seen many times before and since such times, [he] chuckles at me before turning slightly towards me, saying... "what da f*<k is wrong with you?"

Now it is at this time when it should be mentioned that this dude is someone I call 'Patty-boy'... and he is an illusion; he did exist... and then he didn't...

So Patty-boy is turned my way, slightly at first, like he'd expected me... although once again, I'm a bit confused and a bit surprised too because I don't remember choosing to be here in this scene and yet I'm writing this piece of muckish foolishness... but I see him so I know there's 'trouble a-brewing' of sorts...

"Sooo... who da f*<k is this Jaybird dude<??> ...cause I don't remember any such dude although I remember such goofiness" ... and he chuckles his kinda chuckle he does when he thinks he knows something I'm pretending not to know or something... which in this case, is 'may-be' right.

"ahhh... well" ...and I smirk, cause obviously, my illusion is punking on me again cause... well, he can, I guess...

...and again he chuckles... "You're a dick"

"ahhh, well, f*<k you, mannn... maybe you don't remember everything you think you do<??>"

...and he continues to laugh at me... "yeahhh, right... I think I'd remember him if he were there..."

...and I chuckle enough to cut him off cause I'm a bit embarrassed by the situation and don't want to hear his shit right now either... "well, you ever heard of fiction? ...cause it works pretty damn well, if you get my drift"

...and he chuckles just a little... "Yeahhh... I've heard about it but you are too damn dick-da-fied to write any damn good fiction... or truth, for that matter"

"How about this...then<??>" ...and I pause just a bit here for affect... first looking away like I'm about to whisper a secret to him before looking back at him with my hidden words of wisdom... "how about this... how about... I kick your f*<king ass... is that 'dick-da-fied' enough for you"

...and again, he chuckles and says to me mockingly... "yeahhh... and that's my biggest concern<??>"

...and I smirk, just a bit once again... as I reach for my eraser cause I know if he dares to utter another word that I'm going to erase his friggin' mouth for good.

"yeahhh, you're a..."

But he doesn't get to finish his line cause there's a scratch-scratch-scratch of my eraser on the paper and Patty-boy is now an illusionary figure without a mouth.

And I smile at my victory... "Say it again, Mr. Monkey, and I'll bust your friggin' head... or - erase your damn mouth."

...and the curtain falls silently upon a darkened... and now silent stage.

JD and his lost love

There's two guys walking on-down one of those Ocean City streets one afternoon when they spot a couple walking in the other direction on the other side of the street... well, actually JD spots them cause I'm just walking and talking to myself on such occasions cause JD is a dude of few words unless he's using his dry sense of humor or is making fun of something or making-way with a beautiful young lady who grabs his attention when all of a sudden, JD sees the girl on the other side of the street and he knows she's his old girlfriend who'd thrown him out of her apartment after she'd had enough of his shit, I suppose... anyway(s), he's still got a dying flame for her or he possesses a jealousy for her or something like that cause he starts running his mouth loud enough to override me and most anyone else who's around...

"There's that *[lovely lady]* who threw me out" ...which isn't entirely correct phrasing cause his words were more caustic than that.

"What?" I say...

"There's that *[sweetheart]* who threw me out... and she's sucking on him now" ...which again, isn't entirely correct phrasing cause his words were more caustic than that.

...'what *da f*<k*', I think, and 'what a *friggin'* prick JD is being right now' as I spot the couple across the street walking our way but again, on the other side of the street... and I can see the girl is taken a-back by JD's *[loving]* words but the guy she's with, not so much, cause now there's a street challenge going on and it can only be settled one way if this *tither-tather* continues...

So this guy she's with, he's parading along with her in jean cut-offs with no shirt on, showing off his upper torso for all to see and love or fear, I suppose... or at least, for all those *finer rose peddles* drifting along these same OC streets to love, maybe<??>... and/or for all those *stubby guy-like rose stalks* to fear and quake at his bravado, maybe<??>... although I don't really know, but either way, he holds his daring & piercing eyes staring at JD intently as if to be saying 'keep it up asshole, and you'll be under my *ass-thumping gone wild*'. There's nothing like two peacocks putting on a show for themselves and others to see.

"*ssshhh...*" I whisper... "What are you trying to do, JD<??>... get yourself killed?"

"She's the one who threw me out... and for that guy<??>... what *da hell*"

"Okay... okay... okay..." I whisper in a strained voice trying not to be heard by anyone but him... "Just let it go, mannn... cause you are barking up the wrong tree here"

"What's he going to do?" he says...

"How about this... beat your *friggin'* ass... you see the size of that dude?"

"So what... I'm not afraid of him" he says more boastfully now except I know he's out of his element; he's letting his jealousy eat at him in the wrong direction and at the wrong time cause this guy doesn't appear to have the physique of one who cares what JD thinks... in fact, I can see she's holding onto this guy a little tighter and is whispering to him something which seems to be defusing the moment on their side of the rift which is pretty damn sweet given what JD has already said about her in such nasty ways.

It's funny how jealousy of a former lover can eat away at us and make us stupid-nuts when we should probably be moving on but in JD's case, he hasn't really been able to hook up with another young lady to diffuse the memory of her so all he has when it comes to romantic entanglements is the memory of one lost love, her, I suppose.

"Keep quiet, mannn... or he's going to bust your *friggin'* ass... so let it be"

...and for some reason, JD pauses with his personal attacks against his jilted lover although he returns the other parading marauder's glare as she pulls him along while I try to talk some sense into one jealous fool of a boy as we walk along...

...and then for some odd set of reasons and circumstances I don't fully understand... me and her, the two peacemakers, are transported into a free-fall zone type-void where's there's only us... and for some unknown reason, we look at each other out of curiosity maybe, with all this pent-up energy from avoiding this ridiculous collision of sorts... and I notice she's pretty damn hot although not entirely my type, nor me hers either, but in this rough and tumble moment that's been avoided with her macho man more interested in parading like a peacock and my buddy doing whatever fools in love do under such circumstances, [we] rush together - planting our lips together while grabbing on for dear life in a hormonal rush that releases all of our pent-up fearful energy which is now exploding within us... and then... there's a moment of guilt after this cause she's JD's soft spot and what I've just done is smash da *bro-code* (no touching another guy's heart throb until it's all but gone)...

But 'it is' [done] or so I console myself... and she's done with him now so why should the *bro-code* still be in effect?

...cause it is! ...cause he's still not let go of a love that's gone... so there's no touching... and now I feel guilty for my imagined transgressions even though it's only make-believe...

No matter though, cause she decidedly uninclined to spend even a second with me so there's *that going-on* too... and for me, the moment is gone too, although for some reason I hold a touch of fascination for her cause she's someone who's enchanted poor old JD to his very core, so she's intriguing to me for some odd reason... but in the end, it does nothing for either of us and 'it's all gone'...

So she parades away with her preening peacock stud who will one day walk away from her too... all, in the dance of love. But such peacocks as this guy are temporary as she will find out shortly.

...and I walk away with JD who's still lost in love with a girl who's moved on from his touch like it does sometimes when you're in love with a dream who's moved on from you while you foolishly cling to *what can never be again...*

Sooo... I think the peacock won... just saying... at least, in the short term.

...and so, we four people, two people on either side of the street, pass each other by without much more going-on than that, and we never see each other again... but *ahhh*, what an enchanting light she must have been for dear-young JD... *and what an ass JD had been to her this day.*

Carolina Blue at the crab shack blues

Now Carolina-Blue was a sexy reddish-blond hair beauty who seemed to light up an area when she was around; she's sweet and pretty and approachable like some of the other waitresses weren't although if not for JD, Jaybird would have never made contact with her; he's too much of a dweeb to make such a toss.

So Jaybird and I are sitting in the crab house's lunchroom this one morning just eating some free pre-work employee food when she spots *da dangling Jaybird* from across the room and she gives him her pretty smile which makes me gag just a little. It just *kinda* makes me sick when he gets so lucky cause, why him? I'm here for Christ-sake. So as we talk at the morning table I catch Jaybird casting a sly smile her way on occasions and I just want to smack his ass for being such a *dweeber*... but for some reason, he completes the pass and she eventually comes on over to our table...

"Hey..."

"Hey back" says one *dweebish* Jaybird fool with a crooked sly smile going-on.

"My friends and I are having a party tonight upstairs at the apartments... so if you want to come over, I'll see you there"

And Jaybird lights-up even though he's trying to be low-key in his joy cause, 'wowww'... she's a knock-out of a sexy lady and she's asking him to a party where mostly wait-staff are allowed to go so he's almost made a homerun toss here although I have confidence in his abilities to turn this short-term win into a big fumble cause in the end, failure awaits his every turn... well, maybe not although it would be fair to assess this situation as so... but then again, maybe I say 'it' cause I want him to fail so he's not into what I can't imagine getting into... so there's *that going-on* I suppose...

"Sounds good, I'll see you there, if I can make it..."

...'all yeah, he'll see you there if he can make it'... really<??>... pish-posh, who's he kidding... he'll be there *'with bells on'* as they say, if he can muster the nerve to dance-out into those forbidden caverns where the wait-staff plays but I'm betting 'not'... he'll start the journey but in the end, *'he's a no show'*, no doubt about it...

So she leaves after a few more words and her come-on smile is teasingly good at drawing out the wicked in us... hell, she wasn't even talking to me and yet I'm almost wet in anticipation myself... so what the hell... maybe<??> ...it's just me but...

"You're not going are you?" I ask...

"What makes you say that fool... she's hot... and she wants me..."

"*yeahhh*, in your dreams dweeb-boy... you got no chance of dancing with her..."

...and Jaybirds laughs at me and says... "well, I'm on-deck, small-fry... I'm on f*<king deck..."

So lunch turns into a stroll along the boards with some early afternoon beach time before heading back for our shift in the kitchen where we dance to the tunes of the dish-washing machine and the sounds of Blondie's pleasant orders bossing many of the others around.

But come the late evening rush, Jaybird works on Reds, our real boss who Blondie sometimes forgets is our boss, and he's out of the kitchen before we start our late evening cleansing of the joint. But still I have faith, he'll chicken-out, I just know it... cause he's got no guts to dive out onto the edge where the beautiful play at fun.

So I languish in this joint wiping down the place, me and Blondie and a few of his lemmings that follow his lead, cleaning it up for tomorrow's new day.

And afterwards, I head home much later in the evening than I care to, tired and wet from soap & water and the grind of our day in the kitchen... and then afterwards, I park myself on that pathetic stoop of ours just outside our front door and I drink a tall one or two while looking up into the skies for some of those slippery late-night stars that sometimes evade our Ocean City lights... hoping against nothing that Cinderella from a few doors down will come walking on-down the street in that sexy stroll of hers, just turning my head ever so slightly while jerking my chain... or maybe seeing Jaybird coming home *with his tail between his legs* might lighten my mood as well. So... jealousy, maybe<??>

But Cinderella doesn't show this evening even though I know she'd pay me no mind even if she did show... and Bobby must have been busy too cause he's not around... ditto Big Al... and Johnny-boy is up in *Charm City* working cause it's a weekday night... so I sit there and absorb what there is to absorb with no one around to talk shit with and just before I'm about to slip back into the house to tune it all out for the night... here's come Jaybird walking down the street toward our driftwood abode... and I smile a sly smile cause did he<??> ...or didn't he<??>

"So how did you blow it, you dweeb?" I ask.

...and he laughs a giggle like one hiding a hidden treasure...

"So... did you make it with her?"

...and he smiles like a sly-dog hiding a secret and shakes his head... "none of your *friggin'* business..."

And he stops at the stoop and looks at me and my dead beer, "you got another one in there?"

"*yeahhh*, you get it though" I say... and I sit back down on the stoop again.

So he pops up in through the door and grabs two beers out of our refrigerator and pops down on the edge of the front step stoop next to me

"So what's your night like?"

And I laugh just a bit... "what do you think? charming, of course... and, you?"

...and Jaybird smiles the smile of a dirty-dog although I suspect he's throwing me a curveball cause he's got no game. If there's anyone who could swing and miss on such a beautiful light, it's definitely him... well, and me, of course... but I wasn't at bat this time so it's got to be him this time.

"So nothing?" I ask...

"Nothing you need to hear about" he says with a sly smirk of a man in love with a beautiful woman.

"yeah-yeah-yeah... you never even got close to *that thing*..."

...and the boy smiles a deceptive *kinda* smile... "you'll never know..."

"*yeahhh, yeahhh, yeahhh...*"

...and he tips his beer before saying... "I've got some Carolina sunny-like blues coursing through my veins tonight, bro"

And I laugh at his foolishness... "*Yeahhh*, my ass..."

...and *blah-blah-blah*... goes two lost boys. talking shit at each other with no chance of any more detail being exposed or doubtful charges being made which we both know isn't the truth anyway(s)...

...so Jaybird deflects what probing charges I make even though we both know none of it could have ever happened anyway(s), but in a dream of his. So nothing more is known about Jaybird's latest dance which was played-out behind the *screen of the unknown.*

...but I've got my suspicions... cause *'he ain't got no game...'*

(cc) The 'boys of the driftwood' on a boardwalk prowl

Now in one of those chitter-chatter-like ways it all goes sometimes when reflecting on a memory gone by...

Down in the little seaside town of *Ocean City*, a group of boys... four score and a thousand years ago... spent a summer running the streets together, in the chase of fun, girls, and parties although what they eventually found instead, were memories for their old aged amusement.

So there we were in *Ocean City* and when our weekend evenings came around *assuming* we, the *'boys of the driftwood'* weren't still working... or if we were done working and it was still before the midnight hour had expired then we, the *'driftwood boys'*, would prowl the boardwalk after dark looking for some fun which we hoped would include the charms of some sweet young ladies.

But in fairness, we were often abject failures at it and there were some real good reasons for it too, like we were morons... complete and utter morons on the prowl with little to be gained but the laughter in our friendship which in retrospect, wasn't so bad.

So this one night when we had consumed some liquid courage in a bottle or two, we went cruising the boardwalk looking for some fine young ladies who might be susceptible to our charms when we happened upon this group of young ladies who smiled at our initial advances... just enough that we felt encouraged to stop and chat with them for a moment.

So there we were, looking good... and feeling good... and totally full of ourselves... when *Jaybird* lets some dumbshit intro-like words spring forth like so...

"Hi-tty Hi there... young ladies... how do you do tonight? ... cause you are definitely, the brightest stars we've seen out on this boardwalk tonight"

And Johnny-boy laughed in one of his short huffing sort of laughs... as in... or like... 'Really<??> ...*Jaybird*... Are you for real? We can take you out but we just can't let you loose or you'll kill our buzz with the ladies' ...*kinda* laugh.

So in order to break this 'loose-cannon' moment *Jaybird* had created, Johnny-boy says to the young ladies... "Mannn... please excuse my friend, cause he's an idiot" And the *driftwood boys* laughed at 'this bit' cause it was true... and *Jaybird* knew it cause his smoothness at that very moment had not been his finest effort.

Now some of the young ladies just laughed it off as if to say... 'whattt *da hell*<??> ...just another foolish boy with little to offer' although the others just looked and thought, I'm assuming... 'What a dick'... which probably was dead on.

But not to be out done... Bobby would shortly show his charming wit as well.

So the conversation continued... despite *Jaybird's* inadvertent effort to derail this engagement... and somehow the conversation turned towards what our past studies had been in high school... for it was one of those conversations where you're feeling each other out, looking for some common ground on which to build something on when one of the girls says something like... "Yeah... I took French" ...and she asks of us... "Do any of you know French?"

And then Bobby, he shined like the star he was... "Oh yeah" ...he says... "I know how"

And of course, at that moment, we couldn't help ourselves anymore... we fools, the foolish *'boys of the driftwood'*... the foolish boys that we were, we howled *with delight* at the wittiness of his conversational piece for we were the four musketeers of love... okay, maybe there were more with us there that night but nothing could keep us down except for maybe, ourselves.

And this time, Johnny-boy didn't even try to diffuse this latest comment cause it was so foolishly hilarious to us that it was beyond fixing... "French... I know how"

Needless to say... the young ladies departed ever more sure that the banter of the *'driftwood boys'* was, at the very least, worthless & childish... and not worth pursuing any further and so we walked on down the boardwalk laughing to ourselves, actually, howling at the witty banter which we had laid down upon those sweet young ladies almost clueless of the fact that we were walking by ourselves... on down the boardwalk without the charms of those sweet young ladies we had been trying to woo.

But we could not be held down... no way... cause for the *'boys of the driftwood'*, the night was still young and all we had to do was find some other unsuspecting young ladies who could not resist our charms, our coolness, our wit... and we were sure... oh-so sure... that they were out there somewhere, yet to be discovered.

And such was the *'stroll of foolishness'* by the *'boys of the driftwood'* on their boardwalk prowl, on this one night... a *longgg* time ago... in the beautiful seaside town... of *Ocean City*.

JD dances 'OUT' thru a gate

Other than girls, JD's real desire was fishing and he wanted to work down on the fishing boats; he loved fishing and he loved boats... so he thought... 'it would be a gas' to work the fishing boats...

So he quit the restaurant business and left our illustrious crab shack up near 21st street and his buddy Blondie and started trolling the fishing docks for work down on the boats at about noon which of course, is way too late for such work but that's when he woke up and was ready for the world.

Now the chartered fishing boats went out very-early every morning from down in town on bay-side of Ocean City and JD was convinced this was something he'd like to do... something he could do... So as I said, he quit working at the crab shack cause he hated the job and the lack of female companionship he was attracting there and he started going down to the dock every day after his midafternoon rise to see if he could get a job there... NOT in the early mornings when they were preparing to go out because he wasn't a morning person... so later in the afternoon when they returned he'd be down there... hawking a job... and after a few weeks he finally hooked a charter captain into trying him out...

...and he worked for that guy for a short period of time down there and I guess after a few times out he realized it was hard work on fishing boats and not so much fun... cause fun was for the customers... and boat help is hard work doing whatever shitty jobs there is to do out there before casting off in the early morning hours he hated and during the day out on the water... so eventually... not long after starting his employment, it came to an end... and again, he was laying around doing nothing but being in the way using his dry sense of humor to drive guys like Johnny-boy out of his mind which isn't so good to do... but he was still with us, just freeloading...

Now, JD wasn't too bad when he paid his way despite his irritations; he was a funny okay guy... but young... and he could irritate some guys with his dry caustic sense of humor... but I've always been attracted to a dry sense of humor so he amused me more than not and since I wasn't usually the object of his caustic humor, it didn't bother me all that much.

But he used to drive Johnny-boy nuts... and it was just the simple things he did that did it... like maybe JD would say something completely outrageous and Johnny-boy would call him on it... or Johnny-boy would say something stupid and JD would poo-poo his words and they'd be at it again... almost getting into it *time & again*, and again, much like with Blondie-boy. It was like JD just didn't seem to know when to cut-it off. Whether he was nuts *cruising for a bruising* or just a bit naïve I was never totally sure, but Johnny-boy would end up speechless and he'd have to walk out the door to keep himself from blowing up.

So finally, after a few weeks of doing nothing; no work and no girls and no more money to do things... JD realized living *'down de ocean'* wasn't the summer dream he'd bargained for... so I guess in his boredom, he found a way to fetch himself home.

The truth is, I and we were ready for him to go... again, he was a good guy but his dreams were busted and he didn't know what to do with himself any longer so going home was a good idea...

I was at work doing my usual kitchen-dance-shuffle or so when he left... in fact, I never even knew he was leaving... but as the story goes... as JD's got ready to depart out the door for his ride home, Johnny-boy gives him a goodbye wrestle mania drop to the floor for his one last *'good-bye, I love you' kinda* tap... dropping him to the ground saying more or less, in his best way possible... *'I'm da friggin alpha-dog in this dump, NOT you'*... btw: JD wasn't hurt. It was just the *kinda* thing guys do sometimes when wrestling-around is used to *'announce their presence with authority'*; wtf<??> ...now 'that' definitely sounds like some *kinda* silver screen line to me.

...and then Johnny-boy gets up from the wrestle mania drop he'd hit JD with and extends the boy his hand and pulls him up off the floor and pats him on his way out the door with a wink and a word... "I owed you that, boy".

...and with 'that'... JD disappears forever into the summer air although he'd never be forgotten by the rest of the *driftwood boys*.

Note: The line *'Announce [their] presence with authority'* was triggered by a more famous line in the movie *'Bull Durham'*.

de Altoona boys at the crab shack blues

Now there were two brothers in the kitchen who I called *the Altoona boys* cause they were from Altoona PA; imagine that<?? > The older boy was smaller in height and more subdued while the younger boy was more engaging and seemed rather goofy when you first met him but he was more of a really sweet spirit than not; one boy was tripping in a Pennsylvania state *sorta* way while the other one was dancing southward towards a warmer South Florida vibe and they were both in Ocean City to make money for school and nothing else... and this was their primary goal... while mine, and most of us *'down de ocean'* were more interested in a combination of things like making some money while experiencing some *sun & fun* with booze & girls which Ocean City had to offer in the darndest of places...

Now the older Altoona-boy was a wrestler by *high school trade* although oddly enough to me, he told us he wanted to be a chef; he liked cooking and he admitted to it too which was the first time I'd ever heard such comments made from a guy before despite the fact, the world's chefs at the time were mostly men or so I'd been told... but it's something most of us from my neighborhood had never heard said before, at least not too damn often and maybe that's because in our little closed-off part of the world, in general, men did little of the cooking in our homes cause women were stuck doing the majority of it... and yes, while men could usually make a dish or two like my old man for example, it was usually limited to bacon & eggs on Sunday mornings and occasionally my old man would make spaghetti dinner for us when it struck him to do so... but I rarely saw our father cook in our house nor many of my buddies' fathers cook either... it just wasn't usually done, in general that is, so I rarely saw male cooks nor heard of guys professing to want to be cooks or even say they liked cooking which doesn't mean it didn't exist in my neighborhood, I just hadn't seen it or heard it... so when I heard some guy say he likes to cook, well, it surprised me, as in... 'is he a woman?' ...which of course, as *we-all* know, *is &* *was* stupid but again, I'd never seen or heard such a comment made before so it surprised me and I guess I fell back onto my own narrow experiences to make such a stupid-ass idiotic judgment; that's certainly an example of how foolish judgments can be made based on implicitly learned biases or cultural biases defined by one's experiences, right?

We usually think of culture as defined by society's art, architecture, literature, etc., but it's much more than 'that': it's society's implicit & explicit rules and biases as well. That's how segregation and discrimination maintained itself in certain sections of our country for all those years; it was ingrained in society's implicit & explicit rules and thus the cultural norms were maintained. Ditto, my stupid views on cooking at this time of my youth.

Now don't get me wrong... cause other than that, I didn't think *nothing* on this situation other than it was different from what I was used to seeing although if I'd looked around at who was cooking in the restaurant we worked at then guess what I would've seen? That's right, men were doing all of the cooking which may also say something else about cultural biases in reverse, within the restaurant business at least, cause in general, there were no women cooks in this restaurant, as if no women wanted to cook in a restaurant? ...or could cook in a restaurant? Wtf<??>

As for the younger goofy Altoona-boy, he was *kinda* like a *Dudley-do-right* character in the flesh cause he seemed goofy *in look and mannerism* but he was a sweet spirited guy who like his brother, was unafraid to identify his likes and desires as well... at least, some of them anyway(s)... which was interesting to me cause guys don't often divulge themselves to each other too damn often where I'm from but what was really interesting to me was that this sweet goofy dude was into *show-tunes* at a time when *rock & roll* was the cool-music of the day to be associated with and the heavier the metal, the cooler you were... and god help you if you liked pop or country cause that was bad here in the east... but *show-tunes... oh-mannn*, that was considered 'the worse'... the bottom of the barrel... but the younger Altoona-boy knew his *show-tunes* and he'd carry it forth with a *hoot-e-nanny* like flare which just made you laugh along with him…

And his ways must have been contagious in some ways too cause some of the ladies of the restaurant would occasionally look in his direction in amusement and curiosity and *Dudley-do* was either completely clueless of his magical pull on such curious onlookers or he was so focused on the next dollar that he never noticed his distant appeal upon some of the others on the other-side of the aisle.

Now as I mentioned before, this crab shack restaurant used to have free lunches for those who made it up there before working hours started… and for those of us who made it up there… you'd get some good food and get to sit down at some of the employee tables and eat in the company of other co-workers, friends & foes alike.

And oddly enough, as usually was the case... *we-all* ate up in the employees dining area *away-from & before* paying customers arrived for meals and we were usually in our segregated groups cause waiters and waitresses didn't mix with the kitchen help usually, which was us, with few exceptions *here & there*, as has been mentioned...

And most of the time, *Dudley-do* & his brother (*Eddie*) were there for the free meal cause they were there anyway(s), to work. And while the rest of us were there for the same thing *(work & money)* to some extent, we also had girls on our minds... and parties... and good times too, etc... so if the night-before had been too long a night to happily dance out into the morning light for the free meal or if we didn't want to walk all the way up there & back to the apartment before retracing those steps once again later-on when going back to work, then we didn't go; we could have caught the bus up there but the cost ate-away at the benefits of a free meal.

Now for the Altoona-boys and myself... that walk was about twenty blocks or so, about two miles or so... not an insurmountable distance but we'd have to *heave-ho it* up there to eat on time and then trudge on-back twenty blocks or so afterwards... and then after a few hours of off-time, we'd turn around and *heave-ho it* back out to work, twenty more blocks and then back home at night after work. So sometimes, I'd miss out on the fun in the morning and ate at the apartment because it was easier; there's only so much fun that can be tolerated at one time, I suppose. But for the Altoona-boys, it was wasted money not to go so they got themselves *up & over* there for all those 'late breakfast early lunch' free meals every morning before work began.

So this one day, Jaybird & I trudge on up there to grab our meal and we sit down over by the Altoona-boys... and we're gobbling down our meals among all the chitter-chatter going around the table with them and others when somehow the topic of music slips into our conversation... and of course, the cool guys like the heavy metal sounds, etc., etc., etc., it's the seventies after all... when out of the blue, *Dudley-do* says he likes musical tunes... and there's laughter all around the table cause it was so *guy-incorrect* to say such a thing and yet *Dudley-do* didn't seem to care... he just laughed it off... and it goes *on... and on... and on...*

So *Dudley-do* says to us that he likes 'Mary Poppins' & 'The Sound of Music', etc., etc., etc... think Julie Andrew & Dick

VanDyke's musical bits and *da such*... and of course, and again, teenagers, and especially boys in the seventies didn't admit to such a travesty whether we did or didn't like it because you were either *rock & roll*, country or SQUARE... and there was nothing in-between...So when *Dudley-do* admitted to liking 'Mary Poppins'... well, we just had to laugh cause he broke all the rules of male decorum although you had to give him credit for showing such balls... and truth be told, in secret anyway(s)... I always liked the show tunes a bit too although I'd never admit it then as a teenager and especially not to a bunch of werewolves like these guys... in fact, we, in my family had seen all those cute Julie Andrews films aplenty because it was just good sweet fun although again, I'd never admit it out loud to the guys, not a chance... and Julie Andrews was just a musical thrill with that voice of hers... but again, I'd never admit it publicly though... especially around guys... *'no way Jose'* would I do that... but this guy was like a *country bumpkin* who just didn't care about the rules of coolness or he didn't know better... either way... he said... "hey... I like Mary Poppins"... and when others laughed... he did too... with a wonderful laugh echoing through his funny country bumpkin smile... but he didn't fold... he liked it... and *that was that*.

And so *Dudley-do* decides at this moment for some reason, on this day anyway(s)... to break-out in song... with all of us sitting around the table with our near empty food plates in front of us, with some of us stretched back in our chairs after a full meal while others sat forward in their chairs with their arms on the tables still imbued with the thrill of hard *rock & roll* ringing in their head... and he starts to sing it out like so...

A kitchen-hawk... is-as lucky
As lucky... can be...

...and there's a pause cause what *da hell* is this, after all, some of us know the beginning lyrics to the chimney-sweep song and *Dudley-do* is singing an off-Broadway version of it acapella-like in front of us all...

...cause we clean-up your plates & deliver dem too
Washing dem down, all those utensils, we do
And we polish dem up...
and deliver dem - back to you...

...and the guys start to giggle a bit, or at least some of us - cause he's hilarious although the head bangers crow and roll their eyes cause they are too cool for his foolishness... And so there's laughter at the carnage going-on... as in 'wtf is going-on<??>'... and some smile sweetly and some dismiss it all as an *'attack of the nerds'* but *it is what it is and there ain't no more* as some like to say...

"Okay boys... how's it all go?" calls-out *Dudley-do* in a *sing-songy* type way...

A kitchen-hawk... is-as lucky
As lucky... can be...

Cause we dance to our tunes...
As we sing dem out loud
Making our waiters...
And waitresses...
Look so darn good - as we sing at our songs...

...and more of the guys giggle just a bit more at his craziness, or at least some of us do cause he's hilarious at it although again, the head bangers crow and roll their eyes cause they are too cool for his foolishness... and they start to get up and leave the table cause how can one enjoy the silly-ass show tunes of one *Dudley-do* boy who's just a simple bumpkin with a heart of gold?

...and laughter follows, by some of us anyway(s)... and there's some shrieks and heckles... and rolled eyes from non-believers who think anyone singing such musical stuff are nerd-balls of an extreme case... and maybe they were right, but maybe they ain't.

Now *Dudley-do's* brother was more of a heavy metal head too so it must have hurt him to remain seated during this time of play but he was good that way after all, they were brothers in their own band and there's something good about such loyalty if you ask me.

Of course, at this time, I start to notice as I look around the room that some of the good-looking waitresses are looking with amusement on their faces at this sweet country bumpkin who seems oblivious to his attraction and I'm thinking, cause I'm a bit of a werewolf on the prowl sometimes, 'maybe this could work for me?' After all, being friends with a cutie-doll might have some selfish benefits for me<??>

...although 'NOT' is more or less the kitchen God's response... Anyway(s), I elbow Jaybird and he looks at me and then casts a quick look around the room too and he smiles a bit at the sight while some of the waiters get up to leave with our kitchen head-bangers, all with rolled eyes of their own while... the ladies, *ahhh...* not so fast, cause there's something sweet about a sweet spirit who's too damn clueless to the hidden rules of decorum based inside our restaurant walls, that's attractive to them, or so it seems.

...and even though the seemingly implied rule of the crab shack was rather simple in content: all wait staff, and especially the girl-wait staff, did not to pander with such lowly unruly kitchen help as us... what *Dudley-do* had managed to do was open a few of those beautiful waitresses' eyes to his sweet innocence and they smiled and laughed lightly at the cute nerdiness he possessed... although again, it seemed as if *Dudley-do* never really noticed the cute looks he got after his show biz tunes which was a shame but like I said, he was there to work... but *man-oh-man...* he missed out on a few delicious opportunities some of us would have killed for but as they always say, that leaves more joy for the rest of us to enjoy... except of course, there wasn't much for us to enjoy cause *we weren't him...* at least, I wasn't.

So in some ways, I was jealous of him cause his act stole the smiles I looked for but on the other hand, as I've said, it was sweet, so there's *that going-on*, I suppose.

oh-wellll... 'Que Sera, sera...what will be, will be...' and there we go again, *Dudley-do... doing those damn musical numbers again...*

...and then suddenly for no damn good reason I can think of, I find myself in a cloudy mist of smoke in some rundown bar where one old dude sits alone drinking a beer as slowly as illusions might do, and I think to myself, 'what da f*<k - is this?'

...and a trusty face I've seen many times before and since such times, [he] chuckles at me before turning slightly towards me, saying... "what da f*<k is wrong with you?"

So Patty-boy has turned my way, slightly at first, like he expects me... although once again, I'm a bit confused and a bit surprised too because I don't remember choosing to be here in this scene and yet I'm writing this piece of muckish foolishness... but I see him so I know there's 'trouble a-brewing' of sorts...

"Sooo... you're singing show tunes<??> ...in public? ...is there something wrong with you?"

...and I smile a slick-like 'what da f*<k' sorta smile at him and say... "Say it again, Mr. Monkey... and I'll bust your friggin' head with all those musical tunes"

And then he laughs... and then I laugh... and then - there is no-more... except for those musical tunes sing-songing in my head.

A kitchen-hawk... is-as lucky
As lucky... can be...

Note: The line *'Que Sera, sera'* was triggered from a song in a Doris Day movie.

A tall drink of phantom-like heaven

So... there we were this one moment when Jaybird & me, two lost souls, who were delivering plates & utensils to one of the crab shack's food stations when this long neck goose of a beauty who was more of a long-legged blond-haired taste of heaven, pushed on through us...

"Look out boys... I've got meals to fetch"

...and we were bumped aside with the feel of heaven smacking into us and neither of us said a word as we looked upon her with awe at what our eyes did see.

Now I'd first seen her around the kitchen area sucking-up to Blondie occasionally but eventually we talked a bit *here & there* although she was pretty quiet and I didn't usually know what to say which could light a fire between us. And as I said earlier, she seemed different than some of the other girls somehow; she seemed more on the outside looking in and less *'valley-girl'-ish* to me and just more of a beautiful quiet Madonna who stood almost six feet tall with a slender-like statuesque stance that seemed pretty-damn awesome to me and Jaybird. But as I said before, I'd seen her originally in the kitchen area where not too many other waitresses dared venture although she did so in pursuit of Blondie or at least, it seemed that way until he dulled on her a bit because of his *'Lord of the kitchen'* status, I suppose.

"Boys... I've got to get by..." she says to us again as she spins around with plates in her hands while we stood spell-bound for a moment with our jaws dropped down below the waterline like we were looking at the ghost of God herself, in front of us...

"Boys…" she says, as she looks us *up & down* with plates in hand ready to exit the area… "what are you looking at?"

"Heaven" says Jaybird… "just heaven"

…and I laugh …and he smiles sheepishly …and she responds accordingly in a brief moment.

"Hold you tongues, boys" she says with a slight smile before sliding on by.

Now what's funny about this scene, at least to me, was she rarely seemed to talk to anyone much less us and the fact that this God-inspiring creature of 'beautiful' dared to look at us shocked us and tongue-tied us both so badly that there was nothing we could do but give her blank stares like two idiots meeting her sweet stance.

…and then suddenly, oh-so suddenly, like I was dreaming or something… I saw her in a phantom-like Mardi Gras mask for no damn good reason I can think of but still, there she was, masked behind a decorative Mardi Gras mask of sparkling dimensions that changed her into a Goddess looking play-doll which made me drool even more foolishly than before… and then surprisingly, I heard these light & fluffy lyrics play inside the air molecules I breathed-in and out, and again, it was for no damn good reason I can think of except, it did, as she was walking away from us with a beautiful smirk-ish-like look on her face as the music played-on…

"Slip-slidinggg… away… ohhh baby… Slip-slidinggg… awayyy… "

Wtf<??> …and again, I think I've heard such words sung before<??>

Note: The line *'slip sliding away…'* was triggered by the Paul Simon song *'Slip Sliding Away'*.

walking home to the sounds of the ocean

Sometimes when work ended late at night, after we'd cleaned the kitchen up and closed down the restaurant, I'd walk the boardwalk on home from 21st street on down to 2nd street where I'd bear right and head on down towards bayside towards home at the majestic driftwood.

And sometimes, the sounds of the ocean seemed like a frothy cup of joe being whipped around in a fury which was punctuated by the sounds of thunder folding up and over top of itself in an irregular heartbeat *sorta* way, often with differing levels of intensity, some thundering loudly and some rather sanguine... And in the evening, there's always a cold coloring to the sounds which seemed so menacing to me... while in the morning, there's a warmer hue to its feeling, like a warm blanket whispering for you to come near... but in either case, the ocean is a beautiful body not to be trifled with; respect her and she'll usually treat you fairly but dare her and you'll surely die within her cold-hearted grasp.

And while the ocean seemed like it called to me sometimes, with a *come-hither* sort of beckoning that dared me to come closer... still, I feared her wrath even when she seemed so soothing to my touch.

But come the end of my late-night shift, the ocean often times whispered to me like a friend in the dark when I was trekking on down the boardwalk under the overhead lights and summer stars... and when I was late enough, like we often could be after cleaning up the kitchen area, the boards were silent up near where I entered onto it, except for the occasional revelers coming back from their evening out... and of course, the dark ocean sung to me a lullaby as it wrapped itself up and over itself in such a furious *sorta* fake-lullaby way.

And it always seemed to me like the ocean's intensity was never the same most times... cause sometimes, it was damn near deafening while at other times, it lured you so damn near to its edge that you *feared-not* it's wrath which as I've already said, could be a huge mistake to such late-night fools seduced by her deafening charms.

Now unknown to me during most of such treks down the boards, there were usually some big old seagulls sitting up on some of those nearby rooftops at some of those nearby Ocean City boardwalk establishments watching me walking on by... and sometimes, one seagull would say to a second seagull, as he's watching me walking the boards late at night... "you ever seen such a sorry-ass fool looking so lost at play?"

...and the second seagull would look at the first seagull and say... "you outta your mind... I ain't neverrr seen such a sorry-ass fool before!"

"Well... I have" ...says the first seagull to the second, as they both look down on me.

...and after a brief pause, the second seagull would say to the first seagull, after watching me on the boardwalk boards walking away... "true dat..."

...and then... after a pause, they'd both break-out into grand laughter at their funny-ass bird humor.

a sweet kitchen dude & race

Now in the luxury of our 'famous' crab shack *'down de ocean'*, down by the sea somewhere in the eastern corner of that little old *'pleasant land of Living'* of ours... there, in our mists of the kitchen was this dude who was a simple-*sorta* guy for no reason beyond he was probably *'born that way'*; he was different than the rest of us in some ways and I say it with respect.

Now he was just a bit older than most of us, a slender dude whose age was hidden by his youthful face and stature and conversation; he appeared to not be the brightest dude in the world although when he had a clearly defined task to do, he'd hustle through it 'proper enough' to complete the task as required... but god help you if there was any deviation in the task although let's face it, how much deviation can there be as a dish washer... slash... 'dish deliver of plates & things to the various food stations'... or throwing away the trash during the night, etc.,... although our dish washing tasks did involve multiple machines and procedures and *da such* but still, it's mostly brute force work, busy work if you will. Regardless, this guy was a nice-enough *sorta* guy with a sweet disposition and 'a can do' attitude which was pleasant to be around although he had limited comprehension due to a special condition.

But the trouble was, Blondie-boy didn't like failure; he could be *'a dick on the loose' kinda* fellow sometimes; he considered himself one of *'da surfing gods of OC'* as well as our very own self-assigned dish-washing crew boss, of sorts... and he'd lose patience with guys who failed at their tasks like this guy sometimes did. But in retrospect, this guy failed because he had *special needs* although in fairness, we didn't know what that meant then or what it was; he often messed up simple tasks when certain adjustments had to be made and then Blondie would *act the fool* sometimes when things went awry which was a bit unnecessary even if this guy's screw-ups were a bit irritating sometimes... I mean... this guy wasn't working with the same full deck like most of us were, more or less, after all, we weren't Einstein(s) either, but we had 'it' (a full deck) just because we were blessed by God or for non-believers, by virtue of universal nothingness, to have certain analytical tools at our disposal when we wanted to use them... so a lucky star had been placed upon our foreheads and we were blessed more-or-less with more sophisticated abilities to analyze than some others might have, like this dude, who was handed *'a special needs set'* of abilities... but he did his best and what more can you ask for than that<???>

It should be noted that in this era, there were many *'-ism'* used with everyday ignorance; there was racism, sexism, and the dismissal of learning disabilities or *special needs*, etc., as 'stupidity'. In other words, if you had learning or comprehension problems then it was dismissed as stupidity and it defined you. And while today we recognize learning disabilities or *special needs* of some sorts, in our 'yesterdays' you were just labeled 'stupid' instead and then you were blamed for your failures. **Moreover, we didn't really see many people with** *special needs* **in our schools or in our workplaces because they were somehow hidden away in a segregated sorta way or so it seemed. So we didn't really know anything about** learning or comprehension problems which we now associate with *special needs* because society didn't talk about such situations back-then and we did not see such situations very often either. So it was a situation ripe for ignorance.

So what does this *special needs* dude have to do with *racing around the track*? Well, nothing... and yet, everything.

As I've already said, we mostly didn't talk about anything beyond the obvious even in the seventies. We didn't talk about *special needs* and any such things so when it was seen we didn't really know what to do with it nor what it meant for them or us. We were clueless. So, we fell back on street wisdom to explain such things which is nothing more than *'crap-in... and crap-out'*. It's useless crap masquerading as wisdom which is why *special needs* was identified as stupidity; *'crap-in... and crap-out'*.

And the same was true of race issues as well because we rarely interfaced with each other back then so ignorance was our road map to understanding each other. And the same was true of other things in our lives as well, like rape, date rape, and abortion or forced marriages due to premature pregnancy from youthful hormonal explosions, etc... We just never talked about such things as if it didn't exist. It was figured I suppose, that if we didn't acknowledge it, then it didn't exist. But it did exist, at least in the shadows somewhere. And still, we refused to acknowledge it and magically, our parents and us too, I guess, thought this would make it 'not so'. But it was 'so'. It did exist. And our denials didn't make it-all disappear because it was there. And oddly enough, somewhere in the back of our minds, I think some of us must have known something was there. But society stubbornly clung to the notion that anything not shown on *'Leave it to Beaver'* type sitcoms did not exist in society whether it was *so or not* and we followed suit. Which meant of course, we had to rely on street magic for explanations about everything in the unknown categories which as I've already indicated, is just *'crap-in... and crap-out'*.

So we were clueless about most of life outside of our sheltered lives cause ignorance just leaves you clueless. Not wiser. Not protected. Just dumber. And certainly, unable to process life beyond the ordinary sitcom materials we were exposed to.

So again, I return to the idea of: what did this *special needs* dude have to do with *racing around the track*? Well, this *special needs* dude was black. One of the very few black workers in this restaurant of ours or in Ocean City at the time, at least, in the parts of OC we saw. So in this case, with this guy, we were working with two unknowns at the same time where both were going to be defined by the ignorance of street magic because we didn't know anything about either, *race or special needs,* in general that is... So *'crap-in... and crap-out'*.

But that's what segregation does for you. That's what denial & ignorance does for you. It hides what exists so you depend on street magic to tell you things about the unknown which ironically, is all wrong most times.

There's an old saying that goes like this: *'ignorance is bliss'.* But the truth is this: *ignorance is just ignorance.* There are no reasonable thoughts defined in ignorance. But if you like simple and stupid or inaccurate then ignorance is your ticket.

Now I'm not saying there was conscious racism inside this crab shack we worked at, towards him or others, despite our ignorance of *race & special needs,* because I never heard racist talk nor ginned-up *stupidity* bashing in the kitchen despite our ignorance concerning both *race & special needs.* But such segregated situations we lived with made it possible for preconceived racial and other sorts of notions to fester under the surfaces which can poison relationships before they even have a chance to prosper. Lucky for us though, we were still young enough and naive enough to believe in the fairness of *la-la land* type fairytales despite the ignorance of street magic and its *'crap-in... and crap-out'* illogic. *But still...*

So I ask of you now: why would we ever aspire to resurrect the past with all its idiotic blindness & insensitivity like *trump-ism* was/is trying to do today? ...cause our *'yesterday(s)'* were so full of stupidity and ignorance that it's unworthy of ever being considered 'Great'.

Note: the phrase *'born that way'* was obviously triggered by the Lady Gaga song *'Born This Way'*.

detour: troubles in paradise

Now I detour from the story just a bit to describe the backdrop of racism that existed in 'the pleasant land of Living' during the sixties and seventies where we had hidden 'troubles in paradise' if you will, because race was kind of a divider for many of us back then and it existed in Ocean City and throughout the rest of *'the pleasant land of Living'* and the country as well... and so we often-times didn't know each other very well; we were separated by implicit-*segregation-type* rules which shaded what dealings we had with each other inside a dark distrustful veil.

Now on our side of *Charm City* for example, we were divided by main avenues or so; to one side lie the lighter side of the tracks... and to the other side was the darker side of the tracks... and there was a very small mixing bowl area which laid in-between us where sometimes there was peace and sometimes not so much peace.

And oddly enough, the white neighborhoods in our area were rather modest so there didn't seem, in retrospect, to be major differences in our economic status despite the fact there was undoubtedly a difference because of the *'difference in opportunity'* afforded our respective communities. All of us were from what could be considered blue/brown-collar working-class neighborhoods downward towards working-poor neighborhoods so neither side of the tracks could be considered wealthy in any *sorta* way but we were separated none the less.

The first time I ever saw an African American in person, minus the *Arabbers* as they were called, selling their wares (i.e. vegetables & fruit) in the alleys, was this one black female student who was bused into our elementary school with some other white students from another poorer neighborhood *'lower on the food chain'* than us; she was 'the one' unlucky-enough to be shipped our way and the only black student in the group.

As an adult many years removed, I feel for this little girl because she was sent up into our all-white neighborhood as the only black student on the bus and I imagine it wasn't all that straight forward to her as to why. Btw, she was the only black student I would ever go to school with until I was in high school although some junior high schools at the time were desegregating, but this shows how divided we were as a city even in the 1960s & 70s.

Anyway... I remember this African American girl not for anything other than she was the first person shaded differently than me whom I'd met... and she seemed nice enough although other than that, I didn't think on it much. She wasn't the prettiest girl in class, nor the smartest, nor the most athletic probably because she was like the rest of us, a little bit of everything, so I never really noticed her one way or another except for the obvious.

Now on the lighter-side of the tracks I'd occasionally hear the *'N-word'* spoken by adults in the streets but it didn't consciously mean anything no matter what they said because I hadn't met anyone other than the *'homogeneous-us'* except on rare occasions when we intermingled in other parts of the city and again, if it wasn't negative then I just didn't much care all that much about things although there were implied perceptions and problems between us occasionally; there were race based fights sometimes and it went both ways. Racism plays through the direction of hateful people and it causes problems for adults and kids a-like. But the racist attitudes (inferred in the usage of the *N-word*) existed there because when the word was used it was used in negative ways and undoubtedly, it could and probably did influence 'the unknowing' youth like ourselves when (and if) we heard it enough.

So as I said before, we were a whites only mostly blue-collar community with most families owning their own homes so there was stability in our housing with little rental usage and there were no darker colors living with us either, nor other minorities either. And I can only assume this situation was fostered by an implicit race-based segregationist system; there were no *Jim Crow laws* in *'the pleasant land of Living'* as far as I knew. But it was rumored that realtors targeted only white buyers for communities like ours and owners only sold to white families too, regardless of who placed bids on our 'for sale' houses. Political representation in the city was also skewed so black representation was less representative of their numbers for a long time going into this era and therefore, the quality of white public facilities was better than those in black communities. And yet, if a black family wanted to use our 'better' schools they couldn't do it because they didn't live in our community and they weren't allowed to buy into our communities either and therefore, they were denied access to our schools and it was maintained this way because our overwhelming white political representational system kept everything slanted in the direction of white communities like ours. This was what our *systemic racism* looked like, at least on the surface; *systemic racism* is obstacles built into our political & social systems that provides immoveable objects to *equal access for all.*

In 1966 for example, a Democratic gubernatorial candidate in our *'great state'* ran on a slogan which went something like this: *'every man is the king of his castle'*... which seems innocuous enough even if it's a bit sexist (it was 1966 after-all, and that *'-ism'* was also alive as well)... but it turns out this slogan was probably more of a cover for continuing our implicit race-based neighborhoods by enabling real estate's continued use of unspoken racist rules denying minority families the opportunity to buy into our white communities with our better facilities despite civil rights reforms to the contrary. And again, it was *such-unwritten cultural rules as these* which ultimately kept black families locked into underfunded black neighborhoods even if they wanted to move out into other better suited neighborhoods which happened to have better public facilities than their own; again, *'separate was NOT equal'*. It NEVER has been, and NEVER will be. So when the Civil Rights era rolled into the sixties and seventies with the federal government begrudgingly yielding to progressive court mandated changes which filtered down into state & city governments, there was white community resistance to such changes hidden in such non-color-coded language as *'every man is the king of his castle'*.

But such *implicit racism* didn't end there either. Many white residents believed African Americans were more prone to violence and laziness given the higher poverty & violence levels inside poorer black communities, refusing to see our *systemic racist* policies had limited black opportunities in poorer black communities to such an extent that it was a breeding ground for the very vices they feared. So poorer black communities were denied access to good jobs, good schools, and other good public facilities which enabled our modest white communities to thrive without such overt poverty and violence. And make no doubt about this, mass poverty promotes violence because that's how you get what can't be gotten legally or gotten without violence. If you kill mass poverty then you almost always kill or at least drastically reduce violence because poverty & violence go *hand-in-hand,* usually.

So again, this is what *systemic racism* can look like. It's subtle. It's unseen by most unless you are looking for it. It's hidden in words, misconceptions, and blind biases. We tend to blame those whom we lock into untenable situations of poverty & violence & second-class citizenship and then we expect them to live peacefully and successfully despite the unfortunate roadblocks we saddle them with when in fact, it's not possible to do so for the most part (live peacefully or successfully under such unacceptable conditions). It just doesn't work especially inside dense population centers where there's no temporary escape from the poverty or violence or irritations of everyday life. And of course, it got worse cause it was assumed that since poor African-Americans were engulfed by violence and poverty within their communities, that all African-Americans brought such problems with them wherever they went regardless of their affluence which partially explains white flight in the face of racial integration.

So as I've said repeatedly, this is some of what *systemic racism* can look like; it's a system where personal views are racist whether it's subtle or overt in a *'they ain't like us'* mentality enabled & enforced through political, social, economic and environmental systems which limits opportunities and success for discriminated minorities. It's a system where we accept and demand *'Separate but Unequal'* facilities & opportunities based upon blind racist ideas and policies without reasonable remedial actions to fix things. Moreover, such stupid *systemic* hate systems negatively impacted other minority groups as well.

So racism in *'the Pleasant Land of Living'* wasn't as much explicitly enforced or verbally obvious here as has been linked with the deep South during this same time frame (the sixties & seventies) but it existed nonetheless and it was implicit and subtle and *systemic* in its form.

But it would be incomplete of me not to address the race-based problems which existed among our youth at this time & place because not doing so doesn't paint a fair look of the situation either. And despite or because of the *systemic racist* systems I've mentioned above, there were troubles between the races whenever we (young people) occasionally intermingled, but given our race-based suspicions and resentments ingrained in us through society's *implicit racist system*, I guess it's understandable; I knew guys who were white and got their asses beat-up on the corners by groups of young black guys for no good reasons I knew of just like I knew of black guys getting their asses beat-up out on the corners by groups of white guys for no good reasons I knew of either... so *'shit happened'* as they say and sometimes the color of your skin was the only reason it happened. And we were suspicious of each other sometimes because of such encounters which didn't help us build peaceful bridges for deflating racism either.

But in almost every instant where such pathetic displays of racism occurred, it was sparked by groups of *racist-shit-balls* descending upon a single or smaller group of defenseless people not looking for trouble. In other words, gutless *racist f*<ks* used mob mentality to display their ugliness; there was/is no *'manly'* in racism cause racism is gutless & heartless and such hatefulness often needs a mob-blindness to flourish and *'that's all there is to it'*...

But not all race encounters we experienced were negative either cause on the ball fields and in the music halls and in our mixed schools where *we-all* played & learned together sometimes, we had the opportunity to see our one-ness, our humanity, and it taught us, implicitly speaking, through such shared encounters - that 'there was a better way' forward if we only took time to see it.

I'd like to think we can do better than we did in the past. I'd like to think we can live by a simple code of honor which says: *'treat others as you wish to be treated'*. It just seems so simple and yet we often have trouble accepting it and each other's differences whether it be our multi-colored wrappers or our cultural and/ or other superficial differences; we make blind judgments we have no right making and then we bastardize God's light (or 'universal righteousness' for non-believers) when we make such blind stupid choices as hating others we don't even know.

(cc) da doctor of Love
with basketball hops

Now in one of those chitter-chatter-like ways it all goes sometimes when reflecting on a memory that dances between the eastern & western boundaries of one 'pleasant land of living'...

There once was... at least, *once upon a time* within the romantic confines of a *village of violets* that's hidden away somewhere inside the *'pleasant land of living'*... a dude who some of us called *'da-doctor of love'*... actually, just *'da doctor'*; the *'of love'* part was just understood cause he was always schmoozing on *da pretty girls* who walked on-by... And he'd lean in nice and close while walking along-side them, talking and listening to them as if they were the center of his world and we'd all smile and giggle at the spectacle because he worked so damn hard operating on these ladies that it often left us howling like worshiping *jackals of the night*... and thus, Johnny-boy bestowed upon him the call-sign... *'da doctor'*... for being *'a real operator'.*

But *'da doc'*, was first and foremost, a high wire act up in our little village cause he could touch the heavens when he jumped up towards the rim on those basketball courts of ours... and I can still remember getting up to the courts during early weekend mornings to play ball and sometimes when the older guys were up there before the rest of us arrived, they'd all be out there running the courts and *da-doc* would be dancing high in the air, high-up above all the other grounded players who were scurrying around beneath his feet.

And sooner or later, I'd gather myself over by the side of the court silently singing this tune to myself as I watched, with a slight shake *here & there*, hidden away from the others, of course... so they couldn't see my dance... or hear my chant... and I'd chirp-it out like this:

*Say-hey... Jump - Tommy jump... get-off of your feet... Hey-hey...
Jump... Tommy jump... how high can you leap? Hey-hey...
Jump Tommy jump... show us your feet... Hey-hey...*

And so-on and so forth...

But what was really cool about *'da doc'* was this: *'he was a dude for all dudes'*... cause while he'd talk... and laugh... and fool around with his buddies, first and foremost, he'd also entertain those of us who were slightly younger than him but who'd also engage in running and jumping beneath his daring leaps during some of those warm summer days up on the courts and that, as they say... *'ain't so bad'.*

And so it was, some year(s) later... when we were old enough to hunt the boardwalks of Ocean City during those long salty summer weekend nights, looking for the latest summer-love of our lives... sure enough, there he'd be, schmoozing another set of summertime ladies who never had a chance to dodge his smooth delivery. And again, we'd all laugh and yell out towards *'da doc'*... *"heyyy, doctor of love"*... well, not really; it was more like... *"heyyy... doc"* ...cause the other stuff was just understood.

And he'd swivel around, just slightly, of course, so as not to give away his doctor-identity, at least while he was operating... and with a sly smile on his face, he'd node at us... or wink in our direction, and without missing a beat, he'd continue chewing on the ear of the latest beauty walking by his side.

And then I'd silently, ever so silently, so no one else could hear me, [I'd] chirp out these words towards those high-flying ghosts running *up & down* on those courts of ours in the *'village of the violets'*...

Say-hey… Jump - Tommy jump… get-off of your feet… Hey-hey…
Jump… Tommy jump… how high can you leap? Hey-hey…
Jump Tommy jump… show us your feet… Hey-hey…

And so-on and so forth…

dirty Dan and the horror-house dummy

So it happens this one particular night while some of us *driftwood boys* were out entertaining a few of Ocean City's finest young ladies when we decided to dance through some boardwalk rides & games down at the far end of the boardwalk where the carnival rages the loudest under the evenings' bright lights. Now there's this small horror-house down there where small *ships in the night* glide through the horror-house entertaining their riders with so-called scary encounters of the ghostly night.

So on this night, *we-boys* escort a group of lovely ladies into the horror-house hoping I suppose, they'll jump into our arms in fear or something *make-believe* like that, boys - wtf<??> ...and then we'll all get to start a lovely dance together during the rest of the evening... but somewhere along the line this dummy pops out of the dark when it's least expected which is an odd thing to say cause it's a horror-house where things are supposed to be unexpected, anyway(s)... so something pops out and some of us scream-out in fright from the booze and silliness we're making... and before too many seconds have passed us by, old dirty Dan, being filled-up with his best alcohol soaked tricks, jumps out of his royal carriage and pops this sad grim reaper upside his scary-ass head... thrashing and pounding on this poor-poor sweet scary dummy-like creature of such soft stuffing(s) while the other boys & girls laugh at his antics with cheer which is what usually happens with alcohol-soaked fools on such a night.

But despite dirty Dan's dumbass bravado, in the end we failed to win their hearts cause these sweet young ladies were not really fooled by our act so in the end, we, the *driftwood boys,* go home all alone once again because our style was surely lacking in some *sorta* reasonable way... and I imagine, these bright young ladies found other better sorts of entertainment pieces somewhere else along their way even if it was just themselves at play, at least, I figure so... cause we never saw them again. Imagine that?

Beer, cake & Pat-Light

So this one weekend Johnny-boy comes *'down de ocean'* as we from *Charm City* would say so often, to celebrate his birthday.

"Hey, let's go up to my cousins' house... we're going to a party they're having up there"

So me and Bobby join Johnny-boy on a trek up the road to play at a party at this slightly rundown beach house that was still much better than ours. And there amongst the crazy, the music, people, & beer, etc., was this sweet looking young lady with *long-long* straight blond-ish hair that ran down both sides of her face; it was parted in the middle. And she had twinkling eyes which sparkled when she smiled and a smile that lit up the room.

Now I didn't see her right away cause the crazy drowned her out just a bit for me but it wasn't long before I got a glimpse of her through the crazy and I was mesmerized by her. I can't say it was just her looks cause there were others there who were quite stunning too but she stood out to me; she sparkled in a non-showy type way with a sense of humor which was endearing and a charm which was captivating. She seemed smart, personable, and with conversation, she seemed sensitive as well as good looking... but I could also see she could be no-nonsense as well and even Johnny-boy, her cousin, seemed to listen to her when she spoke with a bite in her voice and he was a *friggin'* hard-head too...

But the show must go on as they say, so amongst all the laughter and drinks, etc., comes this pink birthday cake and *we-all hooted & hollered* and drank more beer to down this pink birthday cake which one of these young ladies had made for crunchy-old

Johnny-boy's birthday.

Then this bright light I'd eventually call Pat-Light, for obvious reasons, Johnny-boy's cousin Pat, [she] disappears into the night for her evening shift down at some bar-café setting but as I've suggested, not before I'd been totally entranced by her; I just knew she was a straight shooter with a sweet sense of humor who glistened & gleamed in a very noticeable way.

But the party must go on and we did so although for light-weights like me who could get blasted all too quickly before my time, it became a hazy crazy dance of fun & foolishness which revolved around Johnny-boy's semi-crazy antics.

"Let's go swimming" says one over-drunk foolish boy to a room full of youthful drunk-fools.

"No, we better not"

"*Yeahhh*, it'll be alright… don't be so scared… we'll skinny-dip in the surf"

…now I know this is not a good idea cause we're blasted but I also know when Johnny-boy gets on the rails nothing short of a kick upside the head is going to stop him from doing whatever it is he wants to do and if any girl takes him up on his dare, it's good bye Charlie…

…so Bobby disappears in or around this time too, cause he's got to help close down the restaurant he works at and what's left is Johnny-boy, me, and a few beautiful maidens, one of whom finally takes Johnny-boy up on his dare… and out onto the beach we go, them talking shit and me arguing for some common sense with another or so but Johnny-boy knows all until he doesn't…

And they strip down to the basics and plunge into what appears to be the cold choppy surf talking shit to each other and laughing and carrying-on together as I and a maiden or two watch from the shore pretty damn sure one of us drunken fools may be going into that angry surf trying to drag someone out before they drown, assuming we don't drown too, which can't be too damn good cause one drunken fool helping another drunken fool in the angry ocean surf doesn't really work all that well when you're fighting an angry late-night surf which doesn't care whether you've made a stupid mistake.

...and amongst the drunken playfulness, the sweet maidens disappear one by one as the cold wind batters us until there's only me and two naked fools frolicking in the cold angry ocean surf.

"Come-on in, boy" Johnny-boy yells up to me... "It's fun"

And from the chilly confines of my frozen state of mind, I saw overhead in amongst the stars, a *rocket's red glare with bombs bursting in air*... all the while down below there was only silliness dancing on the edge of idiotic foolishness that wasn't warming my frozen bones all too well.

'*Yeahhh*, not likely' thinks I...and after some more time has passed, I decide to take the coward's way out of this mischief and I too, depart this scene as well, leaving two fools playing dangerously close to their watery grave but I'm too damn cold and tired and drunk to be responsible for their foolishness especially in my fuzzy state of mind. And I reach the maiden's shack where I slip into a drunken coma on the floor as the lights go out... '*good night sweet [fool], good night*'... and again, I think I've heard similar tunes sung somewhere else before.

...and by the way, I think if cousin-Pat hadn't been working that night while Johnny-boy was dancing in the ocean naked and stoned drunk, oh-Lord, I think he would have heard a lot of chilling words coming his way for being so stupid and maybe even I would have heard a bit too, for failing to reign his drunken ass in but... '*it is - as it is*', as they say... and there ain't no more.

So later that night, after Bobby had closed down the restaurant, he shows up again at the maiden's shack.

"hey..." he says to me as I dance on a fuzzy edge of unconsciousness... "where's Johnny-boy?"

"*ahhh*... I left him up on the beach"

"What???"

"On the beach<??>... shit... get-up" he says to me... "let's go check on things"

"Okay"... and I prop myself up with my head clanging about(s) on the edge of consciousness, up upon my unsteady feet I go while I hear Bobby mumbling to himself "shit, I've got 'help' that needs *friggin'* help himself"

...and we trudge on up to the beach with the evening air even cooler than before as the wind blows across us *chillin'* our sorry-ass bones when right there on the edge of the beach nearest the sandy road we walk, hidden just on the other side of a sand dune, is Johnny-boy and his female-dare-me-too young lady, face down in the sand passed out, out cold with little on but the least of things needed to hide the unseen from our view.

"Shit..." whispers Bobby... "Okay, let's get them up and move them back to the house"

And of course, I'm like 'shit'... cause I can barely stand-up straight with this *clangin'* head banging around so robustly that I'm almost sick myself, but I follow his directions and we pick them up, one at a time, and *we-all* stagger back to the shack where Bobby, Johnny-boy and his fair maiden, and I of course, all fall fast asleep on the floor with only Bobby knowing how ridiculous everything really is; I was too blotto to be aware of much. I suppose, cousin Pat comes in afterwards sometime but since I'm *three sheets to the wind*, I don't rightly know.

So the next morning comes and the sun barely shines in through a drizzly morning light and we stir at the commotion in the house with girls coming and going around our dead carcasses... some getting ready for work down at some candy shop they work at, and some not, I suppose, when an angel's voice dances through my head... "You boys doing alright? ...cause you don't look too good from here" she says with a slight laugh.

And Johnny-boy, despite all, seems to jump to life quicker than the rest of us with Bobby in tow and me last of all cause I'm still fuzzy in the head from way-too much alcohol still coursing through my worn-out veins making everything a bit unsteady and unclear.

"It's too rainy for the beach today"

...while I'm thinking... 'it's just too *friggin'* fuzzy for anything'

And life picks up as it does on drizzly grey mornings with guys and gals coming and going getting started on a deary day with light talking and playful recollections of too much beer & wine & pink cake and late-night foolishness in the ocean by our *too-crazy* twosome.

But Johnny-boy is thrilled at his unclear recollections like he is when he's doing dumbass things especially when it involves a prettier one than Bobby & I.

And it's about this time I again recognize just how pretty Pat's shy sweet smile & clear bright eyes are. There's a light about her and I find myself attracted to her more & more as time passes and I look more & more in her direction as the conversation circles around with me saying little cause they-all are friends, not me; I'm an outsider who's only just met them. So morning turns into late morning approaching lunchtime and someone suggests we get ourselves something to eat and then go on over to the Salisbury zoo for some god-forsaken reason unknown to me at the time, but by-god, we are going to be doing something cause Johnny-boy is not one to sit still for long, plus - his hang-over has pretty much dissipated while I'm still dancing with mine and will be dancing with it for most of the day inside my own foggy haze that's hitting me upside my *friggin'* head... so the day will not be wasted, my hangover or not.

And so we jump into our magical robes, after we eat something, and we fly through the drizzly sky until we hit the outskirts of Salisbury where we settle in on a walk through some park near the zoo. And it's drizzly but just barely, so we can walk around pretty much unobstructed by the greyness and wetness. And we talk lightly about things *here & there*; about 'the here & now' and about 'later-on in our lives'. And we share smiles and light banter in a walk of youth all the while my interest is on one apparently shy-like beauty with golden blond hair who's got a shy sweet smile and eyes that glistens with joy... and it all just mesmerizes me, captivates me, and enchants me.

Again, I don't know why we go to Salisbury this day other than it was a drizzly day and we were hung-over, well, at least some of us were and definitely me, anyway(s)... I guess we were a bit bored; *young people get that way sometimes, you know...* and again, this tune has been sung somewhere else before... and when I think of that place (this Salisbury Park) these many days removed from the actual scene, I always think of us being there... the young and dumb and full of ourselves... just walking, talking and carrying on like young people do... and we've filled this park setting in a misty rain with the laughter of youth which only sees youthful sweet dreams straight ahead, all dressed up in pink icing and frothy beer...

... and even though much of the details of such a day escapes my story telling skills... minus of course, my growing intrigue with cousin Pat's bright Light and I'm pretty damn sure there was light flirting done at least on my part, with her, although I did so ever so incognito-like as to not be seen by anyone else, at least as far as I knew, cause I was so secret agent-like as to be undetected by anyone, least of all her... although<??>... maybe she did see my secret glimpses of her as she sauntered along almost like she was floating over her steps with bright eyes that glistened with hope and a smile that lit up this drizzly damp day with more light than there was available to us in the sky, so maybe she knew<??> But either way, she seemed like an angel's delight to me in my fuzzy state of alcohol induced fuzziness... but with a bit of attitude too, which was also intoxicating to me.

Now excuse me my friends, while I kiss the sky... where the light is so bright and shiny... where again, I know similar such words were someone's else's better chosen words<??>

Ahhh, Pat-Light, you are a special light...

Now and again when I look backwards on this time gone by, I see good & bad in our dance. I see the sweet naiveté of youth so sure in our own futures with little idea how life takes different twists & turns which we often don't see coming. And some of us will die younger than we should while others will only touch part of their dreams if any at all. But on this day, we were young and full of youthful laughter & fun, and hope & dreams, and for me, there was a new love for me to see, and we were all so sure of ourselves like youth often is even though we had no idea what lay ahead of us. But on drizzly days whenever I'm *down de ocean* or whenever I pass through Salisbury, I see us all-over again, and I smile... and I cry just a bit, for the lives that were lost too soon.

Notes: The line *'good night sweet [fool]...'* was triggered by the lyric *'Goodnight sweet heart, good night'* by *'The Platters'*. The line *'young people get that way sometimes'* was triggered by something I can't seem to identify now but it's been used somewhere else before. The line *'now excuse me my friend...'* was triggered by a similar better-said *Jimi Hendrix* lyric *'Scuse me while I kiss the sky'*.

de Altoona boys and a bare breasted fool

In *the city* there are always hard-asses who think they are plying their trade as *'hard-asses of the moment'* but rarely do they find their way into a glorious match of equals cause usually they find *'the mild and the weak'* they can attack; *the mild and the weak* whom they can strut their fake bravado shit in front of like mighty peacocks might do in distress.

It just so happens that I was hanging-out with the Altoona boys this one glorious day in the yard of their rented room where they lived for part of the summer; they moved a bit later to another place cause it was a bit cheaper, I think, cause they were all about *'the savings'* but at this time, during this day, they were renting a space in this big old white house who's owners were renting space.

Anyway(s), on this glorious Saturday morning, we three boys were sitting out in these lounging-like chairs in their semi-enclosed backyard with the lady of the house who was renting them their apartment, occasionally showing up to hang her family's clothes on the clothes line.

Now the lady of the house was older than we were but not too old for the boys not to notice or at least, for me not to notice, cause she was a fine-looking older bird than us with an intoxicating look of a younger guy's dream. And our conversation (the boys) was light and fluffy cause the lady of the house was there occasionally so we weren't really using much foul mouth language which the Altoona boys rarely if ever used anyway(s); so me, I guess.

So it's about this time when a bare breasted peacock of a *dick-a-saurus* type struts into the yard with a couple of his coconut stooges in tow who obediently follow him around like blind & stupid-ass bats; they were all walking around the streets just outside the property line like they owned the town or something like that, probably looking for a skirmish to get into when they stumbled upon the Altoona-boys and me sitting in the yard peacefully minding our own business and talking light & fluffy foolishness.

It is then that this bare-breasted blowhard of a peacock spreads his wings and crows stupid-like talk in our direction like a cock-of-a-rock with nothing more going-on than stupid-mud spewing from his mouth, just barking at us backyard boys with dark piercing eyes... and we were stunned at first... and afraid for a bit cause we weren't bothering anyone and weren't looking for a fight and truth be told, we obviously weren't the fighting types cause we'd answered his bark if we'd been like that.

But I tried to maintain my cool, keeping aloof of his mouth as if his threatening words didn't bother me all that much, but as he paraded closer talking about busting our *long-haired hippy* faces, he'd finally grabbed my attention more than I cared to admit.

"You *long-haired hippy* pussies aren't going to do nothing, are you?" yelps this bare-breasted peacock as he's finishing off his rambling shit. Obviously, we had long hair but it was the seventies for God-sakes, so there were bunches of us rocking the 'look' but apparently it was a problem for this dumbass redneck peacock.

...so I'm quaking just a bit from his ferocious barks when suddenly for no reason I can recall, I hear Mikey-boy of 'the Morrel Park variety' and one of our eclectic library boys, stepping around from behind these barking fools and he says to me, "hey, you want to go on up the bar? I've got some extra money."

And this bare-breasted peacock looks Mikey-boy in the face like he's invaded upon his stupid-ass barking territory which he has, and the peacock does so with distain in his face. So Mikey-boy stops short and looks him in the face too.

"You got a problem" says Mikey-boy to this ferocious peacock.

Now you see, Mikey-boy was from Morrell Park inside the *City of Monuments* where, as he'd say it, *'there ain't no damn angels hanging on the corners with me tonight'* cause he & his boys didn't take too damn much crap from no mouthy-ass bare-breasted peacocks talking shit about anything, much less this guy, so he could care less what this asshole had to say nor the size of his bare-breasted muscular physique after all, in Morrell Park, he was just another tree to chop down with an ax.

...then the bare-breasted peacock starts to open his mouth when he sees Mikey-boy is NOT like us. He's gentle in the face and almost angelic looking in some ways and surely non-threatening of build but *we-all* know when a guy says 'you got a [f*<king] problem' then he's not pretending most times, and he's not going to give you any damn ground for free either. In other words, there's a cost to be paid when you play - so be careful my friends... cause *there ain't no angels hanging on the corners of Morrell Park my friends, not ever, and that's especially true with Mike.*

"We got your back" says the peacock's two dipshit soldiers.

...and Mike looks around the peacock to see what he sees and starts to say something like 'f*<k you guys' when suddenly, oh-so suddenly, Johnny-boy shows his face from around the corner too, like a dream run amok cause he's heard some commotion from across the street and he doesn't like it too damn much. And besides, Johnny-boy holds court with us so he's not above shutting the door on fools brushing against his guys in some *kinda* threatening ways.

"Mike, you and Jimmy got a problem going on over here?"

...and the three blowhard peacocks' feathers are now dimmed just a bit cause they know there will be no war here without casualties today and they too, might be counted-down in some of those casualties.

So now that I've been resurrected by this ballsy-ass force which I apparently need to be more of a *friggin'* man, I step up to the plate, putting myself under the chin of this bare-breasted peacock talking shit at us like I'm Clint in full drag or so, and I say, "So... do you feel lucky - punk?" while driving a magnum 44 firmly under his *chinny-chin-chin.*

But dreams are just 'that', illusions with no substance... and suddenly, I'm cast back into reality where this bare-breasted peacock yelps at me again... "Sooo... you *long-haired pussies* going to do anything?" ...and my beautiful momentary delusions of Mikey-boy & Johnny-boy & myself standing guard against these *friggin'* blowhards shit-wads talking shit, *is busted flat in [OC, while] waiting on a train...* and flattened-out too, oh-so sadly. Btw, that line too, contains another's set of *sing-songy* words from somewhere else.

And in the quiet of the moment which passes, as I again, try to be cool under duress like they're not really bothering me all that much while the Altoona boys are doing whatever it is they're doing, a superwoman of sorts, leaps down the back stairs and out from behind the hanging clothes to rescue us in such a way that this bare-breasted blowhard of a peacock who's spread his wings wide and crowed his stupid-ass shit-talk our way like some kind of cock-of-a-rock idiots might do with nothing more than stupid-mud spewing from his mouth, [he] is crushed under her mighty blows of truth and no nonsense.

"Get the hell outta here before I call the police" she says to the peacock boys as she's walking towards them. "This is my backyard and you're not welcome".

So while this peacock and his *dick-a-saurus* crowd had crowed at us while thumping their bare breasted chests like they were whiz-banging pumped-up peacocks or something, they were quickly neutralized by her presence and words. It was as if she'd jumped-out and over the line and delivered one *helluva* crushing blow down upon these puffed-up fools... and she'd crumpled them to the ground like the sorry-ass *dick-a-saurus-es* they were.

...and the bare-breasted peacock's stooges stood there shaking just a bit because of what they heard said to them as their leader was dropped flat before his last syllables had been completely delivered... while I, ever the crusader I might be if I were writing this script, looked-on at these few fools and barked-out support for her as best as I could, as a lounging type guy might do while trying to be oh-so cool... "and don't make me get the hell up out of this chair to make her point with you, either"

So the bare breasted peacock of a *dick-a-saurus* scowls at me under his breath with a little more crowing going along with his retreat, saying a few words like 'I'll see you later' going-on or so, which he scratched onto the surface of the concrete sidewalk just a bit outside this quiet yard as he & his delightful-idiot friends crawled off to hide in the *'mud & blood & beer'* on-down the street somewhere while whimpering something more about 'the next time we meet... it won't be so lucky for you' ...or so... and a *'...blah... blah... blahhh...'*

'Ahhh, F*<k You!!!' I think to myself; *mannn*, it's easy to be a roaring-type crow when superheroes are behind you.

Now anyone who knows anything about the streets, either by fear or not, knows when such crowing goes on it sometimes has a bit of substance to it so you better keep your eyes open and your hammer close at hand or at least, your wheels lubed and ready to roll cause it may not be over. *Ughhh...*

"*Ahhh...* F*<k you boys" I yell after them with some misplaced bravado going-on while our silvery sweet heroin stands guard over our very lives... when she says to me a bit cross, "don't use such language here, boy, or you can go too".

"Yes ma-am" I say, just glad for the heroin-like stance she's just made for us.

And after this ruckus, I stare just a bit at this wonder-lady who's freed us from this idiocy and for some reason now, she seems to have a grander glow about her which beckon's me forth like an unyielding light of magnetism drawing me near which is weird cause she's just hanging some clothes on the line.

And at about the same time, it almost seems as if *Dudley* and Eddie disappear into the shadows of the house almost like they've been written out of this scene we've been sharing and now, there's only two lights glowing, one slightly older but an attractive ass-kicking light with a magnetic pull and one younger duller light drawn to the brighter light like moths to a street lamp.

And all of a sudden, it was like she was a *Princess Warrior Queen* or something... and she kicked and shot her karate-like bullets out from her frame like a Bruce Lee figurine in drag might do if she were alive. And she yelled like they do on TV... "*ahhh -yaaahhh...*" with every thrust she made. And I become transfixed by her glorious light. As in: she was my savior, and my lustful desire, all wrapped-up in one. An inspiring & desirable guardian angel.

...when suddenly, she makes a kick that flies past my head within inches of skinning my cheeks.

"*ahhhh -yaaahhh...*" she yells with pointed authority while looking directly at me with frightening eyes piercing through my skull. And then she smiles slightly at me as her eyes dance lightly across my surprised shocked face.

And in this moment, I'm totally in love with one illusionary *Princess Warrior Queen.*

"Hey... Jimmy, did you hear me?" asks *Dudley.*

"What?" I ask... just a bit surprised and shocked at this turn of events cause now it's not just me and this beautiful light anymore, but it's me and *Dudley*, who's standing near me poking me in the shoulder with Eddie just a few feet beyond him while our wonder-lady is hanging clothes on the clothes line... and the guys seem ready to leave the scene while our wonder-lady turns her head slightly in our direction to see what the commotion is about.

"We're going upstairs... sooo..."

...and I realize... they want to retire from the scene so they can go upstairs to their room and rest before work, I guess... and therefore, I've got to go... like 'get'... and I think 'Shit'... and I was having such a nice walk in the park with this lovely lady and damn if *Dudley* hasn't busted it all to bits before my time to shine has come around... 'well, *I do declare*' thinks me...

"yeah... *yeahhh... yeahhh...* sure"

And I get up out of my chair and start to exit the premises... "later guys" I say... and off I go on my way.

"See you soon..." comes one sweet illusionary female voice from my wonder-lady-like desirous dream swaying behind me... and she's says it with a daring smile that makes me weak in the knees with my own desires bursting loose in my heart and loins...

"See you soon..." I reply...

...*ahhh*, 'to dream large' as they say... '*to dream friggin' large*'.

Notes: the line '*do you feel lucky -punk*' was triggered by a famous line in the *Clint Eastwood* movie '*Dirty Harry*'. The line '*busted flat in [OC, while] waiting on a train*' was triggered by a lyric in the *Kris*

Kristofferson song *'Me and Bobby McGee'*. The line *'mud & blood & beer'* was triggered by a *Johnny Cash* lyric in the song *'A Boy Named Sue'*.

(cc) dancing through
the night

Now in one of those chitter-chatter-like ways it all goes sometimes when reflecting on a dream...

On a lonely darkened street somewhere in an Ocean City town, there's a party being played out in some dumpy Ocean City apartment where there's more kids dancing, drinking and playing then there's room within the apartment... so it overflows out into the street just outside the door.

Now there's a boy in the apartment who's oblivious to the crowd and he's grooving to the musical tunes blasting-out so loudly that almost nothing can be heard that's said between the youngsters on the floor... so all the 'I love you(s)' said between such young lovers are definitely missed out-on, much less all the other less heart-pounding sweetheart words that are exchanged.

...but the boy is oblivious to all the other people in the room as he moves around the floor to the music being played all by his lonesome; his eyes are closed just so... while he glides across the floor in-between the clouds of people decorating the floor as if he's been absorbed by the music itself; as if he's one with the music... and he's glad to be a music-man of sorts, with rhythmic movements which consumes him as if he's the musical notes themselves floating through the air... and he sways to the tunes... and he glides to the tunes... and he swings to the tunes cause he's one with the tunes.

Now at this time, while all this was happening within the apartment... just a bit outside the apartment windows' blasting sounds, there are two old *seagulls* sitting high up on some electrical wires which are strung across the night on the other side of the street... and they've fixated on this boy for some unknown reason... so while they stare down upon this boy in amusement, their thoughts turn to *'what da f*<k is he doing'* ?

...so finally, the one seagull says to the other seagull... "what da hell do you think that boy's doing, anyway(s)?"

...and the other seagull crackles and creeks with laughter, saying kinda sarcastically in return... "I don't know, but that boy ain't got NO damn rhythm, does he?"

And for a moment, there's only silence between the two seagulls... but within seconds, the two seagulls look at each other in amusement before bursting into grand laughter at the mindless dancing boy down below whose rhythmic movements seem altogether un-rhythmic in the eyes of these two odd birds... but... that doesn't stop the boy from dancing through the night either.

dem Imported
friggin' beers...

A late-night bar scene with the *driftwood boys*:

There's a group of wayward *drifting-like boys* who approach a bar railing for some late-night beers in some dark and dank ocean city bar hidden away on some back streets of this town down near the fishing boats when one of the boys says to this gruff bartender, "do you have any imported beers here?"

...and the gruff bartender replies to the boy... "yeah... it's f*<king imported from Milwaukee..."

...and after a pause, the boys erupt into grand laughter before the 'leader of da pack', Johnny-boy, says back to the bartender...

"well sir, then we'll have a round of dem imported *friggin'* beers if you don't mind..."

Pat-Light at the Sand Castle

Somewhere out among the hotels and bars on the beach stands *'a castle in the sands'* casual cafe.. where softer rock or folksy-like music is playing... *kinda* like Joan Baez might do... or Bob Dylan with his softer touch... or maybe even the Eagles. It's just *kinda* smooth and sultry and *da such*...

And a couple of guys order drinks from an angel with long straight blond hair that flows sweetly around her pretty face... and she is serving up drinks to these two deadbeat fools who've decided to visit her this weekend mostly cause I couldn't help myself... we were a little bored and I was wondering if Johnny-boy's cousin-Pat even remembered me cause I just needed to know.

So I'd said to Johnny-boy, "Hey... how about we go on up to the Sand Castle for a bit?"

...and after a pause, Johnny-boy shrugs and says "shit, why not<??>... maybe Pat's up there" ...and so off we go hot-footing it up there in his blue-ish like Nova to a star's kind of show.

And *we-all* smile and kid-around while she makes her rounds between prying eyes who want to steal her away from us even though it's us who captures her occasional playful glances while she's doing her work and we both know it for slightly different reasons, and we both know that tonight, we are the luckiest two fools in all-of this beach town.

It's funny sometimes, just how a sweet smile can light up a room like it does but she does it all with the gaiety of a dance made for two... although - I'd never tell Johnny-boy cause...

Leon's crushing blow

So this one summer evening sometime around the fourth of July time-frame, more or less, I go out to a bar to see an Olympic fight; time has a way of shifting around as we get older, from the actual time-frame to another more floating time-frame so I could be off by a few days... anyway(s), I went on-up to this small old bar up at the end of the boardwalk near the inlet that's shaded green in some ways, to see the Leon Spinks fight for the Olympic gold medal in the light-heavyweight division fight with this heavily favored Cuban fighter who was expected to win.

Now the bar was empty minus a few others sitting there mostly quiet and sucking on their beverage of choice... and this place was a slightly quieter reprieve from all the carnival lights and activity just outside the door of this place... and usually there were just a few old men in there so it wasn't somewhere any of us normally went...

But there was this one dude in there at the bar who kept asking for a 'jellybean' drink... I think it was supposed to be a mix drink or something but the bartender kept replying to his requests by simply saying... "I've never heard of it..."

But this dude was sure it was a 'thing' cause he'd had it up the road a bit somewhere else westward from here along the rails...

"No... it's called a jellybean... you sure you haven't heard of it?"

"Nope..." says the bartender... although finally he relents and says to this dude... "but if you tell me what's in it then I'll make it for you"

"*ahhh*... not sure... but it's really good... it's called a jellybean..."

"Nope... can't help you"

So a bit later still, the same dude reiterates his thought... "damn... I'd love a jellybean right now" ...and this dude shakes his head like he's missing out on some beautiful shade of love or something and the bartender just looks at him with a blank look of disbelief on his face as if he's an idiot or something... and I smile wryly at the bartender's smirk but I say nothing cause 'what *da hell* do I know about such things'... answer: "*absolutely nothing... say it again...*" And again, there's another tune from somewhere else.

But despite this one slightly odd interesting dude, most of the other few guys at the bar were quiet while sucking on their beers and their rather ordinary shots of liquor...

...and besides... I was only there to see this highly anticipated fight in some kind of quiet and while I would've rather shared the moment with some of the guys or so... or that oh-so-sexy neighbor girl of ours, what a thought, huh<??>... or any group of people I knew... tonight, I sat alone at the bar drinking alone while watching the fight... and other than hearing the jellybean man whisper his wishes on occasion... I was alone... and oddly enough, maybe I even relished the 'alone time' to some extent cause sometimes all the activity and craziness of the apartment and work and even our playtime within the carnival settings outside the bar's door could wear on you after a while; just weighing you down in the sticky mud of endless noise of people and lights.

So this rumpled old boy, me... sits at the bar sucking on my beer watching a fight that seems closer than I thought it might be even as this highly respected Cuban fighter mostly peppers Leon in a methodical *sorta* way that he's trained-to-do, and something he's good-at-doing too...

...but when the third round opens at the bell... Leon charges across the ring like one of those mad bulls chasing after some of those wayward dancers in the streets of Pamplona at *'the running of the bulls'* there... and he strikes a thunderbolt of a hit down upon this old Cuban boy... and Leon drops this dude to the floor like a sack of heavy potatoes... and the boys in the bar shriek with joy at this thunderous show of might which Leon has just dished-out upon that Cuban fighter in his mad rush for the gold, or at least I do... cause... *'damnnn*, dreams do come true'; 'odds can be broken and overcome'... cause 'dreams do come true in the USA'... blah, blah, *blahhh...*

...and I wanted to celebrate with someone else at the moment but there's no one else there to really celebrate all my joy with, like the *driftwood boys...* cause it's just me and these other dead-like guys, this bunch of rather sedate beer drinkers who I don't really know so well and who seem so sedate at this unexpected outcome that it surprises me... although there's a moment of subdued pride *we-all* share-in for what this young man has just done.

...and even the jellybean dude is less musing on the subject of his jellybean drink for the moment and that's good too.

Now for me... and for lots of people in the USA, we'd-all thought we'd won that night even though only Leon had actually won, much like we'd all thought we'd won when the USA hockey team beat the Russians just a few years later in 1980... cause they were big upsets... as in BIG upsets... and we rightly, or wrongly, believed we'd all won on both nights as in *'dreams come true'...* but in 1976, it was Leon who'd done it, and we believed we'd all won; we'd all walked into the promised Land that night which *we-all* believed-in, for us to taste, and for him to taste, and for all to taste... but in reality, it was only Leon, a Marine by trade, who had busted his way to the top of Montezuma as only a fighting Marine could do... and it was he who'd applied the crushing victory at the feet of 'liberty and justice for all' except of course, we were still fighting our very own fight for that *'freedom light'* here at home even then, in the seventies, to the consternation of all people with any *sorta* heart and vision for what *'life, liberty and the pursuit of happiness'* values mean... but still, at this moment, all was forgiven... and Leon represented the best *we-all* could be... cause he'd KO'd a much heavily favored Cuban fighter for the Olympic Gold medal and we'd all won except of course, as I said... we hadn't won... he had... cause I was still just sitting there at the bar by myself with a beer in my hand in the relative silence of a rather sedate bar minus my own celebratory yelps at his victory and the victory dance I spun *around & through* in that little old green bar at the end of the boardwalk down near the inlet with only a few old men customers hidden away from the carnival sounds, lights and activities, just outside the door.

Note: The line *'absolutely nothing, say it again...'* was triggered by a lyric in Edwin Starr's song *'War'*; *'War, huh... what is it good for?'*.

(cc) Fourth of July
in Ocean City

Now in one of those chitter-chatter-like ways it all goes sometimes when reflecting on a memory gone by...

Once upon a time... in 'the pleasant land of Living', in a state of mind I call *Pleasantry*... there, in a small ocean-side town of Ocean City, was a group of guys who played the whole summer long chasing the dreams and fantasies which danced in front of their eyes, there, *on the boardwalk... till way past dark...* hmmm, that sounds awfully familiar<??>

So it was on the fourth of July of that year in 1976 during the bicentennial celebration when Johnny-boy flew in from the west after a hard week of humping boxes and packages at the *Charm City* shop he worked at with all these OC fantasies playing in his head; he planned on corralling the boys of the driftwood for parties which abounded around town on this holiday weekend and run they-all did, during this long holiday weekend.

Now added to this situation was this brand-new car Johnny-boy drove into town with; it was clean and bright and new although it was someone else's car... You see, Johnny-boy's father had lent him his new car since Johnny-boy's car was in the shop or so... and since Johnny-boy desperately wanted to play in the land of Ocean City for the holiday weekend with all his fantasies of girls and *rock & roll* and so, he bartered with his father for the car and got it although he knew if he damaged it in anyway, it would come with a steep cost for him. So guard it, he did... and semi-behave, he did, when he had this new ride of his with him.

Now sometime during this holiday weekend, Johnny-boy lassoed a few of the guys *and Bobby's sister* for one of his party trips somewhere in this coastal town and *sooo...* down the back-roads of OC we did go, talking of the evening ahead with all the fine play that was surely to follow where the music played loudly and the liquids flowed easily during the night... and where our fantasies of the night would surely come true.

When suddenly... oh, so suddenly... a light from the darkness struck us like a bolt of lightning might do from the sky up above... and it shot through the stop sign with nary a blink or a pause... and it slammed into the side of this brand-new car with a grand old *friggin'* thud.

Now I digress just a bit here because I saw the crash coming from the rear seat of the car, just before it happened; the impact didn't come so suddenly cause I watched it unfold in a series of small photographic clips that were staggered over a few moments before the impact occurred, as if time had slowed down into small bite-size time-clips like a set of still-shot photographs being shot in succession... and it all played out in a slow moving film stuttered into segments until just before impact when the slow motion of the pre-crash events sped up again into real time... and *bammm...* the light exploded and the car spun around... and when it all came to rest, we looked around at each other and thought... 'Shit, *I want to go home, Toto...* yes, home... Toto... home... my dear one'.

But no matter how hard we clicked our heels we just couldn't go home cause the crash was real... and we were there... and the parties and our fantasies would just have to wait for another day.

So *we-all* unloaded from our car and this blotto young lady who was driving the other car, stumbles out of her car with her friends who were obviously coming from another party, much like the one we were all headed to, and to her credit, she knew her error at once, even if she was in no shape to understand the whole situation... and she apologized profusely and took credit for her mishap which was an honorable thing to do even if accident lawyers would advise against such speak; god forbid we speak the truth.

And lucky for us, no one was hurt except for that brand-new car Johnny-boy was driving, his father's new car, the car his father had lent him with the stipulation that he not go to parties with it so it wouldn't get messed up... but it was all messed up now... and messed up bad... and Johnny-boy looked at it in disbelief cause what was he going to say to his father that would make it all right? ...something that would say it wasn't him this time who had screwed up but someone else who had... cause his father was not sympathetic of *suffering fools* and on this day, Johnny-boy knew he was the *suffering fool* this time, about to be schooled for his mishap.

Now while the boys of the driftwood were buddies, maybe not perfect buddies mind you, but certainly good buddies cause we never jeered at the screw-ups we each made in hurtful and spiteful ways although we were not beyond laughing at our occasional mishaps... but always, afterwards, we'd smack each other on the back and say, after our laughter had been completed, *"you da man, boy... you are... da friggin' man"* ...and we'd all laugh once more together and then move on to the next item on our agenda with our heads held high. But we were careful not to mess with the bull too often and Johnny-boy could be the bull on occasions. So mess with him, we didn't do, too damn often.

So there we were... all standing around the car and the cops arrived and took our statements and he, Johnny-boy, and his blotto-lady, were both in the back seat of the cruiser while we stood close by because we'd been in the accident too.

And of course, Johnny-boy like his old man, was not big

on *suffering fools* either... so while our blotto-young lady was blubbering on about things like blotto people blubber-on about in the back seat of the cop cruiser, much like we would've probably sounded like if we'd made it to some party, Johnny-boy's eyes just glazed over with time passing-by as blotto-girl continued to blubber on... and it seemed like Johnny-boy's life blood was being drained from his body as he slumped in the back seat of this cruiser deflated about his fate... and he seemed to turn another shade of pale white with every word she uttered.

And then came the topper... the thing that made us all laugh, at least to ourselves then because we didn't mess with the bull... so there we were with her and him in the back seat of the cop car and we're off to the side, but close by... and she says to him... all blotto-like... "Listen *mannn*... I'm really sorry about all this shit... but... still, I just want to wish you... *a happy... bi-cen-tennial, mannn... really, mannn... A happy... bi-cen-tennial*".

And man, I almost busted out laughing right there cause it was one of those driftwood moments, one of those mishaps which just seemed like a laughable moment because I knew Johnny-boy's head would burst through the top of that cop-car in any minute now, after such a comment like that, like a rocket ship on steroids.

But somehow he didn't blow even though his eyes turned devil-like red, so I'll give him credit for that... but still the steam boiled out of his ears and we could see it as his pale white color turned hot Satan-like 'red'... like *"red, red wine..."*, and it rose up through his pale white face like a clear bottle being filled from bottom to top... with *red-red wine*... but in this case, it was his face filling up with boiling red blood cresting in a tidal wave of sorts... and then there was this purple-like stuff which pulsated through his arteries, going up into his head and I thought to myself in a moment of light, what a sight was he... *'yes-sir-ee bob'*... what a sight, was he.

Well of course I didn't laugh out loud although I almost did, but I didn't - cause friends don't do that *sorta* thing I suppose... and because I didn't want to wake the bull from his slumber any more than he already had been shook loose... else, I might get whacked upside the head cause as one silver-screen line goes, *he weren't going to hit no girl...* so if I'd done it, if I'd laughed... then he'd whacked me upside my head pretty damn quickly... so I didn't... *'no-sir-ee bob, I didn't'*... I just didn't.

But in all the years since then... whenever we've gotten together, the *driftwood boys*, as rare as it's been in our later years, we'd all laugh about that time together, even Johnny-boy, cause in retrospect, it was hilarious to us, at least afterwards... and we've roared at the remembered/imagined sight of Johnny-boy turning blood red with all that steam pouring out of his ears while he held his tongue cause all he wanted to do, was explode upward into the sky.

Now even though this story is nothing really-special to most people cause it's just a simple moment in the lives of some wayward *driftwood-like boys* and nothing more... I often slip back upon this 'fourth of July' memory whenever a fourth comes along... and I laugh at the sight of us, and for the moment *we-all* shared together.

Notes: The line *'On the boardwalk till way past dark...'* was triggered by a Bruce Springsteen lyric in the song *'4th of July, Asbury Park (Sandy)'*. The line *'I want to go home, Toto'* was triggered by a line in the movie *'The Wizard of Oz'*.

detour: Independence Day

Now I detour from the story just a bit to talk about Independence Day...

So we Americans instituted Independence Day to celebrate our independence from English colonial authority with extreme reverence towards the soldiers who sacrificed so much of their beings (lives & limbs) on the battlefield for our freedom which is *just & right to do* with the exception that little reverence is given to another group of people who fought the same glorious fights here at home in America, oh-so many years later... after all, our soldiers' Revolutionary War & Civil War, and WWII sacrifices, as well as so many others too, didn't end racial bigotry & segregation & discrimination of darker minorities in America nor did it rectify their stolen right to vote denied them through conservative political shenanigans at the hands of bigoted groups of *'deplorable(s)'*.

No, that fight was fought by our American Civil Rights workers who sacrificed their lives and limbs as well, to access what our soldiers couldn't seem to accomplish overseas for us in all the wars they fought in. Now why that is, I don't know. And the same can be spoken about in other countries as well; *we-all* celebrate our own independence with reverence towards our soldiers in uniform forgetting so many others who sacrificed for our freedoms as well, for our independence, and yet since they didn't wear uniforms they seem forgotten all too often. But they got busted bones & asses while fighting for our right to vote, and our right to be *counted & seen* way-too damn often as well. So they too deserve the same respect and reverence as our soldiers in uniform get.

Now this monologue is NOT meant to deny or trivialize our soldiers' contributions or sacrifice for our freedoms as much as it is to augment this conversation. And if you fail to understand what I'm saying then you've probably got *deplorable-type* blindness going-on like so many of those self-serving conservative bigots bastardizing the ideas of freedom & liberty here at home; freedom that includes the right to speak and vote and to be represented without discrimination... and those who fight for such rights are all heroes too, in my mind.

And so while it is *right & just* that we should celebrate this Independence Day holiday, which is dedicated to the proposition *'that all men are created equal; that they are endowed by their Creator with certain unalienable rights; that among these are life, liberty, and the pursuit of happiness'*... where of course, *'men'* in its most perfect state here means *'mankind'*... and where *'the pursuit of happiness'* in its most perfect state, *EXCLUDES* the enslavement of others... cause *then & only then,* is this idea the noble proposition it's supposed to be, we should give thanks to all.

And for those of us lucky enough to have a certain level of freedom, those freedoms came at a cost made through the sacrifice of many. A woman's right to vote and their subsequent civil rights came about because of the huge sacrifices made by women suffragettes; their civil rights were not ascertained by our soldiers' overseas sacrifices. And African American's right to vote and their subsequent civil rights came about because of the huge sacrifices made by Civil Rights workers; their rights were not ascertained by our soldiers' overseas sacrifice although one would think the Civil War's military sacrifice by our Yankee armies would have made those rights more than real but in the end, it wasn't accomplished that way because political shenanigans masquerading as compromises allowed bigotry to reign supreme through our so-called free country despite the huge sacrifices made for such freedom and liberty.

That's why I, on the 4th of July, America's day of Independence, and Juneteenth as well now, give thanks to *all people who fought for freedom, liberty, and justice for all*... because many contributed to our fight against the entrenched hateful bigoted abusers of our freedoms who should be identified as *'the deplorable(s)'* cause it's deplorable to deny others the same freedoms *we-all* wish to enjoy ourselves.

As I said, I believe in the Declaration's magnificent words of *'all men are created equal'* because in the eyes of God, assuming one believes in God, we are all valuable in our own way; we are *'equal in our humanity'*; we are *'equal in God's design'*... and therefore, we are deserving of human respect and the rights of mankind is important for all. And please note that I've taken the term *'man'* in the declaration's line to mean *'mankind'* because if not 'that' then it's only half of a grand phrase with mediocre overtones.

I believe in the Declaration's words which say *'governments are to serve mankind and when they fail to do so, they are to be replaced by another government more representative of its citizens'*. And let's face it, if government's purpose is not to serve its people then what purpose does it have? Mediocrity? Lies? Welfare for the greedy? Pandering to religious fanaticism?

Make NO doubt about this, the Declaration of Independence was truly a magnificently idealistic document claiming the rights of mankind are unassailable and the way to such a goal is through a responsible representative government which is essentially *'of the people, by the people, and for the people'*, free of bigotry and authoritarianism.

It's not the Constitution which is our ultimate American document of freedom because the Constitution compromised the essentials of the Declaration; it accepts slavery and then it accepts non-representative governments for those people it enslaved; this runs counter to the idealistic ideals used to justify the Revolution. The Declaration does NOT make such compromises whether it meant to be as grandiose as it is or not, but it is... and that's what makes it grandiose. Imagine a declaration which said *'all rich white men are free'*. Would it be considered such a grand document about freedom? Somehow, I doubt it.

Although in fairness, the Declaration does unfairly blame England for America's slavery problems in 1776 and let's face it, by then - Americans were certainly responsible for its existence here in America. But other than 'that', it's a grand document claiming the rights of mankind and the role of government in obtaining those rights.

And with that being said, I finish this rambling off with these final words... May we, my country, and the world as a whole, one day realize a truly spectacular *Independence Day for all*... where we are truly free of hate, bigotry and oppression.

One sexy young lady
goes walking by...

So there we were, Jaybird and I, just sitting out on the front stoop while I danced upon some *sailing* dreams that lingered inside my head all the while we sucked on some cold beers to cool our whistles when suddenly... to my love-ravaged surprise, there in the distance strolls this lovely 'sexy lady' from just down the way; our sexy neighbor who had little to say to me most times and yet, there she was just a-walking our way. Actually, she was going to be walking past us on her way home to her trusty abode.

So I started singing to myself, *as incognito-like as I do...*
Here comes my girl...
a-walking down the street
And she's so damn hot...
I'm losing my mind

...and the closer she gets to us, the more ravenous I become, just hungry for the taste I've longed for but would never have in this lifetime or any other lifetime but still, what a sight to behold cause she's so beautiful beyond almost anything I'd ever seen before.

Now what Jaybird thought I do not know but she definitely had four eyes watching her *'walk this way'* as another sound of the day once sang... *'just walk this way'* my dear cause I long for your touch... or even just a smile might do.

And maybe it was Jaybird or our four eyes following her but for some reason unbeknownst to me, she flashes a deafening smile our way as she saunters on by with a slight acknowledgement that sent my soul soaring ever higher which seems odd to me cause I just knew, that if I could just reach the diamond ring which laid below the water's edge then I'd be *'knocking on heaven's door'* as some long-ago rock song once hammered on-through via their glorious sounds of thunder... but then again, if I can't hit the drums with the rhythm needed to play along with the band then why would I think I could swim the long stretches down below the water's edge while looking for heaven's gate, without drowning during my search?

Answer: 'I can't!!!'

Notes: The line *'walk this way'* was triggered by a similar lyric & song *'Walk This Way'* by *Aerosmith*. The line *'knocking on Heaven's door'* was triggered by a Bob Dylan lyric & song *'Knockin' on Heaven's Door'*.

Shaking it with the beach patrol

I was walking down the bench this one sunny morning with my shades on trying to look good and inconspicuous behind those reflecting shades as incognito-like as I could while scoping-out the pretty girls strolling the beaches or frolicking in the ocean waters before me as I occasionally peered up & over at the beach patrol stands trying to see if I saw anyone I knew.

It turns out that I knew several rather cool-dudes who were lifeguards *down de ocean* who held lofty positions of authority and respect on the ocean city beaches although it came with tough responsibilities as well. An Ocean City (OC) beach patrol guard had to be such good swimmers that they could swim a mile or so in the ocean surf with their float-gizmos attached to their arm to qualify for the job or so it was said. I'm sure there were other things as well, that had to be done but the point is, you had to be *'da man'* or *'da woman'* to earn such a spot on the beach patrol.

And it was their responsibilities to save or warn or haul-in stray ocean goers who got in trouble in the ocean surf. So, a big deal.

But once you made it there, mannn, you were *'da man'* in town if you were a guy and all the prettiest girls would grow weak in the knees for your attention. And even if you were just a friend of an OC beach patrol lifeguard, you were guaranteed at least *a look* by the lifeguard's castaways maybe because they were revved up by the lifeguards and so anyone would do afterwards... or maybe because they figured a friend of a lifeguard meant they'd have a chance at sitting with the lifeguard himself at some time down the line, I suppose.

Now I wasn't aware of the benefits of being a female OC beach patrol lifeguard at the time and the truth be told, it was another area where females were probably discriminated against more times than not which meant to make this special group of guys as a female you had to be a lot better than the guys you competed against for the available slots cause otherwise, no dice. That's my guess. Later on, with the dawning of more progressive ages where somethings happened along the correct enlightened path, maybe these biases relented just a bit and females just had to be *'the equal'* of the guys they competed against although my guess is, nothing comes easy when you're breaking stereotypical images in a male dominated world and this was one of those cases. Males dominated this job because it was considered a male dominated role and *'that was that'* in the roaring 70s.

So anyway(s)... whenever I strolled the beaches, I was not beyond yelling over to a lifeguard I knew while trying to be incognito-like cool which of course, I was not no matter how hard I tried. *Geekism is geekism* and *that's that* for most of us.

Now it just so happened that I met this one dude in school one year who worked as a lifeguard *down de ocean*, and that was beyond the few I'd already known from my high school years, and we'd met at the emergency ward when I was there for a broken jaw I'd gotten from a baseball pitch to my face while he'd earned his stay there with a separated shoulder via a lacrosse collision which turned him upside down for a bit.

And he was a good-looking guy who was down to earth and I could tell it was so even though we had few things to say to each other most times cause we shared little in common beyond our shared time together in the emergency room that one afternoon but regardless, thereafter when we saw each other, we'd always take time to share a few words before moving on.

So I knew he was working *down de ocean* this summer as I

strolled along the beaches even if I didn't know where… so while I strolled-along I'd always cast a slight look up in the direction of the lifeguards to see if I saw him or the few others I knew just so I could yell out my hellos. Plus, as I said, I thought maybe some of those beautiful ladies vying for his attention would see me as a consolidation prize of some sort even if I was the lowest of the low for them.

So, as I glanced over to my left this one time, there standing alongside his beach chair was *lacrosse boy* staring off into the watery distance with a few girls nearby of course, playing near enough to him in the hopes of catching his attention.

"Hey Rod" I yelled in his direction… and after a couple more yells he finally cast a wary look in my direction and then nods slightly in my direction.

"How's your shoulder?" I asked as I approached.

"Good" he says while barely looking at me cause his attention was mostly scanning the horizon for wayward swimmers.

"I didn't know you were down this far?"

"Yeah, we make our way down the beach towards the more tourist packed areas with time and skill I guess you could say"

"So how long you've been working down here?"

"Three or so years… but honestly, I'm getting tired of it. It was a gas early-on but now I'm just tired of it"

…and of course, I'm gassed cause I know whenever an OC beach patrol guy walks into a party and he's identified as one of the Ocean City Beach Patrol, then he is *'da man'* and everything seems to open up for him after that but then again, I was probably looking at things through rose-colored glasses cause it's almost never that simple, now is it?

"Really?"

"You can't imagine what people will do out there in the ocean. Just dumb-shit. And I'm just tired of it all, I guess"

...now keep in mind, while I'm looking at him and talking to him, he's always scanning the water's edge looking for dumb-shit things going-on which may need his attention after all, he's expected to NOT lose any swimmers in his sector which stretches from left to right where the other lifeguards have taken-up positions sweeping over their consecutive sectors.

So anyway(s), as I'm standing there in the glory of one cool-ass lifeguard, I'm thinking - 'Jimmy-boy, you must be 'cool' talking to this lifeguard, right<??>'... and I look over at some girls frolicking nearby trying to be irresistible to Rod as my unknown wing-man, and I smile to myself and to the nearby young ladies in a - 'ladies, can I help you?' *kinda* way.

Then suddenly, Rod bolts with his floaty-gizmo in hand, rushing towards the beaches' edge yelling out something to a few swimmers who were getting too close to some nearby rocks that they could be thrown into with the rough surf.

'Wowww' I think. He really is *'da man'*.

...and as he's engaging with the guys in the area trying to warn them off from their impending doom with their continued foolishness in the area, I realize we'd probably spent our few words for the day and maybe, he really does have some more important work to do without having to entertain me and my idiotic visions of riding his fame into some delusional *la-la-land*.

So I turn and walk on up the beach, again trying to look all-so incognito-like & cool even if such a feat cannot be done cause I'm not so very damn cool at all, with or without the mojo coming from some OC Beach Patrol guy.

Gorilla-Tea comes a-calling

Part way through the summer, the youngest of our group appeared in town to fill-out this loose group I call *the driftwood boys*... and so Little gorilla-Tea as I called him sometimes... or Teacup as in *Teeea-Cuppp* when we were animated, cause he could be a talking fool *sonofabitch* sometimes although he could be cool sometimes too, anyway(s), he joins us... and as I said, he was slightly younger than *we-others* of *the driftwood boys*, in age anyway(s)... but not so much in some other ways, I suppose... and he joined us because he was driving our old man nuts during his summer vacation from school so he called in a favor asking for a break from their fighting at home and we, *the driftwood boys,* we told him we'd accept his lost-soul provided he cared for himself without our prying eyes baby-sitting him most of the time...

By the way, there were other names we bestowed on him as well... like *PJ Magillicutty* which we usually cut down in size to something like Cutty... or Cutter, or PJ... or gorilla-Tea which we liked and derived from *'f*<king Maah-gorilla Tea'* which we probably stole from the comics somewhere... and by the way, he looked nothing like a little gorilla or so, but nicknames sometimes stick and I'm not sure why that's so other than in our case, we were idiot boys talking in the foolishness of youth, so all of the above and others were on the table, I suppose.

Now Bobby would say of Jaybird, who was the lead voice in accepting gorilla-Tea into the driftwood abode, at least to others, in a *'what da f*<k' kinda of way'*... "he rounds up the stray-dogs in the neighborhood and brings them-all home"... and gorilla-Tea was just another in a line of stray-dogs he brought home, I

suppose.

So I spent a week walking through various restaurants looking for a gig for gorilla-Tea to work at cause he'd never really worked anywhere much before and he wasn't going to be allowed to freeload off us at our summer shack; so 'it's to work you go' or you can 'go back home'...

So again, I led him along as a job-looking guide and we hit every restaurant in town looking for some *kinda* kitchen help work but we didn't hit on any takers... nothing doing at this time... anyway(s), the day gorilla-Tea was supposed to catch a bus back home to *Charm City* cause he'd failed to fetch himself some work, he walked on-down the boardwalk looking at things one last time before leaving when he finally finds himself a job barking at vacationers to *'come and spend your money with me'* up on the boardwalk at one of those many flim-flam carnival-like game-booths which operates mostly during the evening hours which just worked for him cause he was a night owl; up all night and asleep until way past noon; plus he was a bullshit artist... so there was *that going-on* too.

And yep, gorilla-Tea was always a talker; he could sell ice to Eskimos if he had to, as *the old saying goes*... anyway(s), he found his niche up there on the boardwalk where he'd spend the rest of the summer doing his bit while doing what Bobby and I thought we'd be doing, talking shit and getting girls, but he was way more effective than we were at chasing the pretty ladies and... PAR-TEE!!! ...which is why we sometimes called him Peacock too.

So up on the boardwalk, gorilla-Tea was always trying to schmooze some girls with his brightly colored gorilla-wings on display and he'd bat their concerns *about(s)* until they'd forgotten what it was that troubled them. And he played and sung to all the girls he could convince *'to come his way'* with his youthful bullshit-ass salty charms.

...yeahhh... Bobby use to say of little brother Tea, he had more

girls and more parties and more fun talking shit to strangers than all the rest of us combined... and he did it in a shorter time than we did too, but maybe, that's what gorillas *and/or* peacocks do, I'm just saying.

Now gorilla-Tea played the field for a while until some foolish young girl turned his head around a few times too many and after that, he mostly played her tune whenever he could... and the two were inseparable most of the time for the rest of the summer or at least, it seemed that way to us cause we didn't see him all that much until late at night when he'd stumble into our *'den of imagined iniquity'* and close his eyes.

So time passed and later during the summer, a hurricane was projected to hit and *we-all* decided to leave for a couple of days except of course, for gorilla-Tea, who tried to be our lone holdout; he was a hardhead who was going to ride out the storm but I grabbed his young-ass by the scruff of his neck on the day of our departure and threw him in the back of the car and then *we-all* headed home for a break from the beach and the hurricane coming our way...

And as you can imagine, the buzz the week before had been about the up-and-coming hurricane which was focusing-in on Ocean City during this particular week. Of course, there was the usual Hurricane parties talk which young people engage-in while dancing on the edge of youthful stupidity and of course, the nay-sayers who are not afraid of anything until they're caught inside the eye of the storm and then they can't understand why emergency workers can't save them from their impending doom; wtf, mannn<??> And of course, even amongst the *driftwood boys* there was a bit of a difference of opinion as to what to do as I've said, but for Bobby and me and Big Al, the common-sense thing to do was *'head west, young men'* and get some home cooked meals in us until everything blew over and if the hurricane only turned out to be a glancing blow or a total miss then that was okay too, cause *we'd be back*, as some say.

...so *we-all* jumped into Bobby's small-ass dingy Pinto and we started on up the road towards *Charm City* and away from the incoming storm and Bobby starts telling us this story about his car repairs he'd just had made so his broken-down old car could make it all the way home in one piece... and gorilla-Tea starts in with all his "you got ripped-off" stuff... telling Bobby he'd paid too much for his repairs which may or may not have been necessary, as if he knew<??>

"Mannn, you got ripped-off... my buddy back home did the same thing for a nickel & a song for what you paid... Mannn, they must have seen you coming..."

...and I could see Bobby was seething after a bit of this crap, not at first mind you cause Bobby was a gentle spirit most times but there's nothing like being told you were a chump to get pissed-off just a bit with time.

"*Yeahhh*, mannn, you got ripped off"

"How the hell do you know? You're just sixteen, for God sakes"

"Well, I know about that. My neighbor fixes his car all the time and I'm over there watching and listening and learning so I know more about this then you do"

"*Yeahhh*, somehow you know more about it than this mechanic?"

"No, but he saw you coming, mannn... and he played you like a fool"

...and Bobby finally reaches the tipping point and he reaches over to the radio after a bit of this *kinda* talk and turns up the sounds on this broken piece of musical static with the bass sounds booming-out in an 'out-of-tune' *sorta* way rattling our brains with its nonending *thump-thump-thump* sounds... and he cranked it up so loud that nothing gorilla-Tea said after that, could be heard... and I mean nothing; he was drowned-out and I had to laugh to myself at first cause gorilla-Tea had it coming although I couldn't hear anything worth hearing for a time for many miles on-down the road because of it.

Now there was a moment when I thought Bobby's move was just a bit ignorant but after a bit, after a brief moment of reflection, I knew *we-all* weaken under the pressure of a *know-it-all* telling us shit which may or may-not be true about getting ripped-off. So again, I had to laugh at it all cause it shut gorilla-Tea *da f*<k up...* cause sometimes, gorilla-Tea lacked certain social graces which may have been due to youthful ignorance or his over-confidence on this subject matter but I mean, there's nothing like telling some guy who's giving you a ride home away from potential danger that he's a dumbass who's just been ripped-off, to really piss him off, so it doesn't make sense to do so.

And whether gorilla-Tea was right or not, it doesn't really matter cause you don't piss on a handout... and since I knew nothing about cars then or now except where the engine is... and where the oil goes... and where the battery is... *blah-blah-blah...* and maybe a few other simple-minded things like that, what *'da hell did I know'* about Bobby's situation... answer: *'absolutely nothing'*... so I didn't know squat about whether Bobby had been ripped off on his car repairs or not, but if I had, I wouldn't have told him 'he'd been ripped off' after he was so proud of resolving his auto problems in such a quick hurry so we could escape an incoming hurricane, that's for damn sure...

...but gorilla-Tea, despite his youthful age, he was a *know-it-all*, of sorts ...and again, maybe his youth was a part of it, I don't know... but he didn't get to say much more on our ride home after that given the loud music busting out of those old cheap-ass distorted banging-type speakers drowning him out.

a Yankee Clipper
Great Escape

Bobby and Johnny-boy were the closest of *the driftwood boys* and they were certainly, at times, birds of a feather who flocked together although Johnny-boy was *the leader of the pack* always. They were more *loosey-goose-ier* than Jaybird and the others were, in general that is... and they would head-out carousing about(s) searching for parties often by themselves... and they'd sometimes get themselves into a pickle although again, the undeclared leader of such escapades was Johnny-boy just as he was for all *the driftwood boys* escapades; he was the heart and soul of all carousing for this group.

So one evening Bobby heard about this raging party up at some hotel named after all those Yankee Clipper ships that had plied the seas in pirating *sorta* ways as swiftly as storms might do breaking through our sand swept sand dunes on our outer banks.

Now as usual... a *'teenage wasteland of days past'* swept through this lovely wooden party-place this one night, dripping in booze and the smells of burnt rope tickling the air molecules all within the party rooms of this Yankee Clipper place when a bunch of cops descended upon this establishment to straighten out these wayward young peoples' ways... so Johnny-boy, ever aware of the threat breaking down upon the door, led Bobby to the back bathroom in a rush where they broke out a small window so they could make their great escape, laughing and giggling in panic sorta-ways like school boys do sometimes... after all, if they had to make a call to their parents to be bailed out of jail then there was going to be hell to pay for both of them.

But Bobby, while scared of the cop's rush, wasn't so keen on the idea of squeezing through some tight-ass bathroom window and dropping out of sight given the worse which could happen was they'd be hauled in for a short stay down at the city lockup, if that... although he didn't relish having to call his old man back in *Charm City* if he needed to be bailed out either; his father was a cop there. So he didn't fight Johnny-boy's desires to dash for the finish line through the window no matter how ridiculous it seemed... so after Johnny-boy cleared off the glass, they had but one thing left to do, jump through this tight-ass looking window-frame to see what's on the other side of this Clipper's police lockup.

Now Johnny-boy was a bit of a portly boy so when he jumped up onto the window frame and started to squeeze his bigger-sized ass through that small looking glass hole, he looked a little like someone squeezing ketchup out of a bottle that just won't let go of the last few drops of its special red tomato sauce... but he squeezed... and he squeezed... and he *blew those boys down* as the slogan goes, more or less... all the while there was all this chaos banging around in the next room from cops *a-grabbing* and kids *a-running*... and like a ketchup bottle which usually yields-up its last plop of red sauce after much banging on the bottle's bottom... Johnny-boy fell out of the window and fell to the ground with a grand thud, down into Alice's wonderland of laughter... and after he signaled he was okay, they both laughed at his less than smooth exit for a bit but time was not on their side so...

...so Bobby, ever the diligent companion, jumps up next to make his great escape and although he was thinner than Johnny-boy by a lot, he was also taller and more awkward in some ways... so up and over the window ledge he goes and out of the window he squirms before finally falling through the looking glass window with all the chaos closing in upon him from the other room... and as the boys scrambled to their feet, they both looked around from inside the looking glass theater they were in and what they saw was not even close to what they expected... so they blinked and chuckled like youthful fools might do and then they fled in laughter into the darkness, out beyond the hotel and then down those partially lit streets they ran hiding their grand escape.

Ahhh, those youthful cries of exhilarating laughter when *the best laid plans* of panic finally come true... and *'away... we go...'*

Note: The line *'teenage wasteland'* was triggered by a lyric & song *'Teenage Wasteland'* by *'The Who'*.

Pat-Light & the drive-in show

So somewhere along the line I finally run into Pat-Light again, and maybe it was up at some bar or at some party but either way, we shared some drinks and chitter-chatter while I tried to win the heart of this sweet young lady. And to my surprise, I make some ground in my walk forward and I swing freely for a while before suggesting we should get away from it all for a bit, down to our driftwood palace. And surprisingly to me, she acquiesces to my suggestion.

"Sooo... you want a drink?" I ask.

"Sure"

So I fetch a couple of beers and we sit on the couch appropriately separated for a bit and resume talking about mostly nothing. Now I know the guys were all out this evening so no problem from a 'being alone' standpoint. So I try to be seductively romantic even though I'm about as inept as 'inept' can be before a crusty blue Maryland crustacean steps forward in my head and sings out as loud as he goes... *"for Christ sakes, kiss the girl"*

...and I *hem & haw* for a bit trying to get it right after all, what if she doesn't want to be kissed? What if she just likes me as a friend? Then what happens if I move in too close? Will it kill everything we have even if it's only flirting on my part cause that wouldn't be so good after all, I like her... as a person and as an attraction.

"For Christ-sake, just kiss the girl" sings this crusty blue Maryland crustacean

...but... but... but...<??>

So finally, I move in close to listen to what she's saying although I hear little cause I'm focused on my next step when she says to me... "you know what... you can kiss me if you like"

'Wowww...'

It takes a miracle in some cases to make a dream come true.

Of course, maybe it's just what I thought she said but regardless, in a short bit of time we are *locked & loaded* playing at what young teens do when playing around with the hormonal fire of such naïve kids... with hands moving around the clock and touching what ignites a fire until it's all shattered by noise outside the door... which is when I pull back from the little action we have going-on to see if it's what I hear cause - 'that wouldn't be so damn good, would it?' thinks I...

Now I disengage from this story for just a moment, as I swim through some deep blue waters down below the surface where I encounter a little octopus who's busy feeling around at many new things with his many arms when he smiles at me with one of those pleasing-type smiles one gets when they feel heaven is within one's touch... and the little octopus says to me, 'what's this I've found<?>'

Ahhh... the touch of heaven<??>, I suppose. Where youth & energy engages in the heavenly touch of the unknown where life makes a big splash.

...and now, back to our regularly scheduled show.

"Mannn, that was a rush..." comes the grabbled sounds from the leader of our pack from outside the door and then... my hormonal rush is finally shattered with the sound of his voice... and the door swings open and Johnny-boy & Bobby appear through the door surprised to see us sitting near each other on the couch although we are now separated by just enough even though we're a bit disheveled and appearing to be pleasantly pleased with ourselves just enough to be suspicious to a new pair of eyes...

And Bobby smirks a bit cause he 'suspects' while Johnny-boy is a bit *quizzical* in this surprise... "Sooo... am I missing something<??>" Johnny-boy says to us.

...cause he knows or suspects something is amiss too but he thinks I wouldn't dare be playing where I shouldn't be playing; I guess he hadn't noticed the sweet flirting I'd been doing with this fine young lady, his cousin.

"Hey... sooo... what you two been up to?" I say to the two of them.

"We just got back from our great escape..." says Bobby.

...and Johnny-boy laughs a bit at the thought of the two of them escaping through the window at the Yankee Clipper. And after a moment he returns to us.

"Sooo... what you two been up to then?" says this more suspicious Johnny-boy "cause..."

"Nothing"

...and again, Bobby smirks cause *we-all* know what's happening and it's almost like I've been discovered by a father who wants to know 'what *da hell* are you doing here?' kind of thing going-on cause Johnny-boy is a bit over-protective of his cousin and while he likes me enough, *ahhh*... there are limits, I suppose.

And believe me, I know... cause I'm conscious of the fact that if I cross over a broken bridge there's a cost to be paid although I hadn't thought or planned for it to all happen here or anytime soon.

"Relax cous... I'm alright" says a cheery light from this sweet lioness with a slightly sweet giggle of one who knows she in the 'spot light'.

"Okay, but you'll let me know if he strays off the rails, right?"

...and again cousin-Pat laughs at Johnny-boy's over protection... "Sure" ...and again, with a slight giggle.

"You guys want a beer?" Bobby asks, to break the ice.

"*Yeahhh*" says Johnny-boy, more relaxed now...

"Me too" I say.

"Pat, you want one?"

"*yeahhh*"

...and Bobby grabs and hands out the *brewskis*...

"So what happened?" I ask, trying to break-loose from this moment once & for-all.

"We got caught when the cops busted into the Yankee Clipper" says Bobby... and Johnny-boy cracks-up in laughter, "You should have seen us making our great escape..."

"...and your fat ass squeezing out of that window"

And laughter erupts from those two fools... "yeah, well, you didn't look so damn slick sliding out of that window either"

...and *blah-blah-blah*... it goes on for a while and all I know is I've escaped a close one temporarily and Bobby knows it too in the back of his mind, and Johnny-boy too, but he knows he's sent a clear message of 'be careful of where you tread dude, cause there's consequences for *f*<king-up*' and I've heard it loud & clear... Oh-so, loud & clear, as if it were *'crystal clear'*.

...a kitchen 'douchebag'

"Hey, you *douchebag*... what the hell are you doing?" goes one authoritative voice towards another clueless bastard.

...giggle, giggle, giggle... "*douchebag<??>*"

...giggle, giggle, giggle... goes the sounds of several boys plying the kitchen floor *back & forth* in the dish cleaning area doing our work.

"Hey..." I say to Jaybird.

"What?"

"You *friggin' douchebag*... get... da f*<k... outta here"

...giggle, giggle, giggle...

"Nooo... you, *douchebag*... you... get da f*<k outta here..."

...and *back & forth* it all goes between several *douchebag-talking* boys who, despite our age, really have no idea what a douche is or even why we are saying such shit as '*douchebag, this & that*' other than we've heard it used today and for some reason, it just seems to roll off our tongues so easily...

"Hey, *douchebag*..." goes the yells *back & forth* like a contagious cold between the boys in the kitchen area where the hot water machines are kicking up such a fuss as we're cleaning the *utensils & talking shit,* that the noise blunts our stupid-ass sounding tongues which are mostly lost within all the whirling, whining & banging of all the kitchen cleaning machines which is probably better than not, for everyone else who's working in the kitchen area.

Carolina-Blue at the crab shack blues, once again...

So Jaybird and I were making some of our usual plate & utensils runs from the kitchen cleaning area where we worked, out to one of the various kitchen stations we serviced through the night when we hear the lyrical voice of one Carolina Blue.

"Hey Jay, what's going on?"

...and we looked in unison at this pretty young lady who's got teasing eyes dancing over at Jaybird while she's making her food pickup.

...and Jaybird smiles his shy-like grin much like a *Chessy-cat* might do at this pretty dreamboat and he utters out a low reframed response which even I can't hear; some people just cannot be helped, I suppose.

"You stopping by tonight? We've got a party going on later tonight"

...and I look at his *Chessy-cat* like smile he's got going-on that must be hiding a secret or something else going-on and I almost barf up hairballs of some sorts but in a happy *sorta* way for him, if such can be done.

"Yeah, I'll be there Blue" says this smiling jack-of-all-trades *Chessy-cat* of a clueless dude.

...and she smiles in return in a playful alley-cat *sorta* way that even makes my heart go *thump-thump-thump* in a love-struck way.

"Good, see you then"

And then she's gone with food in hand and on out the door into the restaurant area she goes delivering some tourist's food. And I look at Jaybird with a foolish smirk on my face even though he doesn't return my look almost like he knows I'm staring at him with a foolish 'what *da hell*' kinda grin I do sometimes. But I realize too, at least at this moment anyway(s), just how nice it is to see such cuteness sometimes... and I can't deny it anymore.

So how does that *ughhh*-like song go? *"Love... look at the two of [them]"* ...or something like that<??>

Note: The line '*love... look at the two of [them]*' was triggered by a lyric in the song '*Love. Look at the Two of Us*' by '*The Carpenters*'.

Vietnam and the crab shack blues

So I step outside the rear kitchen door of our restaurant this one evening to dump some trash when I stumble upon this dude outside taking a smoke break. Now he's a very quiet guy who doesn't say all that much about anything and while I'd seen him around for a while, I hadn't interacted with him all that much other than to nod in his direction on occasion like guys do sometimes when casting respect in another's direction. And he wasn't very dynamic or mouthy like Blondie... nor scary-tough like some guys could be or charming of the ladies either... in fact, he was more non-assuming almost like a manila folder type dude and for some reason or other we started talking during the break we had, again, just outside the kitchen door

...and somehow, the subject of Vietnam came up which was not something *we-all* talked about much in those days but it came up occasionally like it did here... and it turns out, he'd been over there as a young soldier for the evacuation of the Saigon Embassy just the year before or so; he was one of the many eighteen year old(s) or so, who were trying to bring order to the anarchy that was called 'the evacuation'... and I stood there wondering what he must have felt... what he must have seen... as just a boy... not an officer with a career ahead of him but as an enlisted boy who signed on and then got thrown into the mist of the last of the Vietnam actions America was involved in, officially at least... and I just couldn't imagine what it was, and I was awed by who he was for what he'd done...

In fact, I was thunder-struck by him cause he didn't seem like the soldier-type if there's such a thing; he wasn't a badass from *here or there* or some other such place and he's wasn't all bravado-like mouthy of a dude either, he was just a shy dude who didn't say much of anything; he just did his work and nothing more... but 'wowww'... I thought... we must seem silly to him for all the odd behaviors we exhibited over matters that 'matter not a bit' to those like him who've seen bigger things in their life.

...which brings me to a few side-stories if you will, that's sort of a detour from the main story but is still relevant in story content...

During the sixties and seventies, the Vietnam War dominated the TV screens here in the States and the lives of many young men and women who took their walk *to & fro* sometimes flashed before our eyes. And there were many who made the walk.

We-all knew of guys who disappeared into the war and when they returned they were changed and not always for the better... and yet some were okay, I suppose... and we knew of guys who talked of and learned strategies to avoid the draft too... and I knew parents in our essentially blue-collar like neighborhood who were war-hawks until our time came to be considered... and then they were more cerebral about things especially as the war worn on, as in, what's the purpose of this war anyway? Will my boy come home f*<ked-up physically and mentally with his future stolen from him because of some idiotic worries about some *'domino theory'*; conservatives at the time feared communism would spread across the oceans and disrupt the American way of life which oddly enough, was just ridiculous fear mongering bullshit. Communism can't spread where there's a good standard of living and freedom. But if you eliminate either of them and/or both [of them] then all ridiculous ideas are placed on the table. So it's rather naive to think our disagreements about the war's purpose was just about patriots and so-called non-patriots arguing because it's just not true.

We had an ex-soldier who lived across the street from me when I was growing up. He was, according to neighborhood rumors, an ex-paratrooper of the Screaming Eagles variety and he was against the war upon his return; he was polite and nice and funny and understanding and a straight up good guy as far as I could tell; he was older than me so we didn't really interact so much.

But I remember the old men in neighborhood saying the metal plate in his head had made him 'mental' (i.e. insane) for not supporting the war in Vietnam... the metal plate he'd earned fighting in Vietnam, the metal plate they did not have in their heads because they were not there... and they had the nerve to judge him as if they had earned the right to do so.

...but they weren't there in Vietnam... he was... so maybe he knew something they didn't know... but in 1969... there was not enough respect for those who knew, for those who saw, and for those 'who knew because they saw'... and that was a grave sin.

Which takes me to avoiding the Vietnam war... In the sixties the war was on TV and reports were coming in even if the so-called liberal press didn't report on the worst of it all although there was plenty bad shit shown... and the young were getting the real message despite the defense industries' pro-war message of 'we aren't losing the war'... and despite the conservative war-hawk's adamant demands that we must fight the *dominos' war*... kids were figuring out the truth ever so slowly and occasionally they developed alternative strategies for avoiding the war.

Now after a while, marriage and kids often helped one out of the war; college did too... and physical ailments like high blood pressure and bone spurs by some of the more gutless 45th-type windbags, often created a way-out of the dust storm too.

I remember this one professor who said he'd handed out a failure to some boy in his class who was then sent off to Vietnam cause the boy's draft deferment was lost due to his class failures... and the boy didn't come back. And somehow the professor found out about it and he said to us, a class of his at the time, that he never failed another student ever again; 'never!!!'... he said, he just couldn't do it anymore especially for some stupid-ass *dominos theory'* which was more fear-fabrication than real...

I knew this one guy who'd heard if you went out several nights before reporting for your physical and got 'totaled' on booze and stuff; consumed lots of alcohol and *'da such'*... your blood pressure would increase beyond acceptable levels. So you'd get *totaled* and then enter the physical arena looking straight but hoping your blood pressure stayed elevated long enough to get you exempted out of the draft. So some guys used such a strategy to try & avoid the draft although sooner or later, the military got wise to such tactics and they tried to keep such prospects for as long as they could, hoping for the blood pressures to normalize as the day wore-on and then presto, they got themselves a new recruit. But this friend of mine, he beat it out the door just before the crash made him eligible.

So it was a cat-and-mouse game which lots of guys knew of whether it was reported-on or not. And it wasn't reported-on in the so-called liberal press either. And I'm guessing there were other strategies used to avoid being drafted as well, like bone spurs which didn't exist but could be bought as an excuse with cash, provided you had it.

I knew this other guy who wasn't going to go to Nam no matter what, period. He was going to Canada if they called him up but eventually he struck a deal with his parents; he'd report to basic training and if he got orders for Nam then he'd disappear before they could bus him off.

So he finished basic and he got orders stateside to perform military armament testing instead of Vietnam so he got to do his patriotic duty without risking his neck in a war he no longer supported but make no doubt about this, he was NOT going to Nam cause he'd already figured out that the reason didn't justify the risk and unless they threw his ass straight on the bus before he could dig a hole out, he wasn't going. So the difference between him and criticized draft dodgers was minimal at best. The war was that unpopular among many of those who were of fighting age; they weren't cowards as much as they weren't going to be used by idiot conservative war-hawks who argued for an indefensible war while most of them kept their asses at home. The Reserves were another out assuming you could find a spot.

But some weren't so lucky... and they punched their tickets and went to the war. I was in a community college class in 1974 or so, a political science class, and the war came up in our discussions... and one thing led to another and a probing question was asked of the students or said about the war which we were mostly opposed to by then... and one student answered the question somehow although it's a bit unclear in my head about the specifics of the question or answer these days, as to what it was about except for the words which would follow the opening comments... and so the teacher's rebuttal to the student answer was something like "...and how do you know so much? ...were you there?"

And the student answered "*yeahh*h..."

...and then there's dead silence for a bit when suddenly this other student breaks the silence by sarcastically asking "...so did you murder anyone when you were over there?"

Now I was thunder-struck when it came out like that because I couldn't imagine saying anything so harsh towards the unfortunate souls who'd done their tours there cause they were generally speaking, grabbed for the war from our neighborhoods whether they wanted to go or not, cause almost all of those we knew who went to war at this time were grabbed for the war through the draft. Btw, by 1974 the draft had been replaced several years earlier with the lottery and forced service in Viet Nam was mostly over, as I recall.

Anyway(s)... this ex-soldier student, who was obviously a little older than us because he was drafted and that was gone by 1974, [he] pauses for a moment before answering in what seemed like a long dead-like quiet, at least, that's what I heard, a long-ass pause... and I couldn't look around at anyone... I just couldn't look... not at the ex-soldier nor at the student with no name who delivered the sarcastic line... and even though by this time, I too, was very much against the war and against any war that wasn't about stopping genocide or fighting for democracy and that's NOT capitalism either, and make no doubt about 'that' because democracy & capitalism are different: one is political and one is economic. My thoughts on war were: 'I'm not fighting to protect corrupt corporate capitalism stealing other peoples' mineral rights & lives to enrich corporate greed & avarice which many blind conservatives seem to support'. And I knew a few guys who were *sent off to foreign lands to go and kill some dudes over-there...'* and they weren't really *knowing corporate stooges* either so I felt bad for them despite my thoughts on the war. btw, I wasn't interested in wars pandering to racial bigotry & fear either.

...and most of these guys from our neighborhoods who were sent to Vietnam were just boys and they did what was expected of them... and they did what they had to do... and many had no idea where Vietnam was when they went either... or why it was... or why we were there... but 'America was good to them' or so they thought, and so it must be okay to go they thought, and it's what we were told to believe-in although in the end, I doubt the war in Vietnam had any real purpose beyond inflating the egos and revenues of the defense industry and their conservative war-hawks who had more bark than thunder which is why they sent others to fight their war in defense of their f*<king make-believe *'dominos'* fears.

So back to this ex-soldier student... so he paused for just a moment longer before answering the question... and then he says... "...*yeahhh*... I suppose I did..."

Well, I'll tell you this... I almost burst into tears cause here was a boy who'd gone to war not because he believed in the propaganda of the conservative war-hawks who kept their weak-ass souls at home while sending American boys from our working-class neighborhoods over there, into their war... but because he got a ticket to go and he thought that was what he was supposed to do at least initially, although later on when he was home with us, it was a big 'N-O', I think... Anyway(s), this guy was now smart enough to realize the difference between killing and murder was a thin-thin line and sometimes people crossed it and sometimes not... and I believe he was now more in line with 'this perspective' than other so-called blind patriotic deniers on such thoughts.

On the other hand, the student asking this sarcastic question was more than lucky, just like me, to have missed out on this horrible opportunity and decision and yet he made such a smart-ass judgment of such guys who were just like us other than they were unable to avoid what we luckily had avoided by time & space; we'd never faced the situation of this war... But in America at this time, you were either pro-war or not and there was little in-between at the time.

Now as for the 'did you commit murder?' remark from a theoretic stance: what's the difference between murder and killing? We think we know the difference but when you kill civilians, women and children unattached to a war, is it killing or murder hidden by a uniform? And when you are occupiers, is it killing or murder that you do?

And for some people, they have easy answers to such questions. Like 'Yes, it is' or 'No it isn't' but 'simple is almost always stupid' despite the 80's popular political line 'keep it simple, stupid'. Cause life isn't simple. It's multifaceted. It's complex. But regardless, we should all agree that killing non-combatant women & children and old & young men is murder, whether one's wearing a uniform or not, cause otherwise we probably lack any reasonable set of morals, conscience, character, or honor.

But it's easy to judge others from a theoretical basis although you never really know what you'd do unless you're there... and then you know; then morality meets the road with reality which is not meant as a way to rationalize away genocide even in the cases where obvious genocide-like actions were committed in Vietnam like in the My Lai massacre where American soldiers, who were mostly young men probably so-damaged by the hell created in this war that they descended upon the My Lai village and raped and killed and burned everything and everyone in front them... and while I imagine some of these soldiers rationalized their actions as necessary to rid the area of Viet Cong, I imagine some of these boys knew, at least after the event, that they were wrong in their hate; that they had indeed committed *'crimes against humanity'* in the rage of uncontrolled war... And they'd committed *murder* regardless of the uniforms they wore and the war they fought in... and now they'd have to live with their sins for the rest of their lives knowing they had killed women and children and the young and the old and for what?

Of course, way too many Vietnamese natives suffered from these horrific actions and they had to live with these results, as victims of these crimes... and let's remember, it was their home, their land, not ours... cause they were being killed and maimed and caught in the cross fire between warring sides... and they probably watched horrified as their neighbors and families were killed right in front of them... and their homes burned down beyond usefulness on their lands, many destroyed by foreigners, by occupiers... so no cupcake there either.

But that's the cost of war, isn't it? ...it's the reality of war, isn't it? At least, I imagine it's so... cause *hell is hell* whether it's *'here on earth'* or in the afterworld, and it ain't so good for anyone stuck in it, at least, I'd imagine it so. And so why should we think My Lai(s) couldn't happen there or anywhere else once war has begun? If you send naive youth into hell then why wouldn't they start to look at the world like Satan might do and for whatever reasons they make-up? ...and then they might treat the world like Satan might do too.

Anyway(s), back to this ex-soldier student I had in my class. I eventually befriended this guy because... *ahhh*, well, I don't rightly know why exactly... maybe I felt guilty for some reason for the accusation made against him even though I didn't make it... or maybe it was because he was one *cool-motherf*<king* dude from a place I respected and feared... either way, I was occasionally his shadow slumping along besides him walking from here to there.

It turns out this guy was from Irvington, a blue-collar home at the time to some of the bad-ass corner boys in America, at least, at the time I was growing up in *Charm City*... and *we-all* knew it... and *we-all* respected those streets when we walked in them... and he was one of those street-wise toughs patrolling the corners who probably barely survived high school... So he went on to work after high school fixing cars and chasing skirts and fighting on the weekends with whomever dared cross his path which wasn't all that much different from many of the others in such blue-collar neighborhoods I knew.

You see, outsiders weren't welcome in such neighborhoods which is *kinda* funny to me in retrospect, cause there was nothing really worth protecting there or little anyway(s)... cause you were living near the edge in some cases... and maybe that's what you're protecting, I don't know<??>... or maybe, it's just something to enliven a normal boring life in blue collar America... again, I don't know.

So Uncle Sam came a-calling for him after a bit and off he went...*'to some foreign land... to go and kill some yellow-dudes over there...'*

...and for some background musical tunes to this line, think of Springsteen's 'Born in the USA' and you got it all...

...and it turns out this guy wasn't so crazy about going to war either... imagine that<??>... why would any young guy want to go fight a war for a *dimwitted domino theory?* And while he didn't tell me much about the war because war veterans rarely tell civilians anything about their experiences and maybe that's because we don't know nor will we ever know or understand what it is... or maybe they just want to forget it because the feeling of hell can only be shared with those who have been in war too, and survived... again, I don't know... but he did tell me this one story which kind of shows the complexity of war in general and this war in particular... and I don't remember what brought the subject up but it came up anyway(s)...

So on one of this guy's last nights in Vietnam before shipping home, he was infantry so he was one of those dudes walking up and down those god forbidden trails in Nam getting picked off one at a time at different times & places while killing and/ or murdering others different than themselves, anyway(s), he went out with his buddies into town drinking and carousing and carrying-on with the Vietnamese girls, I suppose... and *low-and- behold...* he sees his hated sergeant out on the streets sometime during the evening and before the night ends, he silently follows the sergeant into a darkened place where he beats the hell out of him without exposing himself to the man... I suppose, for what this sergeant dude had done somewhere else along the line whether earned or not, I do not know... but he did it... and afterwards, this soldier-boy goes back to camp...

Now later that night, the unit this guy was part of was pulled outside the barracks and forced to stand in line while the army tried to identify the soldier (or soldiers) responsible for beating this sergeant's ass up... so I'm guessing, it (the beating) was pretty bad... and when no one steps forth... they commence checking all the soldiers' hands for evidence of a fight... cuts and bruises and *da such*...

...and so as he's telling me this story, I'm all breathless and all at this moment in his story cause I know he's the culprit... and surely, he's going to get caught... so I breathlessly ask him before he can even finish his story... "sooo, what did you do?"

...and he chuckles just a bit... "I didn't do nothing... I didn't have any cuts and bruises on my hands... cause I beat his body... I never went upstairs... I covered my hands before I hit him and I didn't hit anything that cut or bruised me..."

...and I chuckled a bit at what this guy had done... right or wrong... cause his Irvington upbringing had probably saved his ass in Vietnam combat if that's possible... and now, it had saved him from the brig on one of his last nights in Vietnam.

I remember hearing about 'fragging' on occasions (I think that's what they called it at the time) being done in Vietnam... it was something which leaked out in the news on rare occasions but it was definitely something the so-called liberal press didn't talk much about; it was one of those hidden secrets of sorts, I think... so it was rarely admitted to in the press or openly discussed in public... and when it was, the bad-guys were always identified as the soldiers who did it cause sergeants or officers were never wrong or so it was believed in the press... so their integrity was never questioned when fragging occurred of course, cause it opens up a big riff in the chain of command and it's hard to fight a war that way...

But it also indicates there's something very *'wrong in demark'* as the saying goes... cause soldiers don't usually break the chain of command too damn often I think, cause they're taught NOT to do so... and the consequences are usually pretty damn bad when you do... so to do so means (1) something is criminally wrong with the rank-&-file soldiers OR (2) there's something very wrong with the commands coming down the chain of command; something is considered so repugnant to those on the receiving end like maybe poor decisions which needlessly cost people's lives for less than valid reasons, maybe<??>... I don't know... but what this guy seemed to confirm for me was 'such things' happened in Nam, maybe by fists as his story suggested and maybe by guns as was rumored 'to be'... or maybe it was just that *shit happened'* as we like to say... and maybe something had been very wrong where he'd been for this to happen cause we don't usually beat-up people or our authorities unless something is very wrong, at least, in my opinion... or maybe, he was just bad. Who knows<??> ...although he seemed like an okay guy to me so there was that going-on.

So I was again, surprised and awed by this guy... again, not because I thought of him as right or wrong cause the truth is, I didn't know... but I understand how a sense of heightened or explosive pent-up anger might propel one to kill/hurt a *terrible impediment to fairness* on their way home if given the chance to do so, so I get it, assuming that was the case, again, I don't know...

The point is this: this ex-soldier was just a guy... a boy, a young man when he was sent off to war... no war hero... no bum... no terrible person... just a guy... a boy when he went... a soldier in the field... and a young man on the mend after his return... not better or worse, just a guy... and I liked the *'he'* who had returned... and I didn't really know him all that well either but still I got a very-slight glimpse into him for the very short period of time we shared together no matter how superficial it was, and it was short; so not so much... but as I said, I liked him, for better or worse, I liked him... and he was bigger than life to me, of sorts, and I don't totally know why other than he saw, he did, and he reflected afterwards, and he had a growing intellect with some *kinda* right & wrong sense of fairness going-on by now even if he had a bit of an unscripted rough & tough Clint Eastwood edge to him. But he wasn't *no damn* movie star; there was no script here... he was real... and although I'd never be able to pick him out of a crowd today, I remember him... and I think he will always walk with me in my head no matter where I go...

...and at this point, it just seems like there should be some kinda background musical tunes like Springsteen's 'Born in the USA'... right<??>

So in the end... I return to this crab shanty kitchen dude I was talking to outside the crab shanty kitchen door at the beginning of this chapter cause he too, became larger than life to me much like this ex-soldier student dude I was just talking about had, and not for any other reason other than I imagine he'd seen shit that most of us could never imagine... and while we fretted over doing our jobs at this crab shanty restaurant like Blondie did cause he wished to *'be da lion-man of da kitchen'*, or when we fretted over girlfriends or lovers we'd hope would thrill us during our nights... or when we fretted over being *'da mannn in OC'* at some time or other... or when we fretted over getting good grades in school when we returned to college in the fall semester so we could get good jobs later in life with good wages and a good future after that, etc... he must have known there were things much bigger than *'that'* in the world... things, that make these cares of ours seem small in comparison... cause he'd seen important shit, scary shit... he'd seen fear and relief. So how do you go-on with life after seeing that? ...how do you join in on all our simple-minded rat-race games which means almost nothing after seeing all the other wild shit in the world like *'the evacuation'* ...or *war in the trenches... thattt,* was what amazed me about him, and them, and others... cause I just couldn't imagine... and I can't imagine still.

...and once again and for the final time... it just seems like there should be some kinda background musical tunes bouncing off the ceiling as loud as it goes, like Springsteen's 'Born in the USA'...

(cc) a boardwalk Ferris-wheel ride at night

Now in one of those chitter-chatter-like ways it all goes sometimes when reflecting on a memory gone by...

There's a young couple up on a Ferris-wheel down along the boardwalk of some Ocean City town tucked away *in 'the pleasant land of Living'*; she's all giddy with laughter and fun while he's f*<king scared to death even though he's trying to be stoic like he's cool with everything... *kinda* like Clint Eastwood might be up there in the air. But there's just a single bar across their lap that's holding them in this sky bucket of a seat and he's thinking to himself, 'shit, I could bend this f*<king bar and then what would we do?'

'How safe could this f*<king be?' he wonders ...'you know, being up here in the air with just this single bendable bar between us and falling out of this chair, down to our death way-down below'... it can't be safe, right?

But he keeps a stiff upper lip like cool dudes might do... but if one were to look a bit closer into his eyes they'd see his aloofness is concealing his deep-seated fear cause he's scared to f*<king death up there.

So around and around they go for a bit while she looks down upon the boardwalk below with the delight of a child feasting on candy sprinkles dancing upon a chocolate Sunday cone... and she talks with glee at all she sees of this Ocean City town from way up on top of the world... while her stoic love sees nothing but death below... although in fairness, the glittering lights of this Ocean City town is quite spectacular even for him despite his fear.

But after a while the big wheel lurches to a stop for a few moments while the operator unloads and then loads new couples onto their ride into the sky... and while this height-challenged boy tries to be cool at each stop they make as the unloading and loading is repeated for a bit, his love bounces and churns while straining to see another view as they inch upward during such lurched filled moments... all the while the boy prays that when they stop again, it won't be too high in the sky or on the downward side of the wheel where one can see out as far as the horizon... or... where one can see how far they could fall below...

...but as luck would have it... the wheel stops up near the top and just a bit over the other side, just a bit... and his carefree girlfriend rocks the chair with glee looking out and pointing at the lights down below... so much so that this cool aloof boy finally cracks with excited fear breaking in his voice...

"what the hell are you doing? You're rocking the chair<??>"

...and the girl looks at him for a moment in surprise... "are you scared?"

Well, the last thing this boy wants to say, whether it's true or not, is 'yes, I'm scared'... so he blurts out a big fat "No... I'm not scared... it's just that, you're rocking the chair"

...and she smiles and says with a slight rocking motion that would be oh-so sexy if they weren't so high up in the air..."you mean like this..."

And he grabs onto the back of the seat and says... "good God girl, stop it..."

...and she smiles at her wounded wolf partner who she metaphorically holds in her hands without even a touch... "so you don't like this so much?" ...she says, as she rocks gently in her seat, *back & forth*, again, in such a way that his hormones would be racing if they weren't so damn high up in the sky, held in by this simple bendable bar that's keeping them in a seat which could seemingly, be rocked completely over if you tried.

"Please..." he says as gallantly as any man can say who's scared to f*<king death of a fall... "I'm afraid of this shit, okay?"

...and she smiles sweetly in a rather sexy teasing *sorta* way... "Sooo... you wouldn't want to rock-n-roll just a bit, up here in the air... would you?"

And his face is contorted between laughing at her teasing and crying in fear while trying to maintain some level of manhood that's all but evacuated his body by now... "No..."

...and she smiles delicately... then moves just a bit closer and kisses him on his cheek...

...but of course, the seat bucket moves with any movement she makes so it sways just a little in the carnival-lit sky they dance above and in... so he doesn't really enjoy the moment as he'd like too...

Sooo... *"yeahhh*, okay" ...is all he can say without bursting into frightful tears.

But eventually the wheel's lurching forward and stopping, stops... and then there's a bit more of the continuous roll that occurs on a Ferris-wheel ride before all this *'fun in the sky'* comes to an end with their own unloading... with her all a-twitter from the thrill of the ride... and him, 'oh-so glad to be standing on solid ground' once again.

...but what about 'the sexy' stuff?

Oh yeah... cause now would be a fine time for some of that 'sexy shit', thinks one grateful sure-footed boy.

Bobby and his stogie

Now this one night the *driftwood boys* of Johnny-boy, Bobby and I, were out drinking and carrying-on at some bar with little success at wooing lovely ladies our way when we stumbled outside under the street lights where we were laughing and leaning on whatever we could lean on cause we weren't too steady standing out on own... when Bobby pulls out his late night stogie he sometimes lit up after a night of too much booze... and he lights it up and takes a big pull on that thing when I think to myself... 'you know, that looks alright'

Of course, it isn't [so cool] cause smoking causes cancer and we knew of it then despite big tobacco lies to the contrary, but still, despite this important fact... he just looked cool pulling on his stogie under the dim street lights up above so I said boldly to *da man*... "Bobby, let me have a drag on that..."

So he handed it over and I took my pull and inhaled like I was sucking on heaven's gate... and back and forth it went for a short bit before I excused myself to catch my breath.

Now it turns out I don't handle my booze all that well, in fact... I'm not good at it at all... I mean, at first, I'm great at it... I just *kinda* float up into the sky with *'happy feet'*... but then, when I'm drinking too much, like this night... then I continue on my voyage much-further out into the stratosphere until I'm so far out there that I can't return to earth without crashing head first back to earth, splitting my noggin wide open...

So this is one of those nights... and I am still riding the wave out into the stratosphere when I take my puffs on his cigar... but I'll be crashing back to earth in the very near future, just spinning and spinning around as I enter the gravitational fields before crashing and burning upon impact... and I do it this night as I come splattering back to earth with a splitting headache which feels like someone has buried a hatchet in the middle of my skull and I can't shake the fun of it all no matter what I do... but to make matters worse...

...I've also smoked on that damn cigar of his when I'm not really a smoker, in fact, that's my first drag on a cigarette or cigar of any kind if you will... and the nausea from the smoke, and the feel of the smoke turning around and around in my throat, just mixing in so well with the hatchet buried in my head, it leaves me ecstatic for several days with this haunting fun from our night out on the town.

I imagine I was a blast of fun at work the following day, running those plates *here & there* with the clanging of the dish washing machines we filled and managed, and the noise from the guys talking their shit which just gets so much worse with all such commotion that you just want to die and go to hell to relieve yourself of it-all... yep, it was fun alright...

So I never smoked again... and I mean NEVER... cause it made my hangover so much worse that I never even considered it again. I wish I could say I never got plastered again but I did and I would... and as usual, I'd regret it all so very much, often thinking in retrospect, *'why da f*<k would I do that to myself?'*

...you know, making myself sick when I'd entered the night perfectly healthy... cause it just doesn't make a whole lot of sense especially when there are sick people in the world who'd cut their arms off for another healthy day... Of course, the problem with alcoholic-soaked fun is this: there's lots of fun to be had when you're hanging-out with your friends drinking all those warm & fuzzy drinks bringing out so much laughter and gaiety in its rather intoxicating *sorta* way... but there's always a price to pay for such trips, at least for guys like me.

de Altoona boys and
da basketball blues

Now as I mentioned earlier, I couldn't help but like *da Dudley-do* character cause he was just such a nice and sweet-hearted *kinda* dude who could laugh and carry-on over almost anything, more or less... but in a nice way so no negatives from the guy... and he'd strike out in ways that just seemed okay to be around most times besides being a good worker who worked around the clock which he and his brother did all the time, taking every hour they could get which was exhausting to watch cause they never really saw the glittering sun in Ocean City other than in the morning on their way to meal-time and work... and of course, they might have seen the stars at night which could sometimes be seen shining above you when you were away from the carnival lights shining along the boardwalk during the evening hours.

But the other thing about *Dudley-do* was this... *Dudley-do* was a basketball player... and maybe we shared some of 'that' even though I was just the usual *Charm City* playground basketball player type although on the duller side of things mostly, while *Dudley-do* was supposedly better cause he was a high school basketball player from up Altoona's way which means what exactly<??>... like maybe he was 'better than me, of course'... so I often thought of lacing it up with him, with him leading us, the kitchen mongrels, out onto the court against our crabby shack elitist waiters who thought of themselves as so good at all things athletic and *crow-worthy* and I figured win or lose, we'd do all right fighting at our restaurant job-class-war with him at the helm for all the bragging rights there was down at our sweet little crab shack of ours, so there was *that going-on* too...

So the scene is set: I walk-on up to the basketball courts near the 3rd street ball park area and there's basketball going-on up on the courts with the usual shit-talking running-out of some guys' mouths when I notice some of our crab shanty wait-staff playing ball amongst themselves on one of the half-court sides. So I sit my ass down on some bleachers watching out of curiosity at their game wondering if they were beatable.

Now I knew they were playing today cause talk had run through the kitchen area earlier about some play and I'd pitched my arguments to *Dudley-do* and crew about playing but I didn't know if he'd or they'd come on out to play especially with his work schedule being of paramount concern to him. But, I'd said to him, "it's time to assert your kitchen *b-ball* dominance in the restaurant world" although I *kinda* figured it was wasted on him cause he didn't care about such things nor the potential spin-off opportunities for parties & girls which could come from playing...

So I'm sitting there watching the guys playing knowing they don't know me cause they never looked our way even though I only recognized a few of them cause truth be told, I didn't look their way much either, minus the female wait staff.

"Heyyy" comes a jolly-ass greeting... "So they any good?"

...and I look-up and to my surprise, *Dudley-do* is standing there...

"Not as good as us" I say rather chipper-like.

...and the two of us are looking at their game for a bit, sizing them up when another couple of kitchen mongrels meander on up.

"What's going on?"

...and *Dudley-do* laughs his all shucks *kinda* laugh and giggles like the sweet-heart he is, pointing and telling us what he thinks when one of the guys playing ball sees us gathering and he breaks from the game and walks off the court towards us.

"You guys want to play? We're about done and we can pick-up sides for next game"

"F*<k that" comes another voice, "Let them play five of us" says one of the waiters playing ball.

And I and *Dudley-do* smile out like *Chessy* cats might do... "Sure, whatever..."

But I want the game. I want *Dudley-do* to do them up right like I expect him to do cause we are *'Spartacus... da f*<king KINGs of da kitchen urchins'*

And a few of the wait-staff are ready too. 'Let's do this thing' I say to myself cause I know there's benefits from banging into the top dogs and chilling them down. There's parties and girls and what do we want? Girls...

So the sides are picked and the strutting starts just before the ball is tossed into play and before I know it, *Dudley-do* explodes past some *waiter-dud* defending him up top and then he flies up into the air like a jet on steroids might do, up into the stratosphere... and he crashes down upon the rim with a thunderous slam that shakes the rim and opens our eyes to what none of us had ever expected.

But did I expect 'that', you ask?

No f<king way!* In fact, I was a bit suspicious of him even though I was hopeful of his high school playing abilities but did I expect him to *fly like Mike* (think: 'Michael Jordan' here) up above us grounded dudes? No way! And his explosion past his defender meant they were in trouble cause NO one was going to be fast enough to face him up one-on-one, probably. It was him versus the rest of us except, I was on his team.

So I did a short dance and pointed to *da Dudley-do man* yelling-out "that's how you bring the money!!!" ...and there's laughter from the other kitchen mongrels who now know all we've got to do is play some *kinda* defense and let him kill the waiters' while dancing in the air.

"Yeah, yeah, yeah..." says another annoyed ball player from the waiters side of things who thinks the other defender was just a fool. "I've got him this time" he says and he moves out front where *Dudley-do* has gathered again waiting for the ball to start our half-court second possession where 'winner takes all'.

...and *Dudley-do* drops the ball into position and stares his rival down before jab stepping and pulling up and dropping a deuce from the key. Bammm!!!

...and I roll at the waist and howl upward with extreme enthusiasm cause I know it's now over, before it's even begun... cause *Dudley-do is da friggin man of la muncha* where I mean exactly what I write; he's going to kick these guys' asses way too bad for them ever to strut their shit on the courts no-more.

"You are *Spartacus!!!*" I yell... "Spartacus - *da f*<king KING of da Crab shack*"

...and the kitchen mongrels laugh at what they hear as do a few of the waiters who know what the hell is happening out there while the last dude to be toasted scowls a disbelieving 'I dare you to do it again' *kinda* look but I know it's all over. He's too fast. He's too *high-a-flier* to be stopped and he can shoot too. There's no 'D' for him today other than five of them on him and none on us.

"Hey..." comes a voice that breaks my moment in space... and I look up to see who it is.

"What *yaaa* up to...?"

"Nothing much" I say in return to Jaybird's inquiry.

"So they're playing ball, huh<??>... You?"

"*Nahhh...*" I say... "I don't need to today cause *Dudley-do* is *da man* even though he ain't here so..."

...and Jaybird looks around the court confused cause he doesn't see *Dudley-do* but maybe that's because he's incognito-like today, just hiding in the suit of Mike... or maybe he's my imaginative b-ball warrior dancing above the rims in a '*Spartacus - da f*<king KING of da Crab shack*' sorta way... cause maybe - I'm just day-dreaming again; I seem to do that sometimes.

"Sooo... you want to get something to eat?"

"Sure... where we going?"

"How about up on the corner?"

...so off we go, the two of us, while the game I played inside my head dwindles away as the guys on the court played a dandy of a game behind us.

Now in fairness, I must set the record straight here cause to some extent I haven't. There probably isn't a big difference between the wait staff and the kitchen-help economically speaking or otherwise for that matter, cause we're all white kids from mostly blue-ish to light-colored white collar middle-class areas with most of the wait staff on the slightly better side of us, the kitchen mongrels, but we aren't all that much different minus our supposed crab-shack differences defined in our work statuses... and the clothes we wore to work of course, cause the dish-washing staff was worn & torn in jeans and tee-shirts covered in the grim of wet dishes and food throw-away stuff we had to deal with... and they, the wait staff, were clean and neat in their waiters/waitress outfits which they had to have on for the customers but other than the obvious 'looks' differences, we were really the same... except like I said, our supposed class differences related to our work statuses in this little crab shanty world.

And of course, oddly enough... *Dudley-do* and I never do lace it up together; the summer just slipped away and he worked morning, noon, and night... and I, worked most evenings while stalking the ladies up on the beach during the days without much luck and in the evening too, again, without much success there either... so not all so magically well-done by either of us, I suppose...

But the funny thing though, about sports, is this: it usually cuts across other divides, much like music does. And by that, I mean, good ballplayers recognize each other and usually if you're good enough to play there's a respectful bond that's formed by many of the guys & gals who are playing their games which often times makes up for any other perceived differences in color, financial status, oddness, work status, etc... Most ballplayers I've known follow this credo whether they know it or not, with only a few *shitball* exceptions cause once you've proved yourself on the fields or on the courts, etc., it's like you're entered into *'the club'*... and it opens up opportunities you didn't know existed before. Ditto for music and other similar pursuits.

And I found 'this' to be true at all levels of school too... and at work too, later in life... but one has to put themselves out there to do it which we didn't do *'down de ocean'* with the work staff at that little crabby shack up on 21st street... but if we had, there's no doubt that the number of people we knew would have grown immeasurably because it always did so in all the other cases I knew, so why wouldn't it have worked there too?

Now that doesn't mean I didn't go on up the courts and sometimes join in on some of the *reindeer games* with the guys shooting-it around, cause I did. And sometimes it led into a game and sometimes not.

Talking rot at the bar

So me and Big Al are sitting at this bar that sits just to the left of the laundromat where we are doing our weekly wash. There's a ballgame up on this old TV and we're just mindless looking at it without too much interest in the game itself. We're just killing time while our clothes dance in their tumbler.

"So… you seen Pat-light recently?"

"No…"

…and a few moments tumble by while we watch the commotion on TV without digesting too much of it.

"I think she likes you"

"You think?" I say as I turn slightly his way… "How can you tell?"

"I just think it, that's all…"

…and I turn away back to this inconsequential game up on the TV knowing I'm probably throwing away a real possibility with her cause she's sweet and smart and empathetic and pretty too… and her eyes are alluring beyond belief but for some reason I can't seem to understand, I tend to balk at any girl who seems mildly interested in me beyond a shallow passing interest almost like I want what I can't have…

It's almost a curse or so; if they don't want me then I'm attracted to them and if they dare to think maybe I'm okay then I'm *'oh-no, senorita'*… almost like *'I want until I can see and then I don't know no more'* cause then what<??>… it's like I'm on a steel girder way up high and I'm looking out on the distance beyond me and I'm fine up there for a moment or two but then I see the step I'm supposed to make or at least, want to make and then I'm frozen in my tracks... I can't breathe like I fear what's next when I embrace all the beautiful possibilities there are with all its imperfections as well, and I know, even at this youthful age although not in a 'completed' *sorta* way, that we are all imperfect... we're not as symmetrical as we should be... nor as rounded in our appearance as we ought to be... nor *this or that* or whatever... cause we are imperfect beings and yet for some reason perfection seems so possible to me at this time, almost an expectation of some sorts, as it does for most young people feasting on such illusions.

But it's not. There is no perfection. There is only us. And we are people with hopes and dreams and steadiness and lost-ness and wobbles and sturdiness and everything else that goes along with being human. We are imperfect even in our uniqueness which is quite perfect in an imperfect *sorta* way.

So what's the problem I wonder, beyond my own imperfection?

Answer: I just don't know. But the depth of my emptiness is surely dangling beneath my feet even if I can't think of one good reason for my unsteadiness.

detour: disturbed parts...

Now, I detour from the story just a bit to dance along the path of an 'unknown'...

There's a slightly disturbed young boy who seems to have it all together, at least, on the outside or so it seems to some, most times anyway(s)... but he's often times more of an unexplained volcano imploding on the insides with self-doubt and self-loathing which complicates his youthful travels most of the time especially when he's preoccupied with the expedient and mundane activities of everyday life.

...and there's also this girl who's dealing with her own blindness as to where she must go and how to get there although she's much more stable in her mixture than him... and she possesses a bright smile that melts most of the boys under her gaze much less this clueless boy... and often times, she just seems to make this boy's love-struck toes curl *under & over* with a desire that's as much emotional as it's physical...

...so this couple takes a secret rocket ship ride through the cosmic delights hidden along some spacey dark road one night to 'nowhere' special and when they get there, they dance just a little bit to the music playing in the air although they never really get to touch the holy grail cause one young beautiful rose's thorn seems to fear the glittering unknown of happiness.

And this talking thorn says to this beautiful rose flower...

"Have you ever thought of driving straight into the on-coming lights that dot the roads we travel at night?"

...and this beautiful rose flower recoils just a bit in shock &

surprise cause 'who the hell says such a thing'? …although she doubts his insanity for some reason which may be delusional or maybe not<??>…

But still the question remains… 'who the hell would say such a thing'?

The 'damaged', maybe… a fool, maybe… or a 'slightly disturbed' young man under the pressure of growing-up inside a blank canvass where there exists all the possibilities of the world but with no definitive road map identifying a clearly chosen path like you get in school most times, as to where to go and where not to go…

But even so, why toss in the nuts when this dish of roses is so sweet?

Who the hell knows<??>… but sometimes, it just happens in life, I suppose… or as is often said, *'shit happens'*… and you roll-on by to wherever it goes… although hopefully, not while driving into the on-coming lights of innocent drivers on the roads we travel.

So a void seems to develop beneath their feet as *'the crazy'* falls away into a world most don't truly understand, nor him for that matter, nor I either… somewhere out between the happy and the wretched unknown… and those rose peddles are cut loose to find another sweet home upon a more stable stalk of sanity where the sun might shine brightly cause the thorn knows he's tainted by a spotted disturbed unknown.

But time and space rarely clears away the feelings that once were… and sometimes, events occur which brings it all back into perspective, as to *'what was'*, and *'what wasn't'*… and *'what could have been'*, at least in an unclear *sorta* shimmer of a dream, had it not been for one giant big gaping hole of *disturbing* screwing things up…

…and then suddenly for no good reason, I find myself in a cloudy mist of smoke in some rundown bar where one old dude sits alone

drinking a beer as slowly as illusions might do, and I think to myself, 'what da f*<k - is this?'

...and a trusty face I've seen many times before and since such times, [he] chuckles at me before turning slightly towards me, saying... "what da f*<k is wrong with you?"

Now it is at this time when it should be mentioned that this dude is someone I call 'Patty-boy'... and he is an illusion; he did exist... and then he didn't...

So Patty-boy has turned my way, slightly at first, like he'd expected me... so I'm a bit confused and a bit surprised because I don't remember choosing to be here in this scene and yet I'm writing this piece of muckish foolishness so there's that going on, I suppose... but I see him so I know there's 'trouble a-brewing' of sorts...

...and he laughs a bit at me cause, well... that's what he does...

"Sooo... what da hell is that story supposed to mean? And tell me you didn't say 'that' to some girl. Even you couldn't be that stupid. No way, right? Maybe you were smoking on that screen dude-dad-thing you talked about earlier, or so"... and he laughs at me like so...

And I smirk a bit at his humor... "No... I'm just saying shit and that's all... it's just a story"

...and again, he continues his laughing... "come on... tell your uncle Pat what's you doing there?"

"Nothing... it's just a story and nothing more"

"So you didn't say any such thing to some girl, right?"

...and I say nothing at first although I chuckle nervously, just looking at him unsure of what to say or do.

And he chuckles at me after a bit, partly surprised and partly mystified, I suppose... "Tell me you didn't say 'that'"

...and again I say nothing although again, I chuckle a bit trying to

deflect with a slight embarrassed smirk...

"You did, didn't you?"

"Well..." and I quiver and quake just a bit... "well, you could say... ahh.., that maybe, I had some problems for a bit back then, maybe<??> ...I guess"

"Problems... you were f*<ked up in the head. I thought it was just a story"

"Well... it is but..." and I pause for a moment cause I know there's a bit of truth hidden within the script.

...and Patty-boy looks at me stunned for a moment before he chuckles at me again...

"So you're f*<ked up, right?"

And I laugh back at him just a bit "ahhh yeah, and F*<k you too, mannn..."

"So who was it, this charming young lady who you freaked out?"

"It's nobody... don't worry about... it's just a story with a slight point"

"come-on, tell your uncle Pat who she is..."

And I chuckle just a bit... "F*<k you, mannn..."

"Yeah, like you haven't said that enough already... come-on, who da hell is she?"

...and I pause for a bit, as I gather my thoughts... cause I'm not sure what to say about any of it... cause it's just a story, more or less... Then after a pause I start into my bit...

"Did I ever tell you that Pat-Light died from cancer way-back-when we were on the youngish-adult side of things... and still way too damn young to do so?"

...and then Patty-boy is quiet... cause he figures she was the one

'charming young lady' unfortunate enough to be with a troubled young man on a bad night-out or at least, in this story... and we-all liked Pat, all of us, and Patty-boy knew of her too... and while most times Patty-boy likes to give me shit about things I do wrong and maybe, rightly so, he doesn't this time... he just looks me in the face as I try and avoid him by looking forward at some far-away spot on a wall in a make-believe dimension... but I notice his stare just the same and he says not a word during a slightly elongated silence...

"Pat... she was terrific" he finally says.

"Yeahhh... she was..."

...and I pause for a moment again... and I take a breath... "yeah, I f*<ked that up in some ways much like so many others, I guess" ... and then it all starts to tumble out of me...

I remember when Johnny-boy told me about her death... I had stopped by to see him at a time when I had a long-time relationship falling apart on me and I think I needed to see a sympathetic face even though I was never going to tell him about my troubles... but I just needed to see someone on my side, I guess... someone sympathetic to my plight even if he didn't know everything there was to know... anyway(s), we were downstairs in that basement man-cave like place of his where he'd hide away sometimes, I guess... and he told me Pat got cancer... and he said his uncle told him, after the fact, that it was a good thing Johnny-boy hadn't seen her at the end cause it just ate her up in the end... and I was stunned... my mouth must have fallen down a foot or so... and then my eyes filled with tears like a dam was about to be overrun with rushing waters.

I hadn't seen or thought too much about her in a long while before he told me about it cause we often let the past go with time, I guess, no matter what it is, as I had [done]... and with everything going on at the time, well, it just hit me like a thud when he said it... and as I sat there for a moment... it just all welled up inside me and I almost burst into tears right there in front of him. It was everything I could do not to break down right there in front of him and mannn, I didn't want to do that...

Sooo, I turned my face a little this way & that... in every direction but where he was so as he talked about this or that or Pat, in the moments that followed, he couldn't see that my eyes were so filled with tears, like a dam just about to burst open... cause I knew if he saw it, it would all burst loose in one big rainstorm so I wouldn't make eye contact with him no-more; I just kept moving this way & that so he wouldn't see anything.

...and then there was a momentary pause in our conversation and well, I used it to excuse myself... so I could get out of there before I spilled over the top... and so I got the hell out of there as fast as I could, trying to be nonchalant about things, you know... so as not to lead him to where I was... cause... mannn... as I said, I was on the verge of tears the whole time... and like I said, I didn't want him to see it...

So when I got out to my car... I put the key into the ignition and it all just burst out of me like a friggin' dam bursting wide open or something... and I cried my eyes out for just a bit as I sat in the car but again, I didn't want him to see me sitting out front of his house just balling-it out in the car... so I cleared enough space in my eyes so I could see to drive a bit on down the road... and then I drove down his street just a short piece, maybe a few hundred yards and that was all, just so I was out of his sight... and then I pulled over and I cried... and I cried like a baby... and I sobbed for what seemed like forever I might add, but it wasn't... and there I sat until I cleared enough space from my eyes so I could drive on home.

And as I paused for a moment, I could see Patty-boy had turned his face from me... towards the TV whether it's because he's not interested in what I have to say or whether he's sparing me my embarrassment cause maybe he's seen my latest tears starting to run again... or maybe, it's to hide his own tears from me, I don't rightly know... but we-all loved Pat-Light, all the driftwood boys. Her smile lit up a room... and her shy laugh made you smile cause it was infectious that way... and as far as I knew, everyone loved her and with good reason too.

...and I pause for just a bit more, to gather myself...

"In retrospect... I don't know whether it hit me so hard cause I was already over-sensitized at the time, you know, cause my girl and I, at the time, were breaking up after such a long time together so I was already feeling bad about things I guess... so maybe I was just a bit whiny-assed over-sensitized at the time and therefore, maybe more vulnerable to the tears given such bad news... Of course, I still get choked up by it today whenever I think of her now so maybe, it's just that I thought so highly of her that I couldn't help myself when I heard the bad news... or maybe, just maybe... it's a bit of both... cause she was an angel, at least, best I could tell... although an angel who could get after it when she thought it necessary to [do so], but an angel just the same"

...and again, I pause as I steady my thoughts...

"...no one should have to die that way... getting eaten up that way... especially someone with so much heart. It just seemed so unfair to me... and yes, I know... many-many others suffer similar unfair fates... I get it... but I knew her... and that's why I say it's so... but as one once said up on the silver screen... 'deserve(s)... got nothing to do with it' (from Clint Eastwood's movie 'Unforgiven')"

...it's sad, but sometimes true...

So I look over at Patty-boy... and he says nothing to me at all... He just looks at the TV and not another word passes from me either, at least in this moment... and not a move is made this way or that, he just stares at the TV... so I turn back to staring at the wall in front of me too...

...then I open my mouth again, to say a word or more...

"...there are times... on misty rainy days when I see the group of us again, Johnny-boy and me, and Bobby, and Pat-Light, and the other girls there in that park in Salisbury... and we're just walking around those park grounds on such a misty rainy day with some of us nursing hangovers that were lingering at the time... or at least, me... and we're laughing and playing and amusing ourselves with our wit... and me, I'm intrigued by the looks of one pretty young lady... and her smile... and the way her eyes dance out in front of us like so... and we're playing at a distance and yet, we have no idea of what will be... cause we are young and so full of hopes and dreams and fun and games... and we are filled with all the shit 'the young' are filled with, at least those young-ins who are in love with life before it sometimes wears you down... and we have no idea on that day, that some will live and some will die before their time is done... and some will live with some of their dreams coming true... and some will just get to watch from the sidelines with less than stellar dances in their game..."

...and I pause again, just a bit... and another small tear drops off my cheek... "why is it that the good die so damn young... and the 'dicks of the world', who crush all that is good in life, they just seem to live forever... I don't get it... but it is... and it just seems so sometimes..."

"Sometimes..." and I pause for a moment here cause sometimes, I'm a mouthful of melodrama and melancholy rolled into one, like the great Sarah [Bernhardt] from so many years gone past other than of course, she was somebody... and I am not, so I stop right there... cause sometimes, things are best left unsaid, I think...

...and as the scene comes to a close... as the camera pulls back and away, there's just two dudes sitting at a bar looking forward at some wall with neither sharing another word... where both slowly sip at their beers while a solitary tear rolls down one's cheek that neither wants to see...

Looking down on a 'downbound train'

An evening breeze is blowing in off the ocean and it blows in on across the boardwalk as me and Jaybird are out strolling along the boards blowing off some late evening energy in the boardwalk's light filled darkness while stealing a few looks at some beautiful young ladies who are also strolling on by when we stumbled upon some young ladies we know from *here & there*.

"...hey, what's wrong with your buddy today?" ...asks one young lady... and there are some giggles and laughter all around as if they're hiding behind a comedic scene or something...

"Who?"

"Johnny-boy" ...and there's a pause... and then one of them continues... "he's over at the bar just lost inside himself while the party's going on all around him... he just sits there glum and quiet and doesn't say a word...I mean, what's up with that?"

"He didn't even say a word to us" ...offered up another.

Now Jaybird & I smiled slightly at it cause that's Johnny-boy; he could be the life of the party sometimes and a complete downer sometimes... in fact, he was the only one Jaybird knew who could be as 'bi polar-ish' as maybe himself although Johnny-boy didn't let a little personal depression keep him from going out on the town to the bar if it was a bar-night; he was regimented that way... if it's *'bar-X'* night then he'd appear at bar-X regardless of his state of mind.

On the other hand... Jaybird would just disappear for a while when he was down, sometimes for hours at a time and sometimes for a day or two or more; he'd just disappear socially from the lights of humanity into a gloomy space made for one until something shook the stage and set him on fire and then he'd once again emerge when he saw the bright lights out ahead of him... so they were different that way but still, there was something slightly wrong with both of them, in their own odd *sorta* way, I suppose.

I imagine people handle their depressions differently assuming they have them... and of course, there's different levels of depressions too, I would suppose... and some depressions need clinical attention in order for people to survive and maybe some depressions need just a bit of time to bounce back from although - I don't rightly know because I'm not a psychologist and even though not all psychologists are so perfect as they may think they are, let's face it, in general, car mechanics are better than bakers when it comes to fixing cars and so it is with psychologists too, who are better at handling mental health issues than others like myself, no matter how simple or serious the issues appear to be.

Now when most people talk about 'culture' we seem to be thinking of an area's drink, food, architecture and art, etc... when in fact, culture is more than that; *culture is the beliefs & customs its people share; their implicit and explicit rules they cling to...* and so it was where Jaybird and Johnny-boy came from, and Bobby and me for that matter, where depression was thought of as just another mental weakness to be dealt with by one's self and not a sickness of any kind in need of clinical attention... so the natural response to most mental health issues in our neighborhoods was almost always the same... "get your shit together boy, cause ain't nobody going to help you anyway(s)"... and that's how depression was handled in our neighborhoods. And we didn't know any better either. No one did. Nor was there extra money there to fix such things either.

But did such cultural beliefs fix anything? ...somehow, I doubt it... but that was our culture; our implicit set of rules on how to handle depression: 'just deal with it'. 'Be happy'. 'Knock it the hell off'. It was much the same with alcoholism and drug abuse too. We were told to 'just fix it'. 'Just stop it and don't do it'. But these days we know it's not that simple. You don't fix a broken arm by ignoring it and we shouldn't try and fix depression or suicide thoughts by ignoring it either.

Now Johnny-boy and Jaybird sometimes seemed to fluctuate in their emotional states much like a sine wave; they went from thinking they were *'kings of the world'* one day to slipping down into the depths of depression on another day where maybe they even found it hard to take a breath, like they were drowning underwater with a foot pressing down upon their chests... and in the more dramatic moments, when the hurricanes of depression spun off little tornadoes of whirling crazy-like winds, maybe they, and certainly me, contemplated cutting one's breath short with the sharpest of instruments or catching one's death in a winter's storm which of course, seems just a bit melodramatically off the rails to me...

...but luckily for Jaybird and Johnny-boy and even me to some extent, these emotional fluctuation in moods were much more rare than normal so we could hide our momentary peaks and valleys inside a few days before emerging back into the light of day, minus Johnny-boy who'd go out to the bar at night and hide in plain sight of everyone.

Now whether Johnny-boy actually wrestled with depression-type demons or not, is largely unknown to me cause we'd never talk about such things... but he could be 'up' and he could be 'down'... and when he was 'down', he was off the table... but he was there just the same cause he was regimented that way, so everyone saw it... and we wrestled with it as his friends cause we didn't know what to do during such days cause we didn't know what it was. As I said, depression was never discussed in the open so we didn't know about it... and we couldn't shake him of it either until he came out of it himself, whatever it was... but he usually rose from his doldrums sooner or later, much like Jaybird and I would which is not to say we were the same cause we weren't... it just seemed like they and maybe even me, hid behind a similar type curtain sometimes but what was behind that curtain was largely unknown to us.

Anyway, it didn't surprise me or Jaybird at the girls frank talk cause Johnny-boy could be an odd one sometimes when the time wasn't right, but then again... 'who *da f*<k*... am I'?

As I said before, it turns out that in those days of yore, mental health issues wasn't a high priority for most people in the *driftwood boys'* tiny world sphere... so if you were off, you suffered your demons alone... and you were told to 'kick the horse and jump back on', more or less... probably less, but you get the picture; 'fix it' was all that was said to you... So most people from our neighborhood struggled on through their unstable mental health issues while the *'really troubled'* eventually fell apart in time cause nobody really knew what to do for them and they most often couldn't 'fix it' themselves.

A note to the wise: if you have 'mental health' problems then you should seek professional help to help you handle your 'bungled load'; you'll be better off for it, I think... but then again, I'm nobody... but still, it just seems like a wise thing to do.

So anyway(s)... the girls stood there looking at me and Jaybird as we processed all the thoughts running through our heads which was hidden behind our sheepish & foolish smiles not knowing what to say or do...

"Are you alright?" ...asks one of the girls... *kinda* puzzled at the lost expressions on our faces...

...and I, who was *kinda* lost in Jaybird's shade, chuckled just a bit... "don't worry about him... he's just a fool's bird today..."

...and Jaybird looks at me, puzzled at my comment... as if to say... 'what *da f*<k*, dude?'

...then the girls giggle just a bit at *'the words'* and at Jaybird's confused looks before turning and heading on down the boards... err, on down the boardwalk...

...and Jaybird and I start on back up the boardwalk towards the bar to wrestle Johnny-boy out and maybe get him on home without saying another word...

Big Al and his demons

I mentioned Big Al earlier in the book; he was a wonderful lovely ballsy *kinda* guy with hopes and dreams as large as any of us... but unfortunately, Big-Al would eventually slip into a serious fight with depression later-on in life not too far down the road from our *driftwood days*... and eventually it got so bad that he was given electric shock treatments for it and it just seemed to me, like it killed him long before he killed himself with a gun... of course, who *da f*<k* am I? Answer: Nobody...

It was sad to see the life which had burned so brightly in his eyes finally fade away; his eyes sparkled so brightly when he was happy that you were almost awed by it... and they were so soulful when he was hurt or sad, at least before his depression and his subsequent electric shock treatments and the destruction of all visual clues of his emotions... cause afterwards, after all *this shit,* all visual indications of life all but disappeared from his eyes as far as I could see; his eyes just went blank as if *'nobody was home'*... and it broke my heart... and when he finally shot himself, I couldn't help but feel relieved because NO one should lose himself like he did... and he did, or at least, I think he did... and it just seems, as one song once said, that... *'only the good die young'*

For a man who had eyes that sparkled with excitement and sincerity most of the time, a true romantic who just couldn't seem to find a love anymore, a guy who had a deep lust for life, it was truly heartbreaking to see the life he symbolized drained out of him. I'm truly sorry he didn't find peace in life cause he certainly deserved it.

The simple truth about Big Al was this: Big Al was a beautiful person… and *we-all* loved him and he left us with a lasting smile with his cute albeit, slightly disturbing pie-faced Al story… and we, the *driftwood boys*, would never forget him… none of us… and whenever we used to get together, we'd always share a smile and a laugh and a bit of a tear for Big Al which oddly enough, *we-all* tried to hide from each other cause *'big boys don't cry'* even if we couldn't help it, where similar type words have been sung before…

Now there was another thing I learned from Big Al's demise and it was this: Bobby had lots & lots of heart, more than I ever thought he had. You see, when Big Al slipped into his darkened funk, it was Bobby who went out of his way to see Big Al. It was Bobby who took him out to meet with us for some social contact when Big Al's lights were going out… and he didn't turn away from him like I did, thinking 'I can't watch this anymore'… cause it was heart breaking to watch… but Bobby persevered, he didn't lose hope. He did what he could do.

No, Bobby just tried to help him out as best as he could… not asking to fix the impossible but not giving up to the futility of his efforts either; he just seemed to accept that he would change what he could and he'd live with what he couldn't and it showed me 'heart'… much more 'heart' than I had and a strength I didn't have either…

So I grew to appreciate this aspect of Bobby's character more than he'd know… and to love him for it too… although let's be honest here, Bobby was probably NO saint anymore than the rest of us but he was a good guy with lots of heart and *that ain't so bad,* as many like to say.

…and now I hear in the background, a musical forage into the darkened woods of the unknown from a lonely dude strumming a guitar while groaning-out a simple tune that amounts to this… *'you are unique, my friend… and we will never forget you Big Al, Never, my friend…'*

Notes: the line *'only the good die young'* was triggered by a *Billy Joel* lyric & song *'Only the Good Die Young'.* The line *'big boys don't cry'* was triggered by a similar *Frankie Valli* lyric & song *'Big Girls don't Cry'.* In the final words where I talk of *'a musical forage into the darkened woods'* ending with the words 'you are unique, my friend...', I'm feeling the lyrics in the *Bruce Springsteen* song *'Terry's Song'.*

in the shadows of Ocean City

By the time I was living in Ocean City, I had lost a lot of my interest in most competitive sports we'd played all along the years I was growing up, like baseball and basketball, etc... and of course, by this time, baseball had been replaced by slow pitch softball for most of us guys where we were using the game primarily as a backdrop for drinking beer and carrying-on rather than playing focused ball most times although we could be quite competitive at it too... and so it could be fun to do and I did it sometimes cause I could although it wasn't the same to me as playing baseball had been... but in time, I would learn to relish the carousing associated with slow pitch softball as well.

So during this summer instead of seeking out basketball games up at the park or softball games with workmates in summer leagues played under the sun, all of which would have led to knowing more people and getting invited to more parties than not, which was sort of a mistake because by this time, sports really acted as a door to other socializing activities like parties where there was fun to be had... But instead of doing that, I sometimes retreated into alone-time where I'd throw a lacrosse ball up against the base of the Route 50 bridge which brings all those summer vacationers eastward into Ocean City.

I would take gorilla-Tea's lacrosse stick down there near the bridge area and throw the ball up against the wall endlessly... fetching it in a less than athletic fashion but still I was playing... and then I'd spin and chuck... and turn and fetch... like I knew the game I didn't know... and if you watched me for more than a second or two then you probably knew I didn't know shit about the game but that aside, and for a few minutes at a time, I played the game by myself and it allowed me to daydream in some fun filled fashion... and to dance in the warmth of the summer sun without wasting all my time up on the beach which in many ways seems counter intuitive for being *'down de ocean'*... after all, why do you go to the beach? ...cause - I think: it's to go up on those sandy beaches and dance in the ocean blues with bikini-clad ladies strutting their stuff while wolves like me watched from nearby.

But I was never one for sitting still too long when I was up there; I was walking the shoreline looking at all the sweet decorations dancing all around the ocean's edge while trying to be incognito-like cool which I definitely wasn't... and yes, occasionally I'd dance into the surf with friends, playing and showing off our wears with the finer sex when they were there... but beyond that, I didn't see the purpose of sitting under an umbrella reading a book or something or looking blankly into the hot sunshine while looking at nothing at all.

So yes, occasionally... to avoid the sunny beaches at the ocean's edge, I'd go down there near the bridge where most people didn't go and I'd get lost in my play of one where I'd have some fun in the warm sunshine for a while before disappearing into the dungeons of the kitchen where I worked later in the afternoon and into the evening.

...but ohhh... to be a dancer on the base paths once again... just turning the wheel as fast as it goes... now that would've been the ticket if I'd just listened to the voices in my head... but nooo... I didn't.

...now on occasions there would be several big old seagulls who'd be sitting up on some nearby fence posts near some of those electrical wires that's near the Rte. 50 bridge... and on occasions, one of these seagulls would say to a second seagull... "you ever seen a turtle-ass fool play lacrosse before?"

...and the second seagull would look at the first seagull and say... "you outta your mind... I ain't neverrr seen no turtle-ass fool play no

lacrosse before!"

"Well... I have now" ...says the first seagull to the second.

"nahhh you ain't... cause he ain't playing no lacrosse here"

"well<??> ...what's he doing?" asks the first seagull.

...and then there's silence... "Well, it ain't no lacrosse he's playing, that's for sure"

And after a brief moment of silence, the seagulls burst into grand laughter at the sight of this one lonely turtle-ass fool playing lacrosse by himself down against some concrete bridge wall with nobody else around...

(cc) a worst dinner ever

Now in one of those chitter-chatter-like ways it all goes sometimes when reflecting on a memory gone by...

...I'm guessing, you've had a worst dinner before... something that's just makes you gag... Well, my worst dinner was the one I made with Bobby when we were living *'down de Ocean'* in our driftwood abode a million ago when I was a young bird flying higher than maybe I should've been...

So there we were, living *'down de Ocean'* this one summer and out of boredom or curiosity, we decided to make spaghetti dinner for ourselves... cause we liked spaghetti... and besides eggs, it was something we both could cook or so we thought. The only problem was we learned to make this meal in different ways and when we meshed our ideas together... well, it was awesome... but only in a very negative *sorta* way.

You see, in my house, we learned to brown our ground beef by putting salt in the pan first which of course, I haven't done in a long-time cause meat doesn't need it but in this case, that's the way I learned to do it so I did it that way... so I put some salt in the pan... then I threw in the meat and browned it all up... and then (in our house) we'd pour the grease out (and with it I imagine, a lot of that salty-taste).

Anyway, in Bobby's house, the salt wasn't added in the initial step and so before I could pour the salt and meat grease out, Bobby dumped the tomato sauce into the pan... and now we had all that meat grease and salt mixed in there with the spaghetti sauce... but to amp up this mess even more, Bobby tells me to add in *'a hand full of salt'* to the mix ...and even though

I questioned the idea and the amount cause I knew salt was already in there, he insisted on *'a hand full of salt'* being added... so being in a compromising mode, after all, we were doing this together... I poured... *'a hand full of salt'* into my hand... and then I dumped it into the pan... and *Whaaa-laaa...* we had a mess. Now just think about this for a moment: would you like a little spaghetti sauce with that salt?

Well, come to find out... the expression... *'a hand full of salt'* when applied to cooking... is NOT literal... imagine that<??> Who would have guessed it? ...besides most people other than me, I suppose<??> So you got the idea... since I took it literal and put a real *'hand full of salt'* into the pan... we now had, to recap... the initial salt I put in the pan to brown 'the meat' with, and the meat grease from the cooked meat, and now... a literal *'full-hand full of salt'* had been added... all in this pan of spaghetti sauce. Can you say... yummy???

But we persevered on... after all, how bad could it be we thought<??> ...so Bobby finished up the spaghetti (pasta) and we fixed up our plates with a heaping load of spaghetti sauce cause we were hungry young guys ready to enjoy the meal we'd made... and then we sat down to eat, the two of us. And that first bite... well now, that spaghetti tasted like we'd dipped it into the ocean for an added salty-like flavor... or maybe like we dumped it in the ocean to accentuate its saltiness... cause it was the saltiest stuff I'd ever tasted. To help you with feeling 'this taste'... imagine you are at the Ocean... *hopping & bobbing in the surf...* now take-in a mouth-full of that salty water in your mouth... and hold that taste in there for a moment... and now - add some spaghetti sauce into the mix... and *oh-myyy...* what a taste<??>... *blahhh!!!*

But since we were a little tight on money... you know, with our beer money expenses being untouchable... and since we didn't want to waste our other cash or our efforts from making our spaghetti meal, we persevered onward... eating it... beyond that initial ungodly taste that was... until finally, I gagged-out... and quit. It was terrible... just TERRIBLE!!! I couldn't take it *no more*. And after all these years, and I mean lots of years later cause I'm *friggin'* old now, the only spaghetti meal I've never finished was that spaghetti meal. It was that bad.

So what did I do? I took some of my beer money and went up the street to this greasy spoon sub-shop and I got a greasy Philly cheese steak sub to eat... and oh-my, it was a beautiful sub with not too much saltiness in its bite especially when compared with our spaghetti meal if you can imagine that<??>... in fact, a whole lot less saltiness than in our spaghetti sauce, so it was a wonderful substitute for our horrible spaghetti.

But Bobby finished his plate somehow cause believe me, it was mega-salty... although that's where it all ended... and there was *no seconds* for anyone. We just trashed it all after that. And believe me when I say this... I don't throw food out unless it's really bad... not then, not now... but that stuff tasted just too damn salty even for a cheap-skate like me to keep around and eat later.

And so, I finish-up this *chitter-chatter* by saying this: this was '*my worst tasting dinner*' ever... although in fairness, the camaraderie we had making it... and the laughs we've had since then recalling our cooking calamity always makes for a fun memory to have... and *that's not so bad.*

gorilla-Tea's tattoo

One day I came home from work late at night and I got into a small tiff with gorilla-Tea about something or other that probably shouldn't have even been an issue at all except, I'm over-controlling sometimes and he's often careless...

Now it all started cause I saw he had this patch on his arm which I hadn't seen before; he was hiding it under a longer shirt sleeve but I saw it anyway... I didn't say anything at first cause we had started arguing about some other stuff so it didn't seem overly important to me initially but I can be a little OCD of sorts about some things that are *'different'* even if I don't say anything about it at first... But in time, it just nags at me... and nags at me... until it pops out of my mouth.

So I ask of him... "What's that on your arm?"

"None of your business..."

"What *da f*<k* do you mean? On your arm<??>" ...and I point at the patch... "what's that?"

"It's nothing, so don't worry about it"

"No, right there on your arm, what's that?"

"None of your f*<king business..."

...and I look at him all puzzled-like cause what's the secret? ...so with my arm still stuck out there pointing at his patch, I repeat myself... "No, what's that... on your arm?"

"I done told you... it's none of your damn business"

And I chuckle just a bit... "You know I'm NOT going to let it go...

so fess up... what is it?"

"It's none of your f*<king business..."

...and so I chuckle and then move in to grab at the patch... "No, what's that<??>"

"Get *da f*<k* away from me..." he says... and we tussle a bit back and forth with him pushing me away as I'm fending off his pushes like a defensive end fighting off an offensive tackle while reaching for a prize just beyond my grasp...

...and finally ...after he's batted me away a couple of times and I, him... he, in order to keep my hands from grasping at his patch, says out loud... "it's a f*<king tattoo... So leave it *da f*<k* alone, will *yahhh*..."

So I back up slightly... rather stunned cause in those days tattoos weren't as popular with *'the masses'* like they've become in the years since then; tattoos were mostly used by motorcyclists and enlisted Navy dudes, etc... and there was little brother gorilla-Tea with a tattoo of some type on his arm...

So my jaw drops slightly as I looked at him... and then at his patch... and for a moment, I say nothing... cause I'm stunned... but questions are coming... he knows it... and I know it... cause I can't help myself...

And I spread my arms out in a 'what *da f*<k' kinda* way and say... "When<??> ...and why<??> ...and how much? ...and what *da hell* are the folks [parents] going to say?"

But gorilla-Tea smirks at me like he does and says "I did it today, okay... I got it today... so are we done here?"

"But why?"

"Cause I wanted it"

"But why... aren't you afraid of infection or something?"

And gorilla-Tea laughs at me... "No... "

He thinks of me as an uptight *wuzzy-boy* afraid of 'cutting loose' and to some extent, he's right...

"So how much?" ...I ask

"It's none of your business..."

And I am speechless for a moment cause I know what that means; it costs a lot... "what *da f*<k* do you mean?"

"You heard me..."

And now I laugh just a little cause I know I'm not going to let it go... no f*<king way, and he probably knows I'm not going to let it go, sooo... "come-on... how much<??>... tell your uncle Jimmy, how much?"

And gorilla-Tea tries to walk away from me but I follow him close behind cause *'I just got to know'*... and we banter for a bit, *back & forth* with me pestering him and him deflecting me until he finally relents cause he knows I won't relent until I know...

"I spent the check..."

...and then my jaw drops down again, but this time - it's well below my chest...

"You spent your whole f*<king check on that patch..." I say, pointing at the patch.

"Yeahhh, and don't worry about it... it's my money"

"But it's your whole *friggin'* check..." I say incredulously... "how could you?"

"don't worry about it... it's my f*<king money..."

"Buttt..."

And I'm beside myself cause I'm a saver who'd never spend that much money on anything much less a tattoo and gorilla-Tea, he's a 'live-er' and savings be damn; I save what I make and he spends what he makes... and I'm guessing that somewhere in-between is probably 'the answer'...

"Please tell me you didn't spend your whole week's pay on that damn thing?"

And again gorilla-Tea chuckles at me... "It's my money..."

...and before he can finish, I interrupt him... "but it's your whole f*<king check<??>... how could you not save anything..."

"It's none of your business... it's my f*<king money..."

And I crack and go into a raving tirade about fiscal responsibilities and so-on and so-forth... and he waves me off as we circle around this small room we call our summer home with me badgering him about money and him pushing me away telling me to stop being a tight-ass cheap-ass f*<k afraid to live a little... and *around & around* we go... and where it all ends... nobody knows... except, he didn't change and neither did I.

In fairness, it was an awesome tattoo; it was an iconic spirit yelling out wild-things like screaming eagles might do when tearing at their poor helpless victims from a bad-ass motorcycle... Of course, I wonder in retrospect, maybe that eagle wanted to tear me to pieces for doubting him... but *nahhh*<??>... that couldn't be... could it<??>

Best 'not' cause that means... *da batman will have to come alive again... and ohhh, yeahhh...* then really bad shit happens... *he-he-ho-ho, it's off to bed I go.*

Singing at the Irish Bar

Now out on the Ocean City boardwalk there's an Irish bar and at night there's a music scene played there with live music on occasions although at other times, there's just music playing out of some jukebox like music-machine or so, and people often stayed-out late at night to play inside their illusionary high that alcohol and bar noise and music makes happen all too often in late-night intoxicating sorta ways.

And the driftwood boys would on occasion, enter the bar and drink and carouse with whomever we could convince to carouse with us... and we'd sing there too, when the alcohol deaden our stage fright cause there were times when music spun up inside us and it just had to be played-out even if we were so out of tune that it wrecked musical purists sensibilities which we rarely cared about cause alcohol has a way of deadening it all.

And the king of our octave-bad sounds was Johnny-boy. The rest of us were merely backup singers when enough courage had been drunk inside our human cavities. And the performer who brought the beast out of Johnny-boy was the King himself, Elvis Presley. Now I didn't mine Elvis but he wasn't my musical king like he was for Johnny-boy. But to Johnny-boy, Elvis was *da man*. And when he drank enough courage to loosen his tongue, he'd often jump up onto the tables and belt out Elvis tunes while doing his Vegas show mannerism to a tee.

Now Johnny-boy wasn't slim in the traditional youthful Elvis mold cause he was a bit more portly in youthful ways, but his confidence up on the stage after alcohol had infused his musical talents into illusionary stage stardom, was stargazing... and he'd howl with just enough crap that he carried his backup singers along, most often, Bobby & me, as he piped-out the King's tunes. And when there was a beautiful woman nearby who he was romancing, ahhh, well then, he'd bring out the big guns.

'Wise men say… only fools rush in…' where of course, I'm talking about Elvis' 'Can't help falling in Love' serenade.

…and yes, he was a fool… and we were fools… especially… when we were drinking and carousing and singing and playing fancy with our whimsical visions of love blinding us from any sorta reasonable reality. But sometimes, that's what youth is for.

Sweetened tea from two WV maidens

So this one day in our Ocean City town... Johnny-boy and I were sitting in the apartment just chitter-chattering a bit; he'd just gotten back from this place where some girl, slightly older than him, had taken him down-town, sort of speak... and he came back all giddy and smiley and happy... and really *kinda disgustingly happy* too, I thought, cause *'it weren't me...'*

...well, he's talking about this ordeal with great fanfare while my hormones are running wild just a bit cause *whoa, man...* and I think: I've got to do something about this situation cause I'm sitting here like a loser doing nothing while he's gotten to dance with some lovely young lady playing along with him... so I start thinking to myself, 'what *da hell*, mannn<??>... maybe, *I should write my own story'*...

So after a bit, I step outside into the late afternoon warmth to try and cool down my own run-away hot train when in the mist of the fray, I disappear into the air only to be absorbed by another who's even more ridiculous than me...

For I am hormonally flustered by what Johnny-boy has danced to... and *'what I have not [danced to]'*... 'What *da f*<k?'*... thinks I... and 'why not me?'

...and as I stand up there on the bridge of our ship like a crippled captain of some sorts which in many ways, looks like an apartment stoop at some beach house apartment to many onlookers, and yet to another set, maybe it's a bridge to some *'Sun and Fun'* type ship where I spy out over an ocean of parking lots stretched out before me which often decorates so many

Ocean City small strip malls, and there in the distance are two pretty young ladies coming out of some liquor store just up the ways with a stash of riches they hope will lead to some special *'Sun and Fun' kinda* joyous play themselves, I suppose...

...and the captain of the bridge thinks to himself... *'heyyy... good looking... Whattt... you got brewing... how(s) about playing darts with me'* ...or something like that... where at least some of those words are rather famous from a country tune of some kind.

...and so, the captain sings out these lines over the ocean of parking lots before him to those lovely young ladies... *"heyyy... good looking... whattt... you got brewing... how(s) about playing darts with me..."*

...and at first the ladies are surprised at this foolish serenading line from up there on the ship's bridge... after all, while they are there for some *sun and fun* of their own... who'd expect such a foolish *kinda* show from such an idiot *kinda* guy...

But to my dismay... they shake their heads slightly at me with a touch of laughter and I, the ship's captain, seeing just a bit of hope at the end of my spyglass, sing out again towards these lovely young ladies with more of my *come-hither* idiocy...

...and the ladies look at each other for a moment or two... and giggle a bit more before finally yelling back up to the captain of the bridge... *"sooo...* what do you think you've got that's worth exploring?"

...and a voice from the dark lagoon issues his warnings to these young ladies in a quiet *sorta* way... 'nothing... he's got nothing... beat it, before you're sorry for a wasted time'.

But the fool on the bridge drowns out this dark reply bouncing through the air while *whirling & twirling* about(s) with one of his own... "I've got plenty of dance for you, my good ladies... just give this ship a chance and we'll dance the night away together"

...then the captain whirls around a bit more up there on the ship's bridge like a dancing doll on a stick...

"Okay fool... here's your chance... show us your dance moves?" ...says one of these lovely ladies in a classic *sorta* dare.

So the captain dances about(s) for a bit more, all *debonair* and irresistible and for some reason, who knows why... maybe low self-esteem... or pity for such a foolish captain... or maybe even for a daring kind of amusement... they engage with the captain just a bit more than before... although in time... the captain's dance tires just a bit as it slips below the waves of his lies while the captain stutters and stammers trying to save what's left of his dance which has no substance... and just as he's about to lose the line on these lovely young ladies looking for a good time which probably doesn't involve being serenaded to by such a foolish captain... Johnny-boy emerges from behind the door; he must have smelled the beauty and gaiety of these two lovely ladies who are dancing near the hook of my line but who were about to slip away from the line as well, and disappear into the evening's fading light, *forever more, forever more*... so he emerges from his happy slumber and engages in their repartee... and he sings out his own set of lines which magically captures the two of them in a net of lies which are swimmingly tight and cherry red... although... not nearly as sophisticated as I might assume given his success but aside from that, Johnny-boy has his way with the *language of love* with these ladies at least, on this occasion anyway(s)...

...so Johnny-boy connives them into joining us up at the corner bar & lounge for drinks and music and *da such*, later in the evening... and so we leave this brief encounter sure of our destiny cause we are knightly werewolves out on the prowl.

...and with a little shake... and a little bake... we gather later in the evening and we drink and we play merry-like until late into the evening... drinking and dancing and playing around with words and such other-like play that's made by the young, for the young.

Now these two young ladies are from WV, just in town for a bit of magical Ocean City summer fun and we've paired off as the dance of words lines us up accordingly... and one is a match for Johnny-boy cause she can also drink lots of booze and talk *da-smack-talk* of young love without any fear just like him... you know, where you say you can *'drink dem under the table'* and *'make love like the devil him/herself'*... or whatever... and you mean it, whether you can or not... and she's every bit a match for him cause she's a woman who doesn't back down; a cool *dudette* of a young lady...

And the other young lady is a sweet young lady who it turns out, is a pretty good athlete too... but she's shy like me before I get to know you... So we're paired up like 'so' although the problem with us is that for shy people it's hard to get started running down the tracks when both are hesitant to make the first step; Johnny-boy and his match have no such problems...

Now beyond my initial shyness, for those who get to know me, they usually wish I was still shy again cause once I get to know you then I don't *shut-da-f*<k up* too damn often, usually that is... but to the unknown, I'm as quiet as a mouse when not dancing a jig... So anyway(s), we are paired up and we played off their lead just a bit cause they are the *dynamic ones* and *we-all* have some fun despite it all.

So we drink... and we flirt... and we dance around the bottle of love... and when the evening winds down, we split up more or less, going in different directions except... while I and my lovely young beauty end up alone by ourselves separated by time and place... somehow, Johnny-boy ends up snuggling up tight with his lovely *dudette* of polish-like descent for a bit of time... now how *da hell* does that happen? He's swinging at love while I've fumbled the ball once again, at midfield, as usual...

So again... I've failed to *'write my own story'* while he's writing his own story... *'what da f*<k?'* But when one is lost at the scene without a set of keys that seem to work on the door... *'shit happens'*, as they say... or doesn't, as-is the case here with me.

...anyway(s), one thing leads to another and the next thing I know, I find myself completely alone or at least, I think I am alone cause I have no idea where I am or where the other three have gone once I *come-to* from my visit into *la-la-land*... So I open my blood shot drunken eyes to the world with my head fogged-up with some alcoholic soaked banging going-on inside my brain... and there in the distance, like in a foggy dream, I hear someone trying to make time with some girl in our place of ill-repute; the last thing I'd known was that we'd all separated sometime after the bar scene... but here I was in a very different scenario than I'd expected to be in, like I was in a bad dream or something... cause I hear things... damn, I hear things.

...so somehow, I find myself in a room where some guy is trying to make it with some girl; I don't know how... and I don't know why? ...cause as I said, the last thing I remember, I'd been with Johnny-boy and the West Virginia girls and now, it's me... and two young bloods tussling alone in the same darkened room as me, with myself off to one side of them somewhere in another bed (thank God) while they're trying to dance a tango that's been made for *dem two*; I'm a bit unclear about how it-all happened cause, well... I don't handle liquor all that well so I'm just a bit blotto as in, *I'm a thousand sheets to the wind...* and of course, I'm lucky to not be throwing up on the floor which would have put a *friggin'* damper on their escapade...

...which makes me wonder in retrospect, was it the drugs I never took in such massive portions, or the abusive alcohol I sometimes took in massive portions, or just my delusions that sometimes surfaced at odd times like these<??>

But this problem aside, I think to myself as I'm awakening from my slumber in the room's darkness while hearing these two other voices in the room fooling around... *'ughhh...* I'm in the room too, guys'* ...and... shit... I'm by myself... and I'm thinking... *'what da-hell? what da f*<k is this? ...am I really here?'* ...and am I really in a room with another guy making it with another woman, like a fly on the wall trying to cover up? ...or is this just a bad dream? Maybe, it's just a bad dream<??>...

...and unfortunately, dream or not, I can still hear everything... or at least, I think I hear it all; thank God, I see nothing... cause it's dark and I'm turned in another direction, slightly distracted by my alcohol-soaked cotton-dry mouth and a deep seated alcoholic banging going-on in my head... and of course, it's all because I'm too *friggin'* blotto to understand everything that's going on... but I'm hearing them all the same... so it's like listening to a semi-X rated movie of soft-porn with no picture except there are hormones running wild in the room and *they ain't mine...*

So I say to myself... 'what *da hell* do I do?' ...as in: maybe they don't know I'm here? So if I lay all quiet like, with my eyes closed real tight then maybe it will all just end without it being known I'm here, like it's just a bad dream...

But then I hear the young lady who's fending off this fast-charging persistent bull of a dude in the mist of this movie, telling him... 'we can't... cause he's in the room...'

Ughhh...

'Sooo... shit!!' ...thinks this foolish captain I call myself... for in my foggy state of mind that's been trying to wrap itself around how the evening had ended with me alone in one bed and these two unknowns in another bed clanging around and almost banging the lights out of each other while I'm still in the same room... as I, like a fly on the wall, am trying to disappear from sight as if I'm not really there... but now, the fly swatter is out... and they wish to swat my tired alcohol-soaked ass that's hidden

up in the darkness of the room... so I think to myself, 'oh shit... now what do I do?'

...runnn, my pretty... runnn rabbit, runnn...

Or... 'is this even real?' ...cause maybe, it's just a *friggin'* bad dream?

So after more of their tugging-around goes on in the darkness, I decide I can't hide from this situation any longer... so I've got to depart even though when I do get up to leave, everyone will know I've been there in the room the whole damn time which of course, I know they already know cause I've heard their words... and all because this sea-whore of a piranha of a dude I now recognize by his voice as dirty Dan, cause he sounds like dirty Dan sounds, and he plays like dirty Dan plays, as he feeds on his captive delight while my baggage is thrown all over the floor... but hell, they already know I'm here cause they've wished to swat me like an irritating fly on the wall... sooo... there's no denying the situation anymore, I suppose... *sooo*, I've got to get the hell outta here.

So with all these delightful thoughts running through my banging head while I'm laying there listening to this incessant pleading going-on from this dirty dog of a dude in heat who's pleading with his latest love of his life, for more love regardless of me... and *I in my cap*, decide that I've got to go... cause this bad dream is just too close to be called *'just a bad dream'*; cause it's *friggin'* real, right<??> ...cause I seem to be a blinded spectator with ears which hears way too much shit, I mean, shittt... and *ughhh*...

So I stumble right-side up and off the bed... and I grab what clothes I can find in the darkness of my *inconspicuousness*... and I leave as inconspicuously as I can... *ha-ha, right<??>*... so they won't know I was ever there... again, *ha-ha, yeah*... likely, right?

...cause hell, she knew... and of course, he did too... so I wasn't such an inconspicuous fly on the wall after all... *ughhh...*

...but again I must ask of myself, 'Is this real? ...or is this just a piss-poor dream where I'm playing third fiddle to a youthful dance for two?'

...please, tell me it's a dreammm...

Now one thing you could always say about this dirty Dan of a dude, it was like he was a hound dog sometimes who was in heat... and nothing swayed him from his quest... least of all, me...

...of course, one could ask again... was this real? ...or was it just a 'bad dream gone wild'? ...*kinda* like *'girls gone wild'*... or *'boys gone wild'*... but it's *'me gone wild'* in some heady f*<ked-up dreams *kinda* way, I suppose.

So I leave for a bit... and I head on up to the beach cause what else am I going to do; we are at the beach after all... and there's concrete buildings and streets everywhere around town but who wants to plop down on an empty street corner much less, somehow appear to be inconspicuous sitting there late at night plopped down on some lonely street corner...

So I head for the beach thinking I can get lost in the darkness up there away from the flow of any late-late night life minus the seagulls and stuff... except... of course, you can't sleep on the beach at night in OC... at least, not according to city law.

Now maybe this public policy is for people's protection; protecting them from unnecessary crime which could happen to isolated individuals up on the beach late at night... or maybe, it's just about discouraging vagrancy... and maybe, it's just about encouraging hotel rentals instead... but either way, you can't sleep on the beach at night at least, not if the cops catch you...

So I walk along the boardwalk for what seems like a long bit to me cause I'm hung-over and tired, trying to avoid slipping onto the beach where I risk being confronted by OC cops... but 'I'm tired...' as I've said... I'm tired and hung-over just a bit from the night we've had out at the bars... so I stroll around anyway(s), for as long as I can... hoping dirty Dan will wrap it all up (his flirty escapade) so I can return to the room and fall asleep in my own bed space, in peace, without the wanting sounds of a dog in heat...

So I ramble around town and its wooden boards for a bit longer where there's little life around town at this late morning hour except for the cool evening breezes blowing in off the ocean chilling me just a bit... and finally, in an effort to just disappear from it all and close my eyes away from all possible human contact... I stumble out onto the beach after checking for cops... and I disappear into the darkness of the far reaches of the beach with just the sound of waves crashing down near the edge of the beach; a perfect place to disappear into the sounds of the ocean's lovely night-time music.

And the ocean breeze is blowing its 'way-too-cool' breeze in on top of me so I get a bit cold because I've only got on a tee-shirt protecting me from the cool evening breezes... and of course, the feel of the cool-cool beach sands beneath my feet chills me down a bit too... but I finally slip into a dark spot where I can disappear from life, free to navigate the oceans far away from this crusty shore... and I bundle up tight to fight off the cold thinking, I just have to hunker down for a bit longer until it all blows over... after all, how long can he go on...

...and I'm almost out cold, fast asleep... when a couple of cops point their lights down on top of me and roust me up with their sweet loving words... "no can do, boy... you can't sleep here... get up... and move on"

...shittt... I've been had... what *da f*<k* am I going to do now? ...cause I'm cold and tired with too much booze oozing outta my pores but now I've got to get up... so I do, I get up to my feet... and move-on staggering off the cold sands and walking

some more of the boardwalk and then finally I stumble on down into town for a bit longer before finally saying to myself... 'f*<k it; I'm heading back... He must have wrapped it all up by now cause it seems like I've been out here forever' which may be correct or not cause when you are this tired, times creeps along slower than you think... besides, if not... then 'f*<k him... I'm done with it-all tonight!'

Of course, I'm hoping he's finished with his exploits of love... or they are... or whatever... but no... cause when I fling the door wide-open as inconspicuously as I can... I still hear this dude's longing words of love that seem largely unfulfilled... cause they're still working at it... or whatever... but regardless of whether it's real or not, I'm still hearing their voices in my head...

...so again, I ask of myself, 'Is this real? ...or is this just a dream?'

...wake *da f*<k uppp*, you fool, cause it can't be real, right<??>

...so I decide 'to hell with it'... I'm staying, anyway(s)... so let them go at it all they want but they are not alone and there's nothing I can do about it... so I start out hiding in the darkness again, like a blind fly on the wall might do in a far-away spot in the room... as far from the groans and pleading as I can go... and I turn the other way so I can't see what I hear... but 'I hear', unfortunately... oh my God, do I hear... even though my booze-clouded mind is dulled to what I hear, but still, I hear... yes indeed, I hear...

...of course, one might ask again... 'does he hear what's real? ...or is it all in his head?

Whatever<??> ...but I hear something...

...and so this dude, this dirty Dan of a dude... who's sometimes just way too dirty of a hormonal dude, he continues to try and make time with this lovely lady while I'm in the room... a hell of a thing really, but like I said... dirty Dan was a helluva hound dog when pursuing his love but lucky for me... she's finally had enough of 'this shit' and begs off again cause I'm there...

So finally, I say out loud, "Good God Dan, I'm still here"

"So… get *da f*<k* out!" he replies.

"I've been out… and that's the end of it… so if you're going to continue this dance, just know I'm recording it all in my head for *'guys night out'*" …which if I had to guess, probably does it for his lovely lady.

"I've got to go" she says as she untangles herself from his love infested embrace and then she separates from him completely on the way out the door grabbing her things as she goes.

"I'll see you later" she says to dirty Dan.

"Bye dude" she says to me, I think.

"Come-on mannn, don't go" goes dirty Dan's hormonal pleads.

"Later" I say to this escaping young lady.

And as the door closes I feel a pillow thrown my way… "What *da f*<k*, mannn?"

"What… I left… I walked the streets… and then I got thrown off the beach by the cops… where *da f*<k*, was I to go?"

"Anywhere"

"Anywhere, where?" I ask. We were 'a-ways' from my driftwood escape and besides, in my drunken state, I hadn't really considered it somehow<??> …so here I was, up the road in *nowhere land* with dirty *friggin'* Dan, *ughhh*.

…then he groans to himself and rolls over in the opposite direction from me, facing the outer walls of this love nest of hormonal imbalance…

So yeah… what a night… and I still had no one to dance with but what da-hell, by this time… any hormonal arousal I'd had was long ago tired out and hidden away in my clanging booze-riddled head so sleeping it off wasn't all that bad an aspiration right now although I knew, tomorrow morning - was going to be no garden party, as if tonight was such a party...

Now it would be naive of me to say I wasn't just a little bit pissed-off at dirty Dan's hounding on that sweet young lady while I was still there in the room with nowhere else to go but I guess, 'we are who we are'... or at least, I tell myself that... and we ain't so perfect either; not him, nor me...

...but again, one might ask of me... hell, I even ask of me today... 'did you hear what's real? ...or was it all in your *friggin'* head?' ...and if it's all in my *friggn'* head, then what *da hell* does that say about me? ...*ughhh*!!! I'd rather not know.

So time passes on, of course, and thankfully, I leave behind dirty Dan and our odd evening time together in one scrambled 'I'm left-out' threesome-type action or at least, my connived version of such a scene in my alcoholic soaked state...

...and now we return to our regularly scheduled show with those lovely West Virginia ladies whom we started our sweet evening out with...

This night wasn't the last time Johnny-boy and I intermingled with these lovely WV ladies, oh no... cause we wined and dined these young ladies as young cash-tight boys might do lost in our hormonally imbalanced ways who've got hormones running wild but aren't exactly sure what to do about it all... at least, some of us, like me, anyway(s)...

...so while Johnny-boy and his girl made-their-way on up onto a highway of love, eventually tying some *kinda* knot of some sorts, for a while at least... me and this sweet shy beauty of WV blood were left tottering along some highway made for lost souls cause that's where I often end-up cause I'm mostly clueless... but regardless, I knew she was a charming young lady who was just a bit of a quiet one much like me in many ways and yet not, cause she had a *sweet type of class* I sometimes lacked, but in this case anyway(s), neither of us knew which shoe to step forward with at first, so we danced without making too many steps forward or backward. But when one is lost at *'the scene'* without a set of keys which seems to work at opening a door... or when one is without a 'light' to shine onto the target of one's obsession... *'shit happens'*, as they say... or *it doesn't*, as can be the case sometimes too.

But this much I could always say of this sweet WV young lady I'd danced with, without regret, she was a charming young lady with much love to give; I think the quiet ones are often the truest ones when it comes to love.

So again... I'd failed to *write my own story* while Johnny-boy was busy writing his... 'what *da f*<k?*' And of course, dirty Dan was doing whatever *he* do... *ughhh,* and how the hell did he get into this story anyway(s)?

...and then suddenly for no damn good reason I can think of, I find myself in a cloudy mist of smoke in some rundown bar where one old dude sits alone drinking a beer as slowly as illusions might do, and I think to myself, 'what da f<k - is this?'*

...and a trusty face I've seen many times before and since such times, [he] chuckles at me before turning slightly towards me, saying... "what da f<k is wrong with you?"*

Now it is at this time when it should be mentioned that this dude is someone I call 'Patty-boy'... and he is an illusion; he did exist... and then he didn't...

So Patty-boy has turned my way, slightly at first, like he expects me... although once again, I'm a bit confused and a bit surprised too because I don't remember choosing to be here in this scene and yet I'm writing this piece of muckish foolishness... but I see him so I know there's 'trouble a-brewing' of sorts...

"You're a f<king fool, you know that?" he says with that make-*

believe sorta chuckle of his. "There is no way you and I are related in any sorta way cause you're a f*<king fool"

...and I smile a slight smile as I catch-up on the scene before I speak the words I long to say...

"Yeahhh<??> ...well, how about this Mr. Monkey? How about I just kick your friggin' ass just a little bit, then will I be fool enough for you?"

And Patty-boy laughs like he does while I smirk a make-believe ass-kicking type smirk which is deceptive cause I can't kick-ass 'so good' and I know he's partially correct; I am a f*<king fool sometimes... but what can I do?

"Try being less of a fool"

...and again, I say to him... "Well, how about this Mr. Monkey, how about I bust your freakin' head"

...and Patty-boy laughs again and starts into more shit when I, tired of all this crap from an illusion I apparently can't control too damn well, pull-out an eraser from my pocket again, thinking, 'it's time to say good night my friend' ...and the next thing the universe hears is the 'scratch-scratch-scratch' of my eraser against the sheets of paper I etch this story on and... whaaa-laaa... Patty-boy has no more mouth... he exists in the illusionary form but without any friggin' mouth to talk his shit at me anymore.

"good night, my friend... cause you ain't got nothin' more to say tonight"

And the curtain falls-down on Patty-boy and me talkin' shit over 'nothing at all'.

Note: The line 'heyyyy... good looking...' was triggered by a Hank Williams' lyric & song 'Hey, Good Lookin''.

Pickin' up a drunken fool

So I come into our shaggy-ass apartment this one late-afternoon when I see Bobby getting all spiffed-up to go out on the town.

"What *da hell*, Bobby... what you got going-on?"

"Gotta date with a waitress at the restaurant"

"Can't get enough of a good time, huh?"

...and Bobby smiles cause he's a man of few words.

And I stop as I sit down on our rickety couch... *"Lookin'* good, man"

...and Bobby smiles... "See you later" ...and out the door he goes.

Then time passes and I'm chowing down on a cheap-ass sub-sandwich from up the ways with a *brewsky* in hand just minding my own business when Bobby comes back through the door with a drunken fool of an idiot Johnny-boy in hand, who's all but unstable without Bobby standing him up.

"Hey Jimmy, help me get this load of shit over to the bed"

"yeah... yeah... *yeahhh*..." and I hop up and grab Johnny's other side and we maneuver him into the bedroom where we just push him over and onto the bed and he's talking some shit between periods of nothing.

"What's that smell?" I ask.

"It's me... and him... he threw-up after I picked him up"

"*ughhh*..." and it's then when I see some left-over throw-up on Bobby's shirt... then I look down at this human blub of a guy on the bed.

"He's breathing, right?" I ask after some moments of silence from Johnny-boy, as I bend over to see if he's landed okay so as to keep his drunken ass' breathing going-on.

"F*<k him... I just missed my date cause of him"

"What?" ...and I laugh just a bit cause that's what I do in such situations... "What you mean?"

...and Bobby meanders around in an impatient *sorta* stroll... "I'm going down the road and who do I see over on the side of the road throwing-up?" ...and he points towards the bedroom where Johnny-boy lays washed out...

"F*<king Johnny-boy... and I looked a second time to make sure it was him cause, shit, I've got a date to get to... and I'm thinking, what do I do: keep going? ...or stop and help his old drunken ass?

And I laugh cause, well, what can you do?

"So I circle the damn block and stop near where he is and gather him up and throw him into the car and damn if he doesn't throw-up in the car and on me while I'm driving him back here... so his damn smelly slop is everywhere in the car after that... disgusting... I mean, how am I supposed to go pick up Julie now when the car is a mess and I'm already late... I mean, what the hell... I should have left his drunken fool-ass there on the corner and picked him up at the end of the night"

...and I'm laughing now cause, well, it's funny... after all, Bobby has finally just lassoed himself a fine sweet young lady who's interested in him and might make him feel fine tonight and what's he faced with this evening? Either helping his buddy off the curb and possibly missing his date? ...OR... Leaving his buddy behind and making his date?

But since Bobby is a decent *sorta* guy he's probably thinking, I'm guessing... 'I'll pick him up off the street corner and drop him off at the apartment, and then *beat-feet* to my date and maybe I'll just be a few minutes late which may have worked for him had Johnny-boy not thrown-up all over the car and then some on Bobby too... so as they say... 'no good deed goes unrewarded', *ughhh.*

"I should have left the *motherf*<ker* on the damn corner" Bobby says as he's tearing off his slightly smelly thrown-up-on shirt from his body...

'So you're doing the driftwood dangling thing now?' I think to myself while watching his disco-ball strip... then he heads for the frig and grabs a beer and storms out the door onto the stoop outside our front door and doesn't say a thing after that to me... I guess - it's just not the time or place to do so...

…riding a bike into nowhere(s)-ville

So this one evening I rounded the corner headed towards our illustrious home when I see Bobby and Johnny-boy talking shit outside the apartment while one or the other is riding this bike down the stoop stairs and across the sidewalk and into the street.

"You *douchebag*… what *da f*<k* you doing" yells one to the other.

…and laughter bursts out between them… "You *friggin' douche*"

…you see, Jaybird and I had brought home that expression several weeks ago and occasionally we'd beat the hell out of it for no reason I can think of other than we were *douchebags* ourselves.

So as I approach, smirking at their idiocy, one of them points in my direction… "*douchebaggg* alert"

…laughter & laughter & laughter…

"I ain't no *friggin' douchebag*… get outta here… so where's *da douchebag*?"

"He… be over there" points one of the boys… and laughter, laughter, and more stupid-ass laughter.

Sometimes it doesn't take much to make idiots boys burst into laughter over almost anything but then again, 'they weren't hurting nobody' so there's that much going-on, I guess. Plus, alcohol makes most of us stupid when we drink too much.

"Drive that truck, Johnny-boy" says Bobby as Johnny-boy runs up the few stairs to the stoop as he pushes the screen door aside while grasping the bike in hand with plans of launching himself out the door and across the short stoop, down the few steps (two or three) to & across the concrete sidewalk, and then down into the street while trying to side-step the telephone poll just to the left of his launch.

"Wowww... you *da man!!!*" yells Bobby with a drunken crackle or two as Johnny-boy runs this obstacle course... and then Johnny-boy cracks up when he falls drunkenly into the street on the bike.

And the boys break up at their foolishness.

"You want a run, Jimmy?"

...and I just shake my head cause I'm not drunk enough to be doing and talking such stupid shit just yet.

"No, you *douchebags* keep doing what you're doing"

"You got a beer left?" I ask.

"Yep, grab me one from the *refrig* too, will *yaaa*?" yells Johnny-boy from his flatten position on a dark abandoned side-street.

"Sure, you Bobby?"

...and he looks down at his almost finished bottle before yelling out his approval, "yeah, me too"

...and he guzzles down the last of what he's got in his hands while I roll into the apartment to get more magic stupidity for three stupid boys playing in the dark on a mostly abandoned street corner.

I guess it takes all kinds to be such stupid-ass *douchebags* fools, I suppose. But then again, we weren't hurting nobody so there's that going-on, I suppose.

Jaybird takes a powder

Eventually *'the mundane'* from work comes to an end and let's face it, kitchen work is mundane more times than not with lots of *rinse & repeat* going-on. But occasionally with *the mundane*, there's a sweetness that exists too. And while the mundane is often buried in the back of our memories, it's oftentimes just the sweetness that remains in our memories. And in work places, there's often good& bad times with petty disagreements which often irritates us more than not, but if it doesn't explode in our faces then it's really not so bad when we reminisce back on things with sentimentality from our advancing years and other life experiences.

So up at the crab shack on 21st street, there was fun *with & without the mundane* mindless kitchen tasks we performed with slight irritations we occasionally inflicted upon each other but it was an okay work place with odd personalities fitting together in rather nice ways more times than not. There was the *omega man* who was a hoot. And the *Altoona boys* were too. And even *Blondie* and his crew of *ditto-like* followers were a-okay more times than not. And there were more than a few others who were okay as well. And of course, the sweeter side of things were very-okay by me even if I only looked more times than played in the light. And we shared some work. And we shared some laughs. And we shared some slights & fun. And we even managed to do what we did without too many wild explosions going-on. And with time to reflect, what is remembered of such times has sweetened a bit with time.

Now Jaybird left Ocean City and the restaurant up on 21st street as quickly as he came; he just disappeared one evening after working most of his last shift sometime in mid/late August.

Maybe saying good bye to the guys for one last time was not his thing so he didn't stay around until the end of his shift just in case crocodiles were playing during one last dance, don't know. Of course, you wouldn't think it was a big deal because we were all just 'strays' on a summer working adventure and that's all it was, passing ships at sea. Or maybe, he was just sick of working and playing in Ocean City and he just wanted to leave<??> Who knows?

Regardless, Jaybird was the first of the *driftwood boys* in town and the first to go as well. Anyway(s), the rest of the troops persevered-on until summer came to a close with most of us shoving off for college with a few bucks in hand and summer memories to hold onto going-into those fall dances at school. And yet a few more remained at work through the labor day holidays and into the last of the late September days which was used by late-vacationers for their own affordable fun before all the summer help eventually moved onto other adventures somewhere else during the late fall and winter time frames when Ocean City mostly closed up with the crab shack's operations eventually reduced and maybe even closed-down for the season, I suppose. I was gone before the late September days so I don't actually know about the crab shack's seasonal closure schedule although most of Ocean City at this time anyway(s), closed down sometime after September like a sleeping summer giant taking a snooze.

But... there was a time when *we-all* danced to oddly played tunes with more smiles than not, at least, as far as I can remember... or dream-up... or play-with in-words... or whatever it is...

...a last view of the boardwalk

So work up at the crab shack was over for me come the latter part of August... and then playing up on the beach was over for me too, just before the Labor Day holiday... and my nights out under the Ocean City carnival lights were now over for me as well cause it was time to go home and rejoin the world stage...

So the last night before I was set to go home, I went up to the boardwalk to do some people watching on my last night *'down at de ocean'*... and I walked along away(s) and stopped at some boardwalk railing near some empty benches where I could slump myself into viewing mode, all incognito-like and all... again, just watching the people walking on by when I thought I spied our lovely sexy neighbor girl who'd just look through me most times as if I didn't even exist most of the time this summer... and she was doing her rather hot saunter through the aimless crowds on her way back from a long shift slinging pizzas, I supposed... and as usual, I couldn't take my eyes off her...

And she looked so athletic; beautiful and confident and so sure of herself... with a slight bow-legged-ness in her stride as if she'd played lacrosse or something like that... or maybe even cycled... but there was something athletic about her and *man-oh-mannn*, she was wrapped-up just right.

So again, I can't take my eyes off her... and I watch her weave her way through the crowd in her sexy sauntering way she usually did and the hunger in my soul deflects any sorrow I have at my impending departure from this little city down by the shore that I both relished and despised by this time in the game... when I start thinking to myself in an odd *sing-songy sorta* way...

So in the rocket's bright glare...
I see the plain truth
I'm just a friggin' fool - for wanting her so

And now, I've been left sitting all alone...
Lost in her shadow, blind and alone
And I realize to my late surprise...
I've been looking for love when it just ain't there...

But Lust... ahhh, now that's been there... in spades & more

...and yet, the more I watch her disappearing into the crowd, the more sorrowful I become at my defined departure, almost despondent, knowing I'll never get the ravenous taste I've longed for in this lifetime or any other lifetime, out of my mouth... but still, what a sight to behold...

And maybe it's my hunger which does it, but I thought I saw a slight glint of a smile from this lovely lady as she disappeared for the last time from my sight, just a brief glint of a look from over her shoulders back towards me that's probably tainted by my own blind lustful desires for her which sends my soul soaring so high because I knew - if I could just reach-out and touch the diamond nugget lying just below the water's edge then surely I'd be *'knocking on heaven's door',* as another long-ago rocker once serenaded us with in some glorious sounds of muted thunder... but then again, if I can't hit the drums with the rhythm needed to play along with the band then why should I ever think I could swim the long stretches needed to reach my goal down below the water's edge without drowning before touching *heaven's door*... especially, when I know I just can't make such a trek without drowning...

...and then suddenly... she's gone inside the crowd... and there's just me on the edge of a crowd of people playing under the lights of the Ocean City carnival meant to entertain us-all with joy for just the few days we're *'down de ocean'* during the summer.

woe is me... cause summer is over...

But I remain sitting on the boardwalk railing for just a bit longer, just people-watching while reflecting on my summer gone by as I watch all kinds of people strolling along, families, and girls and guys strutting their stuff, all in a mad summer parade of different sizes and shapes, some big and some small, some pretty and some not, but all seemingly ready to enjoy the carnival atmosphere of one Ocean City boardwalk at night with the lights and sounds and ocean breezes blowing across them from the ocean's front. And I smile at what I see.

Then after a bit more time passes me by, I get up & off the railing I've been sitting on and start my rumbling stumbling stroll on back to our driftwood delight cause... *yep, summer is over...* and it's time to go home.

Now unknown to me at this time, there's several big old seagulls sitting up on some nearby roof tops at some of those nearby Ocean City boardwalk establishments... and the one seagull says to another seagull, as he's watching me... "you ever seen such a sorry-ass fool looking so lost at play?"

...and the other seagull looks at the first seagull and says... "you outta your mind... I ain't neverrr seen such a sorry-ass fool like that before!"

"Well, look at him" ...says the first seagull to the second, as they both look down on me.

...and then, after a bit... all of the seagulls break-out into grand laughter at their funny-ass bird humor.

Note: The line *'knocking on Heaven's door'* was triggered by a *Bob Dylan* lyric & song *'Knockin' on Heaven's Door'*.

Summer's over: Leaving town

It's morning time drifting towards the mid-day time frame and I'm nervously pacing the floor of the driftwood apartment waiting on gorilla-Tea to show. He knew we were heading out this morning but he's always on his own schedule and *da hell be damn on others*, I suppose.

"Where's he at" says Tommy-Jay; he's our brother who's made the trip down this morning to pick us up for our trip home.

"I'm ready to go"

"I know... I know... I know... just a bit longer. I told him we were leaving this morning so I don't know what his problem is"

But sometime this morning, gorilla-Tea had disappeared out into town probably telling his crew of young misfits good-bye or so while we waited around on his sorry-ass. Bobby had already gone out towards work. Ditto, Big Al, who's been gone for hours at his early morning shift at the bakery. So it's just me and Tommy-Jay now prowling around the floors of our driftwood abode waiting on our lone holdout but sooner or later, as the clock ticks towards noon, Tommy-Jay says to me... "It's time... you coming... or am I leaving you behind?"

"You ain't doing shit... just wait"

But Tommy-Jay walks on out to the car and jumps in and turns over the engine.

"Come on Tommy-Jay, just hold your ass up for a bit longer"

... and Tommy-Jay *fidgets* a bit more with things in the car as I fling my duffle bag with my Ocean City clothes into the back seat.

Meanwhile, Tommy-Jay's got the radio on now while popping his foot nervously on the car floor impatiently waiting for us to get our shit together cause he's had enough of our shit and our OC pad... and he's ready to go... He eventually turns off the engine with a grumble but keeps the music playing.

And truth be told, by this time, I was pretty damn ready to go too; I was ready for some down-time now too... but not gorilla-Tea for some reason cause he'd had such a blast *'down de ocean'* that pulling him away from all his summer fun was like pulling an alligator off its waterlogged dinner... not so easy.

So I continue making excuses for gorilla-Tea cause I know or at least expect, he's going to get his ass back so we can leave... but Tommy-Jay has had enough of both of us by now so it looked like he was on a horse trying to gallop away while I'm hanging onto the horse's tail trying to restrain them from leaving. And while I'm holding onto to that tail, I'm bellowing down deep inside for gorilla-Tea to get his ass over-here while cursing his name under my breath...

...but eventually... gorilla-Tea finally shows around the corner and I start bellowing for him to move his ass... and Tommy-Jay now kicks the engine over and starts gunning it cause it's time to go... and gorilla-Tea still hasn't got the message cause he's just sauntering down the sidewalk like he's got all the time in the world...

"You got your stuff?" ...I yell in his direction cause he's got nothing in his hands... just the clothes on his back...

"I got it all" ...he says, like there's nothing left behind.

"But you got nothing<??>" ...I say, mystified... cause I know he's got to have some other clothes left behind, at least, some underwear, right... of course, that's before I knew he'd been taking Bobby's underwear all summer long rather than washing

235

his own so... 'what *da hell* do I know?" ...'*absolutely, nothing... say it again...*'

"I don't need nothing" ...he says, as he walks on up to the car trying to get past me into the shot-gun seat...

"Ohhh, nooo... you don't... I've got shot-gun, dude" ...as I push him backwards into the back seat...

...and then he shoots out his arms trying to wrestle me away from the car so he can jump into my spot but I'm older and bigger at this time so I *fend-him-off* laughing at his feeble attempts at stealing my spot...

...and Tommy-Jay yells to us both... "let's go you f*<kers... this train is a-leaving the station..."

...and gorilla-Tea and I yell at him to "cool his tool" ...and *back & forth* things go until we finally tumble into place in the car *scratching & a-clawing* and making a mess of noise talking shit to each other with gorilla-Tea and my voice dominating the scratchy discourse between us-all cause... we always do... all the while Tommy-Jay is f*<king around with an itchy trigger foot waiting to bust his way outta of this place...

...and then... like magic had finally touched this sweet moment of havoc... a hot footed melody starts bouncing off the roof tops as we edged out into the streets with *Springsteen's 'Cadillac Ranch'* hitting the sound waves in a mish-mash of a way inside our dusty old green used Chevy Impala we lovingly called our f*<king road hog Cadillac... and I reach on over and crank up the tunes as loud as it goes before slumping back in my seat singing in my croaked voice while Tommy-Jay yells for sanity or at least some level of civility... when gorilla-Tea takes this moment to reach forward over my seat to pound-down on top of my head from behind, punishing me for grabbing the 'shot-gun' seat and shouting for me to blast the tunes even louder than I'm already playing them...

...and *around-n-around* we go, punching and popping and yelping and singing and carrying-on like out-of-control family does.

...and so *out the door* we went, like *the disaster* we were... and over towards the OC bridge we went towards our westward-ho of a destination trip, again, all yelling and screaming and fighting in one busted-up old green Chevy Impala like the derelicts we were, all the while our frighteningly loud sounds were blasting *rock-n-roll* majestically forth from our dysfunctional ride like we were a *rock-n-roll* band in motion with absolutely no vocals worth hearing by anyone but ourselves... although... I imagine, we might have been heard by someone...

...and summer was over

...and life was now headed on down the tracks, westward-ho we were... back to *Charm City* and our beautiful village of Violets which was (and is) hidden away on the southwestern side of such *Charming type things*, all the while we were... *'Tearing up the highway like [a rock-n-roll band might do] ...'* where I do believe I've heard a less bastardized version of these words sung before.

Note: The line *'absolutely nothing, say it again...'* was triggered by a lyric in Edwin Starr's song *'War'*; *'War, huh... what is it good for?'*. The line *'tearing up the highway...'* was triggered by a Bruce Springsteen lyric in the song *'Cadillac Ranch'*.

An Epilogue Wrap

I first gave thoughts of writing this book many years ago when I was first approaching the beginnings of my old age. I guess nostalgia creeps in with age sometimes and then we reflect back on times and stories gone by. Anyway(s), here I am many years later-still and I've finally finished what I started to write in my head so many years ago; a story about friendship and play with just a bit of other stuff thrown into the mix, *here & there*.

But first, I feel compelled to make certain 'afterthoughts' concerning the book. I offer much thanks to my wife, daughter, family and friends for brightening my days over the many years I've spent traveling from *'there to here'*. And I give a special 'thanks' to one sweet Betty-dear for her many contributions to my work.

Moreover, I apologize for any editing errors which may still exist in this book. We acted as our own editors which can be a bit problematic at times so I could have missed finding a few errors during the editing process; I often see *'what I meant to write rather than what I actually wrote'* when editing, *ughhh...* So yes, it's possible there are still a few mistakes within the story I've told but it's been reviewed as much as it could be without 'just saying No'. So *'it is'* what *'it is'* and there *ain't* no more.

Now this story was told in a more semi-disjointed sequential story-telling-like chain of events with bits & pieces of fancy dancing through the pages rather than in (what I might consider) a normal sequential storyline. The recipe for this madness was first ignited when I read the book *'up the down stair case'* which used a sequential narrative augmented by scattered pieces of information from such diverse sources as work memos, diary entries, and letters passed between characters, etc. And at first it seemed a bit disjointed to me although I quickly learned to appreciate the flavor of the story when told through this method. And even though I don't actually use such entries as memos & letters, etc., to tell this story, I did tell the story through characters and scenes and *chitter-chatters* and *detours* that are sometimes shorter-type mini-stories linked together in an effort to tell one longer story about friendship and life during a youthful dance through the streets of Ocean City during the summer of 1976, the *bicentennial year of the USA*. So to some extent, the book *'up the down stair case'* made me aware that I did NOT have to tell my story through normal sequential narrative methods utilized in so many other books and therefore, the tone of this story was born; an eclectic disjointed mish-mosh of shorter-type stories linked together into a whole story.

And as I suggested earlier in the prologue, this story has a *bit of fictionalized truth* hidden within its characters and events. So I should make the following disclaimer: all characters & events in this book, even those seemingly based on what appears to be real people & places, are told from a fictional standpoint and therefore, they are fictional by design. The point is: this story is NOT biographically correct and it shouldn't be viewed in any such way because I've fictionalized most characters & scenes in some way or another, throughout the book. The exceptions to my *fictionalizing* are in the social commentaries I buried in some of the detours.

But it would be inexcusable of me to not offer my deepest gratitude to all those sweet characters, real or not, in their fictional states or not, who danced a bit with me through the stories I've written because without them, the stories do not exist... nor would I retain such sweet memories, at least, where a bit of truth exists.

...which brings me to *this final thought*: It turns out that most relationships are like ships passing in the night... or in the day...

or whatever... and I don't mean it in a bad way either, it's just that we are here one day and then the next day we are but a memory in time and space... and if it's good then it's a pleasant memory one returns to when time allows us to do so and if not then...<??>

And *pleasant* is the case with so many of *these characters* in this story... As for the *driftwood boys*, well, they will always be near & dear to my heart. Sometimes, even *the ordinary is extraordinary* when you take time to reflect-back on *good times* gone by.

...which brings me to my sequential-type wrap-up of these storybook characters who made up the *driftwood boys*...

JD disappeared into '*the rest of his life*' almost before we knew he was there; I hope he found peace and contentment.

Pie-faced Al departed this world way-too early for such a fine man... and I, and the rest of the *driftwood boys*, all dearly hope he found *the peace* he was looking for... '*I know we'll see you again big man, sometime later, on the other bless-it side of it-all*'.

And a bit later still, *Gorilla-Tea* walked away as well, into a storm he hadn't expected to hit so damn hard but it did, and he's been missed throughout the years since his departure although I know, like the old silver screen line goes, '*I know I'll see you again... this side... or the other*'.

Then *Pat-Light*, a sweet diamond of Light who brightened our & my heart with her special charms, she too, departed this world much earlier than she should have due to a horrible sickness but we & I, will never forget her, ever... '*I hope I see you again lovely lady... somewhere, on the other bless-it side of it all*'.

Years later still, as we were crossing into old age, the leader in our silly-ass *band of brothers*, *Johnny-boy*, who brought us together early-on, and who in our latter years walked much further to the right-side of me than not, but who still found time to share in our memories with laughter at our times gone by, [he too] passed on... '*I know I'll see you again my friend... somewhere -*

on the other bless-it side of it-all'.

As for *Bobby*, we're all who are left of the *driftwood boys* these days and he's become a trusted dear friend over the many years since our summer together *down de ocean* at the *driftwood* mansion. And while we share more *'todays'* together than we can remember *'yesterdays'*, we still, when prompted, will occasionally share laughter at our *driftwood* summer days we spent together and the joys we left behind... and that, as they say... *'ain't so damn bad'*...

And as for *Jaybird & da dangler & dirty dan and all da other such fictional-like dudes & dudettes who danced through this story* as well... well, *they-all* just melted-away into the fictional pages of time but then again, *we-all* do something-like that with time...

As for me, well, *I am - what I am,* as they say, and *there ain't no more... well, other than maybe our youthful & foolish line: 'I am Spartacus!!! ...da friggin' KING... of da Kitchen urchins' ...or not, maybe<??>*

btw, Tommy-Jay was like an honorary *driftwood boy* even though he never stayed very long whenever he stopped by. But he made his dreams come true despite obstacles thrown in his way. It's nice to know good guys win sometimes.

And now... I'll close-off this book with this one last sweet tidbit:

Bless-it are the sweet-hearts who've enriched our lives in so many ways over all the years we've walked this earth... and of course, to the peace-makers... who've left their damn guns at home.

Notes: The line *'I know I'll see you again...'* was triggered by the same/similar line in the movie *'The Town'*.

Made in the USA
Middletown, DE
30 March 2023

27282755R00139